She Got It

Nicole Jackson

Contact Info:

Author Nicole Jackson | **Facebook**

nicole3317@att.net

Acknowledgements

This has been a long time coming. She Got It was my debut book, my humble introduction into the literary world. I was nervous and I completely underestimated the power of my pen. The love I have received from readers has been overwhelmingly pleasant. My dreams are coming to fruition, and there is simply no better feeling. Yes, Ms. Loud Mouth Know it All Nicole Jackson is officially an author, and I want to thank the very people who made it possible. So, this goes out to all my loyal readers, my mama, Nene, my twin brothers Travaris and Trevon, my cousins, LaTonya, Yolanda, Bubble Gum, my grandma Momo, and my friends that have either sat and read or listened to my stories, or were the actual inspirations for the storylines before they were ever published such as: Michelle, Tamara, Jessica, and Jammie. And last but certainly no least I have to thank my baby, my boo, my headache, the only one I'll empty my pockets for, Khyran and the man that stepped in to pick up the next nigga's slack, Dexter. I do this for us.

Prologue

"Girl, that nigga aint trying to hear that shit." Kathy spat, as she and her best friend Yolanda entered their house.

"No, he didn't mean that. He was just talkin' shit, because he was in the front of his brothers." Yolanda shook her head. She couldn't grasp the concept that her number one trick didn't want to fuck with her anymore.

It was as if Yolanda hadn't seen herself in the mirror in years. She was once a thick beautiful light skinned woman, with long and full hair, but was now a shadow of her former self. Her teeth were rotten to the core. Her hair was so nappy that it was beginning to form as dreads, and she was so skinny that her breasts were now like loose skin. Yet, she thought that any man would be crazy to turn her away. You couldn't tell her that she didn't have it going on.

Yolanda was switching hard in her worn out sundress that was so low cut that it revealed the bones sitting in the middle of her chest. She'd worn her wig for so long that there was lent on every other strand. Her lips were adorned with the deepest red lipstick she could find. She had no problem strutting in her three inch heels, while the back of her feet exposed the fact that she hadn't bathed in days.

"So, what if the nigga really don't come by here tonight?" Kathy questioned, as she took a seat on the couch that Yolanda retrieved from the side of the road.

"That nigga is coming. But if by some small chance he don't we'll just have to make our way down Jensen."

"Jensen? Bitch, I keep telling you that I aint going over there no time soon. That crazy bitch Alex pulled a knife out on me over the last trick I had. I aint trying to spend the next month in the Harris County jail."

"Well, I heard that her ass in locked up, anyway. And besides I'm not letting her or nah other motherfucka stop me from getting my hit." Yolanda retorted, as she picked up lent off the floor and examined it. "Bitch, I thought that I had found something." she laughed, as she flicked the lent off her finger.

"Mama, we're hungry." Crystal whined, as she stuck her head out of the bedroom that she shared with her younger sister Falen.

"Take your ass back in that fucking room!" Yolanda barked.

Crystal immediately ducked back inside the room. "I told you that she was gonna say that!" she snapped at Falen.

"So, I don't care. I'm still hungry, shit." Falen pouted. She was known to have a very foul mouth, and cussed like a sailor. So, often many were taken aback by the way the nine year old girl talked.

"Well, go borrow some noodles from your little friend next door." Crystal told her.

"Booby aint home." Falen frowned, with her thumb in her mouth.

"How you know?"

"Cause I saw him leave with his friends."

"You sure do keep up with him." Crystal rolled her eyes at her sister. She hated how their neighbor would go out of his way for Falen. He'd buy her candy, give her food whenever he could, but she couldn't get a damn thing from him. There always seemed to be a person willing to do for her sister.

"Why you worried?" Falen asked, as she snaked her neck around, while her thumb remained in her mouth. "You just mad cause he won't give your black self nothing."

"I don't want nothing from his ass, you little pissy bitch." Crystal lashed.

"Fuck you." Falen gave her the finger, as she took a seat on their bare mattress that rested on their roach infested floor. She continued to suck her thumb, and twirl a few strands of her hair around her finger.

"No, fuck yourself. You do it better."

"Crystal, shut up. That's why that man was sucking on your little tittys." Falen teased.

That hit a soft spot. Crystal hated when Yolanda would let Mr. John suck her breasts for money. He'd done it so many times that she was now used to it. She'd just close her eyes and wait for it to be over. "Oh, don't worry cause he gon suck on yours next."

"No he won' cause I will cut his ass first."

"Falen, please. You won't do nothing."

"Yes I would. I…" Falen stopped talking when there was a loud knock at the front door.

"Who is it?" Kathy asked, as she walked over to the door.

"John." a voice said from the other side.

Kathy turned to face Yolanda. "Yo, he came!" she said, excitedly knowing that they were a few steps away from getting a hit.

"Well, let him in, bitch." Yolanda urged, standing up, trying to fix her dress.

Kathy damn near snatched the door off the hinges, attempting to open it. "Come in." she told John as she stepped aside.

John entered the shotgun house and peered around. Everything was still filthy just like the last time he'd visited. In fact the extra-large Magnum condom he used with Yolanda was still sitting in the corner of the room. Those damn crack heads just didn't give a damn, and that's why he chose to strap up every time he touched them.

There was just something about fucking nasty women. He couldn't get enough of it. He was a decent looking man with a nice build, but women like Yolanda just provided something that his woman couldn't.

"So, what's up Yolanda?" he frowned. She'd come

to him earlier that day, begging for some money, while he hung with his boys near the Kelly Courts. His people around the way didn't know that he got down with her, so needless to say he was beyond embarrassed.

"You know what's up, daddy. I wanted to give you something." Yolanda gave him a huge rotten smile.

"What the fuck can you give me besides gingivitis, with your yuck mouth ass!" John snapped.

"Baby, don't be that way. You know that I'll make it worth your while."

"Didn't I tell you that I was tired of your stanking ass pussy?"

The look of desperation couldn't be missed, as her eyes pleaded with him. "Well, how about two for one? You can have the both of us for the price of one." Kathy spoke up.

John took a hard look at her. She carried a huge ass around, despite her crack addiction. The thing was that she was rumored to be HIV positive. He didn't know if it was true, but it was a chance that he wasn't willing to take. Shit, he had to draw the line somewhere. He did have a woman at home.

"Hell, no. I don't care if you was fucking for free." John shook his head. His wheels began spinning. It was obvious that they were willing to do anything at that point.

"Okay, so let me suck that big dick for you, baby." Yolanda pleaded.

"No, I aint feeling that. But I would give you fifty dollars for something else, though."

Yolanda damn near pissed on herself out of excitement. "What is it? I'll do anything daddy."

He bit his bottom lip. "I want your daughter."

"My daughter? You wanna suck her titties again?" Yolanda questioned, ready to give in to his demands.

"No." John shook his head. "That's only worth

twenty. I want to fuck her."

"Hell no!" Kathy interrupted. "She's worth more than fifty dollars. You should at least make it a hundred."

"Wait a minute, bitch! How the hell are you gon negotiate when that is my daughter?"

"Well, I'm just saying. She gotta fuck sooner or later. At least now we can get a hit and some food around here." Kathy tried to reason.

"Well, it don't matter cause the most I'm paying is seventy." John added.

"Seventy? Come on daddy you can do better than that." Yolanda pleaded.

"That's all. You know what, fuck this. I'm out." he snapped, as he threw his hands up and headed for the door.

"Wait, baby!" Yolanda begged as she grabbed his hand.

"Let me go!" he yelled as he snatched his hand away. "Seventy dollars. Take it or leave it." he gritted.

"Okay, okay." she gave in.

Crystal and Falen had their ears glued to the door and had heard the entire conversation.   "I'm not doing nothing with that man." Crystal trembled.

Falen stood not knowing what to say. True; her sister got on her nerves but never did she want to see her harmed. "Let's just climb out the window, Crystal." she whispered.

"Come on." Crystal uttered shakily, as she grabbed Falen's hand.
Just as she was lifting the window the bedroom door swung open. "What the fuck is you doing?" Yolanda shouted.

Crystal nervously turned to face her mama. "We was just looking out the window."

Yolanda eyed them suspiciously. "Whatever. Well, come here for a minute. I need to tell you something."

Feeling like she didn't have a choice, Crystal followed her mama to the next room. Falen sat on the mattress, feeling helpless. She wanted to help her sister so badly. A few minutes after Crystal left the room she could here light sobbing. Eventually, the light sobbing turned into loud cries, with a squeaking mattress.

It seemed like John was moaning and humping for hours. Falen paced the room waiting for her sister to return. She wanted to rescue Crystal, but knew that there was little that a nine year old such as herself could do. She then started to fear that she could be next. Her anxiety was so intense that she was too afraid to step outside of the room. So, after holding her piss for over an hour she finally pissed all over herself.

Minutes passed and Falen stood frozen, standing in a puddle of urine. Finally, the mattress stopped squeaking. Then she heard several footsteps moving around, and the front door slam shut. Ten minutes after that Crystal returned to their room.

"Is he gone?" Falen asked.

Crystal was like a zombie as the tears streamed down her face. She hadn't even noticed that the room reeked of piss, as she sat on the mattress. She was so distraught that she just buried her face inside of her palms, as she wept.

Falen decided that she'd comfort her sister. So, she took a seat right next to Crystal and wrapped her arms around her. "It's going to be okay." she cried.

Crystal relaxed in her sisters' embrace, until her senses kicked in. "What the hell is that smell?" she sniffed the air. "Uh, get your pissy ass off of me!" she snapped as she pushed Falen to the dirty floor.

Chapter 1

From Pillow to Post

"I don't know what the fuck you think this is! Get your ass up!" Crystal yelled at Falen.

"Damn, can I get a little sleep?" Falen griped.

"Hell, no! Bitch, it's ten o'clock and my kids wanna watch TV."

"Fuck." Falen mumbled, as she rose from the tattered couch.

She made her way to the bathroom to brush her teeth. As always, it reeked of urine. She was so tired of living in that shabby ass apartment, with her dumb ass sister.

"Look, at yourself, bitch." Falen shook her head, as she stared at her image in the smeared mirror. Her long bushy hair was in a ponytail, and she still had matter in the corner of her eyes. Her t-shirt had a red juice stain that seemed to be waving at her.

As Falen began brushing her teeth there was a loud knock on the door. She continued to brush, as if she didn't hear it.

"Damn, can you hurry the fuck up?" Jeremy yelled through the door. Crystal's boyfriend was always trying to run shit, although he didn't pay a single bill in the apartment.

Falen continued to brush her teeth, and then gave herself a quick wash off. There was no way in hell that she was putting her feet, or any other part of her body inside that tub. The dirt and grime was so thick that the tub would never be clean again.

When she finally opened the door Jeremy was standing there with a mean scowl on his face.

"Got damn, it took you long enough."

"Whatever." she rolled her eyes, as he stomped

inside the bathroom and slammed the door.

Falen made her way back to the living room, where Crystal's best friend Janah was now hanging.

"What's up Falen? When are you going to do something with that head of yours?" Janah jested.

"You aint never lied. Her ass is walking around here with a poodle on top of her head." Crystal giggled.

"Ha ha ha." Falen sarcastically replied. Everyone enjoyed having a laugh at her expense.

"Well, anyways, finish telling me about that fine ass nigga." Crystal told Janah.

"Oh yeah, bitch *Tino* was all up on me!" Janah boasted, putting emphases on one the biggest ballers in Houston name.

Falen simply rolled her eyes at those simple ass bitches. Janah was going on and on about a man that probably hadn't given her a second thought. All the chicks in the projects salivated over Tino, and Janah was no exception. They may as well have been lusting after some big time rapper, because that man was damn for sure unavailable to any chick that resided in The Kelly Courts.

More than likely, Janah was telling a whole slew of lies, in which she was known to do. It wasn't that she was unattractive, but she loved to stretch the truth. Her nice round ass turned plenty of heads, but she was barely average in the facial department. If it wasn't for the fact that she stole and wrote hot checks a lot of men wouldn't give her a second glance. She wore plenty of Gucci and True Religion, which gave her a slight edge, but let her tell it every nigga in Houston, Texas wanted her.

Falen decided to tune out Beavis and Butthead. Crystal was the only fool dumb enough to believe a word that Janah was saying. To Crystal Janah was a boss bitch that went for hers, but the reality was that she was a good thief that ran her mouth too much. Janah would lie about anything from men giving her things to how they treated her. Anybody with a lick of common sense could see through her lies, but that was the same reason that Crystal fell for them.

"Falen, fix the kids some breakfast." Crystal commanded.

"Damn, was that a question or a statement?" Falen snapped.

"I'm *asking* you to fix the breakfast." Crystal cleared it up. She knew how far to go with her younger sister.

As Falen headed for the kitchen Janah turned her nose up at her. Over the years she'd developed a strong dislike for Falen. She hated everything about her from her bowlegged stance to her wild and curly hair. So, she did everything within her power to bring her down. A majority of the slugs she threw went over Crystal's head, or at least she thought.

Crystal was a chocolate tone with the same curly hair as Falen. She was thick, but still had a rather nice shape. After three kids she'd put on some extra pounds, which made her insecure. That was one of the main reasons why she and Falen didn't get along. It seemed that every time she got herself a new man they were eyeing her little sister.

Falen had a coke bottle figure, with a smooth brown caramel complexion. Still, she was invisible to most men with any money or status. Her shabby appearance always deterred them, before they even got a closer glimpse. She was nineteen and had always been unpopular, because of the way she dressed and wore her hair. Growing up in a house with a crack head didn't allow many luxuries, so she and Crystal never had much.

For years they floated from relative to relatives' houses. Their mama had left them on their own a while ago. Then once Crystal became pregnant with her second baby she was old enough to apply for public housing. So, she got her first apartment in the Kelly Courts, and allowed her little sister to come along. That was a much needed income in the household. She was able to collect food stamps and a welfare check for Falen for two years. Just recently, she'd finished high school, so the welfare office cut off her check. This caused Crystal to throw extra shade her way. She felt that Falen's presence had to be beneficial in some kind of way for her to continue to the live there.

Falen knew that she needed to do something and quickly. It was just a matter of time before Crystal would kick her out. It seemed as though her mere presence was getting on her sister's nerves. Women became that way when they couldn't seem to hold on to a man.

Crystal swore that Falen was the reason why her relationships were always short lived. She claimed that all of the men's main complaint was Falen, but Falen knew better. Whenever, Crystal's money or drugs dried up, then so did her relationships. The girl was a huge target for users and abusers.

"Ant Falen, you have a stain on your shirt." Little Ken pointed out, as Falen scrubbed the dishes.

Falen took a long look at her nephew before replying, "Yeah, just like the stains you have in your drawers."

"Whatever, wooly head!" Little Ken spat, as he trotted out of the kitchen.

"Bad ass bastard." Falen mumbled to herself. Her nephew always managed to work her nerves, but he was the most tolerable because for some odd reason he reminded her of her best friend.

"Say Falen, you seen my brush?" Jeremy asked as he entered the kitchen.

"Nope."

"Well, somebody knows where it's at." he mumbled, as he attempted to reach over her and retrieve a blunt inside the cabinet above her head. He was so close that she could feel his hard on. "Excuse you." he whispered into her ear.

"No, excuse you." she snapped.

"Why you always so mean to a nigga? I'm your future brother-in-law, girl. We need to get to know each other." he smiled.

Falen wanted to slap that smile right off of his face. He seemed so ugly to her. He was decent enough physically, but his ways were very unattractive. There he was yellow, tall, slim, and full of shit. Since the day he moved in he'd been hitting on her. There was no use in telling Crystal, because every time she attempted to do so the tables were turned around on her. Crystal would swear that Falen must have come on to him first, because that's exactly what she'd claimed all the other times.

"Look, I don't need to know shit about you." Falen rolled her eyes.

Crystal entered the kitchen at the tail end of the conversation. "Falen, why are you always catching a attitude with people?"

"Whatever." Falen mumbled.

"See, that's why your ass need to find somewhere else to stay. You can have all the attitude you want in your own house."

She turned to face her sister. "Crystal please. If you want me gone, just say it. Be a woman about yours. Just stop throwing these slugs like the coward that you are." Falen seethed.

"Bitch, aint no coward standing in these shoes. You the one living on somebody's couch, without a pot to piss in or a window to throw it out of." Crystal lashed, as she stepped in Falen's face.

"Crystal, you better move." Falen stated, unfazed.

"Make me, bitch."

"Okay, okay. Baby, let her make it." Jeremy

chuckled, as he pulled Crystal away.

"Bitch, you lucky he saved your dog ass." Crystal spat, as she allowed Jeremy to lead her away.

Falen was not moved by her sister's performance. Crystal may have been three years older and fifty pounds heavier, but she knew that Falen could mop the floor with her ass. Falen was known to lay out chicks twice her size. Hell, she'd rescued Crystal from a few ass whippings. So, she knew that Crystal's little tirade was all show for her man.

After cleaning the kitchen Falen was finally able to cook pancakes and bacon. As soon as she took the last pancake out the pan, Janah grabbed it. Although, she'd cooked, there wasn't any left for her. Instead of arguing about it, she decided to take a walk and check the mailbox.

The day was sunny, and the atmosphere was humid. There were plenty of people hanging out, creating a ruckus. The local knuckleheads were shooting dice on the sidewalk, so Falen had to step around them. She hated walking past a huge crowd of niggas, because she always felt self-conscious. So, without thinking she began tugging at her long t-shirt to insure that the guys could not see her thighs or ass.

By the time she made it to the mailbox she was wishing that she'd waited, until the sunset. The only reason she was so anxious about checking the mail was because she was expecting a letter from Booby, her best friend. He was in state jail for possession, and wrote her once a week.

When she opened the box she found the letter that she'd been waiting for. She couldn't wait to sit down and read it.

"Bitch, what's that?" a deep voice questioned, startling her.

She spun around to find her second best friend, Toya. "Girl, you damn near gave me a heart attack." Falen sighed, as she held her chest.

"Bitch kill the dramatics." Toya giggled. "But no for real, what is that?" she asked, referring to the letter in Falen's hand.

Falen took a look at her hand. "Oh, this? Well, this is Booby's letter." she smiled.

"Oh, his bitch ass." Toya sighed as she blew out hot air.

For all the years that Falen had known Toya she never liked Booby. She swore that he was a shiest individual who would kill his own grandma if the price was right. Although, many shared this view, Falen saw him in a different light. He was always there for her and often took up for her when people tried to make fun of her. He even helped her buy her school clothes once. He'd done more than any other person in her life, so for that she tried to give him her virginity.

The night they shared was so special to her and she couldn't have asked for a better partner. She would always keep those memories close to her heart, even though she only saw him as a big brother figure.

"I don't know why you don't like him. He's cool people."

"Falen, you are so damn naïve. That nigga aint no good and one day you will see for yourself."

Falen rolled her eyes. "Anyways, where was you coming from?"

"The store. That's where I saw Tino's fine ass flying by with a bitch on the back of his motorcycle."

"So, what? You and Janah is getting on my nerves with this *Tino* shit."

"Oh, Falen please. You know that you lust after his ass too."

"No I don't. I mean, yeah, he's cute but there are too many bitches chasing after him. Who would want a man that could fuck your entire crew if he wanted to? I aint lining up to get fucked by his ass." Falen snorted.

"What's good Falen, you can't speak?" Joe asked her as they made it to Crystal's front door.

"Hey, Joe." she waved.

Toya' eyes went back and forth between the two. "Bitch, Joe always goes out of his way to speak to you. I think he likes you." she whispered.

"No, he don't."

"Whatever, Falen. You kill me with this shit. Why can't a fine ass nigga like him like you?"

Falen didn't reply, as she stared off into space. Why in the hell would Joe be interested in her? The nigga carried a strong resemblance to the rapper Young Buck without the braids. He drove a damn cocaine white Navigator, sitting on twenty fours. Joe was the man to see around Kelly Courts. He and his cousin Tino had been in the dope game since the age of fourteen and fifteen. So, at just twenty-eight and twenty-nine they were running shit. Every broad that lived there threw pussy at them. Both men were highly attractive even without the money. So, there was no way in hell that Joe was feeling her.

Joe had taken a liking to her after he'd witnessed her handle two females by herself. He would've never thought that a chick with a face as pretty as hers could throw down like that. Even though, she didn't say much to the females around the way she still managed to hold her own. So, after that day he developed a new found respect for her.

As Falen and Toya entered the apartment Jeremy was leaving out. He gave the both of them a wicked smirk, and was on his way. Crystal was sitting on the couch with a pitiful look on her face.

"Falen, by the end of the week you have to go." she spat.

"For what?" Falen questioned with utter confusion.

"You're causing too many problems for me and my man."

"What? I barely say two words to the nigga. Where is all this shit coming from?"

"Look, I'm tired of talking about it! Find you somewhere to stay by Friday."

"You know what; fuck you and this raggedy ass apartment! I can leave right now. You aint hurting me. Hell, a homeless person lives cleaner than this!"

"Okay, well then, bitch, get your *homeless* ass out my house!" Crystal roared.

"You aint said nothing but a word." Falen spat, as she hurried upstairs to gather her things.

What was really sad was that all of her belongings fit into one duffel bag.

"I don't need that bitch." she mumbled, as she held back the tears.

Toya felt so sorry for her friend. "Falen, you can stay with me. I'll work out something with my mama."

"You will?" Falen perked up.

"Yeah, come on." Toya instructed, as she guided her out of Crystal's apartment. "Girl, your sister aint gon have no luck, treating you like this. So, don't even worry about it." she said as she glanced back at Crystal.

"Whatever, bitch! Nobody told you to bring your yellow ass in my house in the first place!" Crystal yelled as she slammed the door behind them.

"Bitch!" Toya yelled at the closed door.

"Okay, so we're going to get up early and look for some jobs." Falen nodded.

"Yep." Toya agreed.

The two friends were both lying in Toya's bed,

talking about everything under the sun. They both felt that their lives needed some drastic changes. Although, Falen was grateful that Toya's mom, Gloria, allowed her to stay, she knew that all good things didn't last forever. So, they were trying to find a way to support themselves, so that they could move out on their own.

"Oh, shit! I almost forgot to read Booby's letter." Falen said as she reached for her duffel bag.

Toya rolled her eyes, as her girl ripped open the letter, as if it contained a million bucks.

Falen could hardly contain herself as she read the letter aloud. "Pretty Falen, how is the world treating you? I hope it's being kind. Well, as for me I'm okay. I'm just counting down the days until I get out this bitch. A nigga really misses your ass. The only thing that keeps me sane in here is picturing your beautiful smile. I enjoyed the last letter and poem you wrote me. That shit was deep. It really got me to thinking, you feel me? I thought back on the first night we got together in a physical way…." Falen trailed off.

"No, bitch don't try to skip over that shit. He was talking about yall getting physical. I want to hear this, since you swear that he's just your *brother*." Toya teased.

Falen rolled her eyes, but continued to read. "I can still remember that night that you allowed me to take your virginity. I never thought that we would ever go there, but I am so glad that we did. I'm so proud that you shared such a special part of yourself with me. That's why I love you. You put trust in me when no one else would. You have the ability to see a man's soul and not judge. Plenty of people could take a lesson from you. But on a more positive note, I have six months left and then I'll be back to hold shit down for you. I know Crystal's been getting on your nerves. Who knows maybe we can come together and get our own shit. Write me back and tell me what you feel about that."

"Girl, I didn't know that the nigga could write." Toya giggled. "But for real, he do like you. But I still say he's not to be trusted."

"We're just friends and I know as a friend that he has my back, so I aint trying to hear what you talking about."

"Just friends, Falen? That man is trying to make plans to be with you. That wasn't a just friends' letter."

"No, you're misreading things. We've always talked about getting a place together, so that I could escape the drama that surrounds me at home. He just wants to be there for me. The sex thing only happened once, and I aint trying to do that shit again. It hurt too bad."

"Girl, you are a mess. You're the only nineteen year old that I know that only had sex once. He never tried to hit it again?"

"Yeah, but I would come up with excuses. Then he got locked up."

"He must've been bad at it, because if it was good you wouldn't have minded giving him seconds."

"Whatever." Falen rolled her eyes.

"And didn't Crystal fuck with him for a little while?"

"That's what she was claiming at one time, but he denies it."

Crystal smirked. "Shit, I'd deny it too, if I was him."

Chapter 2

They're Taking Notice

"Toya, I think these people are staring at my ass." Falen complained as they walked down the sidewalk.

"Girl, chill out. There is nothing wrong with those jeans. They fit just right." Toya giggled.

They'd both just come from placing applications in at all the eateries around the city. Toya dressed Falen for the day. She chose some skin tight dark denim skinny jeans and a white race back muscle shirt. She'd even purchased her friend a new pair of thong slides to wear. The jeans were hugging her sharp hips and plush backside, so since they'd gotten off the bus, cars had been blowing their horns non-stop.

Falen was very uncomfortable with the extra attention. That was the main reason she often opted the long t-shirts. She couldn't believe that she allowed Toya to convince her to wear her long and curly hair down.

By the time they reached the front of Kelly Courts Falen was ready to run in the house and change clothes.

"Daaamn, who is that?" J-Dog, a small time hustler, asked his boy.

"That's Falen's fine ass. She be trying to hide that body under those big ass shirts." Trae replied.

Falen hated when niggas talked about her, as if she couldn't hear them. She was so wrapped up in their conversation that she didn't realize that Toya was walking past the apartments.

"Where are we going?" she finally asked.

"I'm about to go over here behind the store to see if somebody got some Xanax."

"You trying to get fucked up today?" Falen lifted a brow.

"Yeah, you getting fucked up too." Toya informed her.

"Thanks for letting me know." Falen piped, sarcastically.

Once they made it behind the store they found a whole crew of old skools just chilling, playing dominoes, or shooting dice. Falen didn't feel comfortable there with all the stares, so she stood on the narrow street with her arms folded. She watched as Toya approached an older man with a cowboy hat, and slid him a twenty.

Hoonk! Falen almost jumped out of her skin when she heard the loud horn in her ear. She turned to find Tino with Joe, riding shotgun in his Escalade. She quickly moved into the shallow ditch to allow them to pass.

"Damn, who is that?" Tino gawked, as he stopped his truck in the middle of the street.

Joe had to get a closer look. "That's Falen's little sexy ass." he smiled.

"Damn, I didn't know that she had a body like that." Tino licked his lips. "She a little bowlegged stallion."

"Where you been at, nigga?" Joe asked his cousin. He'd noticed Falen's sex appeal a while ago. "I'm just letting her ripen a bit, before I get at her."

Falen stood there with a confused look on her face. She didn't know why Tino was still sitting in the middle of the narrow street, blocking traffic.

"How you doing, Ms. Falen?" Tino finally asked her. Joe gave his cousin a strange look. Even though, technically Falen was fair game, he'd already expressed his interest. All he could do was shake his head. Tino was being typical Tino, not giving a damn. If he saw a fine bitch, he had to fuck a fine bitch.

"I'm okay."

"Why you looking so mean?"

"I'm not." she realized that she was unconsciously

frowning, and gave him a grin.

"That's much better. You got a pretty smile."

"Thanks."

"What are you doing back here?"

"I'm with my girl." she gestured towards Toya, who was now engaged in a conversation with her uncle.

"Oh, you talking about Greg's sister."

"Yeah." she nodded.

"I didn't know that yall run together."

"Come on, man!" some man yelled as he honked his horn at Tino's truck.

"You better get out of these people's way." Falen warned.

"I know that his bitch ass aint blowing at us?!" Joe barked as he hopped out of the truck, and stomped over to the car behind them. "If you in so much of a hurry then back your bitch ass up, and go another way!"

The driver realized who he was dealing with, and immediately placed his car in reverse.

"How old are you lil mama?" Tino asked, never bothering to acknowledge the ruckus behind him.

Falen had to shake her head at his laid back style. "I'm nineteen."

"That's old enough." he eyed her hungrily.

"What yall talking about?" Joe interrupted, as he climbed back in the truck.

"Shit." Tino replied.

At the corner of Falen's eye she could see a female approaching them. She turned to see Janah.

"What's up, T?" she asked as she swayed up to the driver's side of the truck, totally preventing any further communication between Tino and Falen.

Tino frowned. "What's up, my nigga? I aint trying to be rude, but I was trying to talk to lil mama."

"Oh, well let me move out yall way." Janah

mumbled, embarrassed as hell.

"Yeah, I'll holla at you later." Tino dismissed her, as she walked away. He then opened his door and stepped out.

Falen had never noticed just how tall Tino was. He was at least 6'6, with a slender but cut build. His tapered fade was freshly lined up and exhibited an ocean of waves. He had a neatly trimmed goatee, thick eyebrows, and long full lashes. His eyes were light brown and he shared a bowlegged stance like her. He was rocking the hell out of a white tee and blue jean Armani shorts, with some crisp white Forces. The piece and chain around his neck was damn near blinding.

"Can I get a hug?" he asked her, with lust-filled eyes. From where he was standing she could smell his cologne.

"I guess." she shrugged, nervously.

Tino lifted her small frame off her feet, as he took her into his arms. He then grabbed a handful of ass. Toya couldn't believe her eyes, as her best friend got felt up by the most wanted nigga in the hood.

"Your ass is light." he chucked as he released her. All eyes were on them.

Falen couldn't contain the smile that invaded her face.

"Look, I gotta go, but let me give you my number." he turned to Joe. "Say main, pass me a pen and a piece of paper."

"Oh it's like that, Falen? You gon give my kinfolk some play when I been trying to get at you?" Joe teased, even though deep down he was dead serious.

"It aint like that." she giggled.

"Anyways, nigga pass me the paper and shit." Tino interrupted, becoming annoyed for some reason.

"Here." Joe tossed him the pen and paper.

Tino jotted down his number, and then placed it in

her hand. "You make sure that you call a nigga."

"Okay." she nodded, as her heart fluttered.

Falen stood and watched as Tino hopped back into his truck, and he and Joe drove off. She couldn't believe that he tried to talk to her. Falen Bright didn't get that kind of attention from men of Tino's caliber. Did the jeans do that much for her?

"Bitch, you did *that*." Toya laughed, as she came over and hugged her neck.

"Get off me." Falen giggled.

"Falen be pulling them niggas, boy." Toya teased. "So, what was my sister over here saying to Tino?"

"Nothing really. She spoke to him, and he told her that we were holding a conversation."

"Oh, yeah? Now you know that her black ass gon be hating."

"Aint nobody thinking about Janah."

As the two friends made their way back across the street several guys continued to holler. They both ignored all the cat calls and continued to walk. Once they made it to the section of the apartments where Toya lived they found Janah and Crystal sitting on the porch.

"Look at these busted bitches." Toya said so that only Falen could hear her.

"You stupid." Falen laughed.

Crystal took one look at her sister in those jeans and said, "I see we're wearing other people's shit now. Aint those your jeans, Janah?"

"No, those are Falen's jeans. I gave them to her." Toya spoke up.

Janah rolled her eyes. "*Crystal,* I could have sworn that you asked me a question, but nah, those aint my jeans. You know I don't wear Roca Wear."

"Oh, don't try to act like you above somebody. If you didn't steal you wouldn't even be able to afford Roca

Wear or anything else for that matter." Toya read Janah.

"Okay, get embarrassed out here." Janah warned. She too was mean with those hands and Toya knew that.

"Whatever, come on, Falen. Let's go in the house. It's too much hating going on out here." Toya said as the stepped inside the apartment.

Falen closed the door behind them and they headed up the stairs. They had to pass Greg up to get to Toya's room.

"What's up, Falen? You looking good today." Greg smiled.

"Oh, hey, boy." Falen spoke back.

"Damn, is Falen the only person you see, nigga?" Toya teased.

"Oh, what's good, baby sis?"

"Nothing, big head." Toya laughed, as she and Falen walked inside her bedroom.

"I am so tired of our hating ass sisters." Toya vented, as she collapsed on top of her bed.

Toya and Janah were sisters that couldn't stand each other. Janah was twenty-one and two years older than Toya. They were like night and day. Toya was slim, tall, and light skinned, while Janah was an average height with dark skin. Janah secretly resented her younger sister, because of her light skin complexion. It was clear that they had different fathers and people always referred to Toya as the pretty one. She was simply misguided by the people around her. It seemed to her that most people felt that lighter was better, especially the men. Her dark skin complexion was an insecurity for her that she seldom talked about. However, the resentment she carried for her sister became more evident, as they became older. So, Janah tried to work extra hard to outdo her sister. She'd get her hair fixed once a week and stay decked out in the latest fashions. She'd do anything to get the dough to stunt on her sister. It was a known fact that Janah would sneak off with older men to go on what she liked to call a date. She'd pay any price to outshine Toya, and those designer threads provided the perfect camouflage to hide the battered little girl she was deep down inside.

"Yeah, I might end up having to hurt one of those bitches." Falen sighed.

"You should've seen the look on Janah's face when Tino hugged you. That shit was priceless." Toya laughed uncontrollably.

Falen found herself laughing as well.

"Do you think that I should call him?"

"Does a bear shit in the woods and wipes his ass with a fluffy white rabbit?"

Falen's head fell back with laughter. "You stupid."

"So, that slut was actually hugging him?" Crystal asked Janah.

"Yeah. She was practically throwing herself on him. He looked like he wanted to push her ass off of him." Janah lied. She couldn't believe that Falen's little dusty ass was hollering at Tino.

"You see, bitch, that's why I put her ass out. She is not to be trusted. She just heard you talking about him the other day, but that didn't stop her from trying to flirt with him. You need to tell your mama to put her ass out."

"Oh, trust me, I will be having a talk with Gloria. Toya got my mama blinded, you know, trying to make her feel sorry for Falen."

"Yeah, let Ms. Gloria know that my sister is a dirty bitch."

"I will."

"And did you see how tight those jeans were? That bitch gon fuck around and catch a yeast infection." Crystal cringed.

"Bitch, did I? You know those pants are good and pissy." Janah added.

"What hoe yall hating on now?" Greg asked as he stepped out on the porch.

Crystal suddenly became nervous. She always had a major crush on Greg, but he never seemed to notice.

"Don't worry about all that. But say, bro, I might have a lick for you." Janah whispered.

"Oh, yeah?" Greg nodded, as he caressed his chin hairs. His younger sister would always come to him when she'd find a new sucker that he and his boys could rob.

"Where the nigga from?" Greg asked.

Before Janah could reply Toya and Falen stepped out on to the porch, and then on to the sidewalk.

"Where yall going?" Greg asked them, as he undressed Falen with his eyes.

"Damn, you nosy." Falen shook her head.

"To the store." Toya told him.

"That's all your big head ass had to say." Greg shouted to Falen's retreating back. He turned to Crystal. "Man, your sister got a *fat* ass"

"Greg take your bitch ass on. Don't nobody wanna hear that shit." Janah snapped.

"Quit hating. If Falen dressed like that more often, I guarantee you that all the niggas would try to be down." Greg went on.

"Including you, huh?" Crystal asked, although she didn't want an answer.

"Hell, yeah. She look good in whatever she wear. Her ass is just mean. She never did like me like that." Greg admitted, crushing Crystal's spirit.

Falen and Toya were enjoying the night's fresh air, as they hung out on Toya's front porch. There were still plenty of people outside. Both girls were feeling good, having popped two handle bars each.

"I believe I can fly. I can't believe I'm this damn high." Falen sang.

Toya loved to see her friend fucked up. The drugs brought out her animated side. Someone was bumping the hell out of R. Kelly's *Feeling on Your Booty* and Falen was riding the beat. Her moves were hypnotizing and caught plenty of spectators' attention.

"Bitch, are you sure that you've only had sex once in your life?"

"Put my life on it and hope to die. Stick a thousand needles in my eye." Falen slurred, as she continued to dance on the sidewalk.

"Sexy, I thought that you was gon call a nigga." a voice called out.

Falen glanced to her right and saw Tino approaching them. The pills had her loose as a goose, so there was no nervousness.

"I was getting around to it." she said with her hands on her hips.

"You aint moving quick enough for me." Tino whispered, as he moved into her personal space. He was expecting for her to back away, but to his surprise she stood her ground.

"Uh, don't you think that you need to back up?"

"Make me." he said just above a whisper.

All the chicken heads outside were green with envy. They all wanted Tino and there he was choosing a bitch that couldn't even dress. Usually, Tino was too laid back to even pursue a woman, so what he was doing at that very moment was out of character for him. He just couldn't help himself. Falen was one of the most natural beautiful chicks that he'd ever seen. Her long curly mane gave her an exotic appeal. Her light brown eyes drew him in. Falen just had this crazy sex appeal that left him curious. He wanted to know her in a *deep* way. Then the fact that he was wasted probably played a part in it as well.

"Tino, move." Falen whined, never moving an inch.

"No, tell me why you didn't call."

"Cause I'll call when I feel like it."

"You know what, I got your little ass." Tino retorted as he swept her off her feet.

"Put me down!" Falen screamed as she kicked her legs.

Just then, Janah walked on the scene. She couldn't believe her eyes. Tino was a get money nigga who rarely displayed a smile. He was known to be ruthless in the streets, but was now playing around with Falen as if she was a long lost love.

"Tino, put me down!" Falen screamed. She was laughing so hard that tears were falling from her eyes. No man had ever made her smile like that. Not even Booby.

Finally, Tino placed Falen back on her feet. He then slapped her on the ass.

"Now, maybe you'll have some act right."

"Uh, Toya did you smell that?" Janah asked out of nowhere.

"Smell what?" Toya asked confused.

"When he was swinging Falen around, something was smelling like fish."

That comment stopped Falen dead in her tracks. "What did you say?"

"I *said* that your stanky pussy smells like fish!" Janah blasted for everyone to hear.

"Say, lil mama that was uncalled for." Tino tried to wave Janah off.

"*Lil Mama*? My name wasn't *Lil Mama* the other

night!" Janah fumed.

"I didn't need to know your name to get my dick sucked." Tino lashed.

"Fuck you! You's a hoe ass nigga anyways. Fucking with trash like her says a lot about you."

"Trash? So, I'm trash, Janah? Who was the one pregnant by their step daddy? Who's the bitch that had to steal everything that she owns? Who's selling their pussy for a fresh hairdo? Bitch, you better watch your mouth!" Falen barked. She was beyond fired up.

"Falen, don't entertain that shit." Tino attempted to cool the situation.

"Yeah, you better tell that homeless bitch something! Cause I'm this close to sliding the bitch." Janah shouted, drawing even more attention.

Falen had heard enough. She was tired of ignoring Janah's blatant disrespect. She was tired of the bitch underestimating her, period. So, she kicked off her slides and ran up on her. There was nothing feminine about the way Falen fought. She leaned in and gave Janah a mean slug that dazed her.

"Oh shit! A fight!" some young boy yelled. With that everybody ran to catch the action.

Joe had told Tino all about Falen and how she got down, still he was amazed at how she was handling Janah. He'd witnessed Janah whip a few bitches, so he thought that she'd win that fight with little effort.

Falen was throwing blow after blow, and Janah was struggling to get one in. She became desperate and started pulling Falen's hair.

"Bitch, let my hair go!" Falen gritted as she laid into her.

Since, Janah refused to release Falen's hair she shoved her head down, as it came crashing into her knee.

"She's fucking Janah up!" Ms. Brown shrieked.

"Okay, okay. That's enough, little mama." Tino said as he pulled Falen off of Janah.

Toya stood there with a grin on her face. She was glad that somebody had finally whipped her sister. She just never imagined that it would take her best friend to get the job done.

Janah was beyond embarrassed, as she made her way inside their apartment. Their mama Gloria had witnessed the entire fight. She knew that her daughter was at fault, but blood was thicker than water. So, that's why she didn't attempt to stop Janah, as she threw Falen's clothes out on the sidewalk.

"Bitch, find somewhere else to stay!" Janah yelled.

"Mama, I know that you aint gon let her do this?!" Toya screamed.

"Well, Toya what do you want me to do? It's either Falen or your sister, because they both can't stay here together." Gloria tried to explain.

"Fuck that stupid bitch! Let one of her tricks take her in." Toya snapped.

"Lil Mama, don't talk to your mama like that." Tino said to Toya. "Falen, get your stuff. I can take you wherever you need to go."

"Okay." Falen nodded as she gathered her things. What other choice did she have?

Chapter 3

The Big Man's Attention

"So, Ms. Falen where do I need to take you?" Tino asked as they sat in his Escalade.

She didn't know what to say. How could she tell him that she had nowhere to go?

"Hello. Earth to Falen." he waved his hand.

"Oh, um I really don't know." she gave him a nervous smile.

"You don't know what?" he asked confused.

Falen stared out the window, because she didn't want him to see the tears rolling down her face. "I don't have anywhere to go."

He furrowed his brows. "You're joking right?"

She shook her head. "I wish."

"Damn. So, you don't have at least one person in your family that can look out for you?"

"No, I don't have much family. And the family that I do have we aint that close."

"Aint that some shit. What happened to you staying with your sister?"

"She didn't want me there anymore."

"Damn, that's cold blooded."

Tino took a minute to think. He couldn't just leave her out in the cold but at the same time she couldn't go home with him, either.

"I tell you what. I can put you up in a room for a few. Is that cool?" he asked her.

At that moment anything was better than spending a night on the streets. "I'd appreciate anything you can do for me." she broke down and cried her eyes out. She didn't care what he thought of her. It wasn't going to change her circumstances.

"Hey, hey, don't cry. You just need to get your shit together, so that you won't have to live with jealous ass hoes that just want to put you down."

"You right." she agreed as she dried her eyes.

"Is the motel right off 59 and Cavalcade cool?" he asked, as he placed his truck in drive.

"Wherever you take me is fine."

As Tino drove her to the motel, he continued to question her about her family. She gave him the same answers each time. He could tell that Falen and Crystal's problems were surrounded around jealousy. Although, people may not have realized it; he paid attention to many from the hood. He may have never noticed Falen sexually until then, but he had noticed her. Outside of that, he'd done his homework, so he knew exactly who Crystal was. The moment Joe gave him the low he knew the sisters' dilemma. Crystal was a nobody headed nowhere fast. Falen was more like a diamond in the rough, just waiting to be discovered.

Once Tino pulled up at the motel he hopped out and went inside the office. There he paid for a room for two weeks. He walked out with the key card and a bucket of ice.

"Are you hungry?" he asked Falen, as he eased back in the truck.

"A little." she lied, trying not to sound greedy. She was starving and those bars had increased her appetite. Her nerves were beginning to kick in. Tino had this magnetic aura that was very intimidating. His truck was the newest model, he wore the finest clothes, and she really felt like a peasant in his presence.

"Okay, well let's go put your stuff in the room and then go find you something to eat."

Falen sat back and allowed Tino to take over. She felt fully exposed, but was grateful that he didn't make her feel any less. He pulled in front of Hank's, a fish market, and hopped out.

"Come on." He motioned with his head.

Falen slowly followed him. He slowed down so that she could walk ahead of him. He then stepped in front of her to hold the door open for her. Falen thought that he was being the perfect gentlemen, but the truth was he could never get enough of watching that ass pass.

"What you wanna eat?" he asked as they both checked out the handwritten menu.

"Umm…I want some…shrimp."

"That's it?" he asked her.

"And a eggroll."

"That's it?"

"Well…make that two eggrolls…and some oysters." Falen let out, saying fuck it. Hell, she was homeless and he knew it. There was no sense in having pride now. Who knew when she'd have food again?

Tino smiled. "Ay, let me get that fifteen shrimp, ten oysters, and two eggrolls."

"Okay." The old Asian cashier nodded. "You want something to drink?"

Tino glanced at Falen. "You thirsty?"

She nodded.

"Okay, give her a large lemonade."

"Okay." He nodded.

"Are we sharing the food?" Falen asked, thinking that he couldn't be ordering all that food for her.

"Naw." He stroked his waves. "This for you. I just ate."

"Oh." Falen sighed even though she was internally smiling. She couldn't wait to stuff her face.

"Hey, Tino." A chick sitting at a table spoke. She and two other girls were there waiting on their order.

He turned and spotted his baby's mama's cousin, Newnie. She was a local freak that had sucked his dick a few times. "Oh, what's up, New?"

"Shit, you tell me." She said with a raised brow. She recognized Falen's face from the Kelly Courts. She knew that she was just a local hood rat, and wanted to know what the hell she was doing with Tino.

"Gotta eat to live." He rubbed his washboard stomach.

"I know that's right." She grinned.

"Girl, what is he doing here with that little young hoe?" Newnie's friend whispered in her ear.

She sucked her teeth. "Shit, that's what I wanna know."

Falen knew that the broads were talking about her. She was used to that and really didn't give a flying fuck. People were always going to talk.

"Maybe that's his cousin or something." Newnie's friend offered.

They all watched as Tino's iced out hand gently rested on the small of Falen's back.

Newnie snarled. "Nah, that little hoe aint his cousin."

As soon as they got Falen's food they hopped back into his truck. The aroma from the seafood was making Falen's mouth water.

Tino could tell that she was hungry. Usually, he hated for people to eat in his car, but that night he decided to make an exception. "You can eat your food. You aint gotta wait."

Falen glanced at him. She wanted more than anything to eat, but was a little embarrassed to eat in front of him. She wanted to pig out. "I can wait." She told him.

"Naw, go ahead cause we still gotta swing by the store.

Falen shrugged it off. She wasn't about to let her stomach growl just to be cute in front of him. She opened her plate and dug in.

Tino pulled out a blunt and fired it up while she ate.

Before either of them knew it they were in Wal-Mart's parking lot. He patiently waited for her to finish eating then, "Come on." He told her as he slid out of the truck.

"What are we doing here?" she asked sounding confused, but still followed him.

"I know you gon need some shit while in that room." He offered as they both walked into the store.

Two hours later Falen felt that she had much more than she needed. He'd bought her things to sleep in, snacks, and anything else he thought she needed.

It was past midnight when they found themselves pulling back into the motel's parking lot. Falen was more than grateful. For at least two weeks she'd have guaranteed food and shelter.

"Thank you so much, Tino." she said, as she leaned over and gave him a warm hug.

"You're welcome, lil mama. Well, let me help you with all these bags." he said as he released her.

Within two minutes, Tino loaded all the bags inside the room. Falen was kind of hoping that it would have taken him longer. She wasn't looking forward to being alone in a motel room.

"Well, that's everything. I'm about to haul ass, mama." he yawned, as he headed towards the door. "Oh, I almost forgot." he smiled, as he reached in his pocket and pulled out a fat knot. He peeled back five hundred dollar bills and one fifty. "Here."

"What's that?" she asked him.

"Just a little change to help you out. You know, like for emergencies. Maybe you can use a little to look for a job."

"Tino, you've done more than enough for me, so I can't take this."

"Girl please, you need this." he said as he took her hand and placed the six bills in it.

"Well, thank you." she spoke, as she gazed into his eyes.

"Okay then, can a nigga get a hug or something, damn."

"Sure." she smiled as she wrapped her arms around his thin midsection.

Tino had to kneel down to place his lips on hers. Falen wasn't expecting that, but she welcomed it. The bars had her feeling bold, as she slithered her tongue into his mouth. He greedily took her in. He then allowed his hands to roam her body freely. She was so soft.

Falen had never wanted a man the way she desired Tino. He'd ignited something inside that she never knew existed. So, she didn't resist, as their bodies fell into the bed. Tino lifted her muscle shirt and unsnapped her bra, with ease. He took her left nipple into his mouth, as she squirmed. With his free hand he undid her jeans, just like the pro he was.

Tino was able to maneuver her tight jeans down to the middle of her thighs. He moved her thong aside and tried to place a finger in her pussy. He couldn't believe that her vagina was able to grip that single finger.

"Damn baby, are you a virgin?"

"No." she moaned. "I had sex once before."

"Just one time?"

"Yeah." she gasped as he tried to stick his finger deeper inside of her.

"OOOH, I gotta get me some of this." he said excitedly. When he took her to the room he had no intentions of sleeping with her, but right then he had to have her. Tino's weakness was tight and wet pussy.

He broke their kiss to take off his shirt. Falen's heart rate sped up, as she realized what was about to happen. She was about to sleep with Tino Wiltz. And man, was Tino fine. He had washboard abs with those fit slits on each side, separating his stomach from his waist. You'd swear he lived in the gym.

"Lift up, baby." he told her as he pulled her jeans completely off. Then her panties right after that.

Tino eyed her bald kitty cat, and swore that it was calling his name. He loved how moist she felt as he played in her wetness.

"You ready for me?" he asked her.

"I guess." she moaned.

"You guess?" he halted "No, I need you to know." he said seriously, as he removed his finger from her pussy.

"Why did you stop?"

"Answer me first."

"Okay, yes."

"Okay what?"

"Okay, I'm ready for you."

Tino nodded, then pushed her legs further apart. He leaned in, kissing her inner thigh. Falen became wetter, as he made her body feel things she'd never felt before. His kisses landed everywhere, but on her secret treasure. She figured he was just trying to arouse her. Surely, *Tino* wasn't going to go down on *her*. Slowly, he inched closer to her second pair of lips. He moved in puckering his lips to her. The feeling sent a chill down her spine. He used his tongue to separate her pussy lips. She clawed his back, as he wrapped his lips around her clit and began sucking the life out of her.

"Oh my God." she moaned. "T..T..Tino!"

Tino enjoyed pleasing her. He liked the innocence that she still possessed. He definitely dug how her body responded to him.

"Tino, what are you doing to me?" she panted, as she lost control of her body. She tried with all her might, but the feeling was too great. Her knees buckled, as she clenched the sheets. That was her first orgasm ever.

Tino lifted his head, then straddled her. His face was still saturated with her juices. He eased his tongue into her mouth to let her taste herself. Suddenly, Falen had the urge to touch his dick, so she reached down and grabbed his pipe through his jeans. The size made her a little nervous.

Tino rose off her, pulled off his jeans, and then his boxers. His dick sprung up, and waved at her.

Falen's eyes grew two sizes larger. "I don't think that I can take all of that."

"I'll be gentle." he promised, as he straddled her again.

After several kisses he had Falen dizzy, so she didn't realize that he had the head of his piece at her entrance. Finally, he tried to enter her. Her body was rejecting his dick.

"Are you sure that nigga broke you in?"

"I guess he did." she let out, sounding similar to a five year old girl. She wasn't expecting for it to hurt so badly. Booby felt like a pinch in comparison.

"Did you bleed?"

"Not that I know of." she gasped. "Oww. Take your time."

"I got you, just relax." he whispered, as he placed both hands under her arms, then grabbed her shoulders. He then gave her a hard thrust.

"Oww!" she cried out.

She screamed so loud that if he hadn't gotten completely inside he would've just stopped. "You screaming like a nigga killing you."

"You are, *nigga.*"

"I got you, lil mama. Just let me get in this right. I promise you'll enjoy it." he stroked her.

Tino was trying desperately to hold back. He didn't care what Falen *thought*. He knew virgin's pussy when he felt it. His dick had found itself a home. He couldn't contain himself. He hungrily took her left breast into his mouth, never missing a stroke.

"Umm." Falen moaned as her eyes rolled into the back of her head, while attempting to ignore the pain.

"Cum with me, Falen." he urged, as he gazed into her eyes. "Cum for daddy."

She was experiencing pain and pleasure all at the same time. Falen didn't think that another climax was possible, yet five strokes later she screamed, "Oh God, Tino. I'm cumming!"

"Yeah, that's right, cum on this dick." he growled, as he pumped harder.

Falen was so excited that she began working her hips. "Uh, you fucking me back? Daddy likes that. Fuck that dick."

Tino tried to hang in but when she starting working that kitty on him he couldn't take it. Before he could stop himself, he released everything he had inside of her. Minutes later, they were both passed out, while he was still knee deep inside of her.

Tino slowly opened his eyes. To his surprise he was face to face with her. He then realized that he was still in a motel room, lying between Falen's thighs. After catching his bearings he pulled himself out of her warmth, and noticed the red substance on his dick. It was her blood. He knew that she must have been tapped, when he felt himself break her hymen.

For a few seconds he stood above her, taking in her beauty. Looking at her never grew old. She was the shit, and he could tell that she didn't even know it.

Her body had so many dips and curves. She was definitely model status...for *King* Magazine.

He looked at his watch, and saw that he'd slept

through the night. He knew there'd be drama when he arrived home.

"Tight pussy will do that to a nigga." he mumbled to himself, as he tipped into the bathroom.

He was about to take a quick shower then head out, until he thought about it. "I might as well get a nut for the road."

"Falen!" he called out.

"Yeah." she answered sleepily.

"Come here."

Falen drug herself out the bed. "Yeah, what's up?" she asked as she stood in the doorway of the bathroom.

"Can you take a shower with me, before I go?"

"I guess." she blushed.

"You guess? That's the least you can do after you bled on my dick." he joked, looking down at his piece.

"No I didn't." she shook her head.

"Yes you did. Look." he said as he wagged his long instrument at her.

"Damn, that's my shit?" she asked in shock.

"Yeah, but don't worry. That's normal." he reassured her. "Now climb your ass in this shower."

She didn't hesitate to hop in. He made her feel so comfortable that she wrapped her arms around his neck and gave him a long kiss.

"Umm." he indulged. He wasn't much of a kisser, but it was just something about Falen. "Your lips are so soft." he whispered.

"Yours too." she smiled.

They were wrapped into each other and time became lost. Before Tino knew it he'd stayed another two hours. Falen may have been inexperienced, but that pussy was still the shit. The fact that she hadn't been around made him feel comfortable doing whatever he wanted; without the fear of catching anything. So, he worked her and slowly but surely she worked him as well.

The shower was no longer producing hot water, but they kept it steamy. They grunted and groaned, without realizing that the water had turned cold. Tino was showing Falen things that she'd only heard about. She realized that she had so much to learn. After stretching her walls out he finally decided to dress and leave. Although, she was satisfied, Falen hated to see him walk out the door.

"Falen, I don't care what you say. You had to fuck that nigga for him to do all of that shit for you." Booby seethed.

He'd been in a bitchy mood since Falen told him that Tino helped her out. She was trying to figure out why he had an attitude. It wasn't like they were a couple. So what if she did fuck Tino?

"Look, let's just change the subject, okay."

"No, let's talk about this. I think that you should go back to Crystal's, because if you continue to depend on that nigga he'll expect something in return."

Falen rolled her eyes. "Booby, look at me. I am not going back to Crystal for any kind of help. She hates me. It's sad but it's true. I'm grown so she doesn't have to deal with me anymore. I'm in this by myself. You can't help me, even if you wanted to. I have to do what I gotta do to make it. If Tino hadn't helped me when he did I would have slept on the streets that night. That's just how crucial the situation was for me."

"Well, let me holla at Crystal. She'll listen to me."

"I don't want to live with her and that nasty attitude she carries around."

"I hear you, Falen. But you are smart so don't limit yourself. You say that you have that room for two weeks, so you need to look for a job every day. Two weeks will fly by and you'll find yourself back in the same predicament."

"I know. I been putting applications in everywhere. Somebody has to call back."

Booby just sat back and observed Falen. Something had changed about her. She couldn't look him in the eyes. She wasn't telling the entire truth. He had a feeling that she was hiding something. That something had to be about Tino.

He took in her physical appearance. She would usually visit him in long shirts or loose jeans. Deep down, he preferred her that way. Those form fitting clothes that she was rocking was drawing too much attention. Every few seconds he'd catch another inmate sneaking a peek at Falen's goods.

There was nothing expensive about Falen's ensemble. She had on some Old Navy purple skinny jeans with a hot pink shirt that was given to her by Toya. It was her body that brought out the outfit. Her curves could make anything look good.

"What's with the new gear?" he asked her.

"Oh this? Toya gave this to me. The jeans were too short for her."

"Don't you think it's a little too tight?"

"I mean, no. You know that I don't usually wear stuff like this, but people keep telling me that I look nicer this way."

"What people?"

"You know people. Toya, Greg, Tasha. You know, people."

"Whatever. You got to be careful, Falen. A lot of niggas know that you haven't experienced much and will try to take advantage of that."

She sucked her teeth. "Well, I aint worried about no niggas so that won't be a problem." Falen was tired of having that same conversation with Booby. It seemed that his only concern was who she's talking to.

"James, visit's over." the C.O. told Booby.

"Well, okay I'll see you later." she smiled, glad that the awkward visit was over. She stood and proceeded to leave.

"Wait." he said as he grabbed her hand. He pulled her closer and gave her a long kiss.

"So, Falen are you going to tell your *best* friend where you've been staying?" Toya badgered, as she braided Falen's hair on Ms. Brown's porch.

"I told you. Down the street."

"Where bitch?" Toya popped her with the comb. "And with who?"

"Ouch, bitch. That hurt." Falen whined, as she rubbed her shoulder.

"Well, you better tell me, before I pop your ass again." Toya threatened.

"Okay, damn. I got a room. It's paid up for two weeks."

"Tino paid for that?"

"Yep."

"What else did he pay for?" Toya asked with a raised brow.

"He just bought me some food, stuff to sleep in, and some hair products."

"What you mean, he just? He sure did do a lot."

"Yeah, he did." Falen shrugged her shoulders.

Toya pulled her hair, and made her look up at her.

"Bitch, did you fuck Tino?"

"Girl, let my hair go."

"No. Tell me what happened. You know that we don't keep secrets. I'm still pissed that you just told me about you and Booby."

"Toya, let my hair go."

"No!"

"Okay, okay." Falen took a deep breath. "We did it."

"Are you serious?"

"Yeah."

Toya released her hair. "So, how was it?"

"Hmm, it was good." she smiled as she patted her hair to see if it was still rooted to her scalp.

Toya did a little dance in her seat. "Oh shit, Falen's in the big leagues now."

"Girl, please. I mean, I had fun but I aint trying to read too deep into that. I'm sure he gets pussy all the time, so what makes me special?"

"Falen, I'm not telling you that the nigga is trying to marry you tomorrow, but damn, give yourself some sort of credit. He went after you. How many bitches around here can actually say that?"

"I feel you, but I'm not about to play myself. Why get my hopes up high for a man that aint gon ever be mines? I think that he has a girlfriend somewhere."

"He probably does, but what does that have to do with you?"

"Everything. I aint trying to be his little play thing. I takes shit more serious than that. What I gave him was special, and I can't just pretend that it was no big deal."

"You act as if it was your first time."

"Shit, maybe it was. When Booby tried to penetrate me it was hurting so bad that I kept stopping him. He never got completely inside of me."

"No shit? So, Tino popped your cherry?"

"I guess, if that's what you want to call it."

"So, have you called him today?" Toya wanted to know.

"No, cause I aint trying to be a bug-a-boo."

"Falen, your ass is crazy. Let's go call him."

"For what?"

"To say what's up."

"I'll pass. Just finish my hair so that we can burn."

Toya decided to let it go. She knew how stubborn Falen could be. She refused to recognize her own strength and beauty. That was something that life would have to teach her.

Toya asked Falen to tag along, while she visited an old boyfriend. So, they walked to the corner store, because they needed change to catch the bus. As usual, there were niggas hanging out front. Once again, Falen began feeling self-conscious about her clothes. The belly shirt that Toya begged her to wear was a bit bold for her taste.

"Sup, Falen." Wayne spoke.

Falen gave him a quick smile. It was amazing how a wardrobe change affected those niggas.

"Here those niggas come!" shouted Shameka, a local hood rat.

Everyone looked up and saw a gang of dudes, riding up on sports bikes. Leading the pack was Tino. He had a long haired freak, holding on tight as she rode on the back of his bike. Falen's heart dropped down to her stomach.

"Look at that trick he got with him." Toya whispered to Falen.

"Fuck him." Falen rolled her eyes. "Come on, let's get this change." she pouted, as she snatched the store's door open. Toya followed behind her.

"I'm a get me a soda. You want something, Falen?" Toya asked.

Just then the chick that was riding with Tino stepped in the store. She was pretty. She was light skinned, slim, with long hair. The chick was decked out in Ed Hardy and sported Chanel shades on top of her head. Her presence made Falen feel so small.

"I am *so* thirsty." the chick announced to no one in particular as she grabbed two bottles of water.

Toya took a good look at the broad. She decided that she was cute, but her girl had her beat. She just wished that Falen could see that. She could see it in Falen's eyes that she was intimidated by that material girl.

"Falen, do you want something?" Toya asked again.

"Yeah, get me a Hawaiian Punch." Falen said as she headed out the store. She needed some space to think.

As soon as Falen stepped outside Tino spotted her. He hadn't realized that she was there. She was wearing the hell out of those skinny jeans and belly shirt. He had to adjust his dick in his pants after laying eyes on her.

"What's up, Falen?" he spoke.

"Hey." she replied blandly.

He got off his bike and stepped up to her. "That's all you gon say to a nigga?"

"I spoke. What else do you want me to say? I don't want no problems with your woman."

"Oh, so that's why you tripping? That's just a friend." he chuckled.

She didn't see a damn thing funny. "Well, it was nice seeing you again." she told him as she attempted to walk away. He grabbed her hand, preventing her from leaving.

"Where are you going?" he asked as he pulled her closer to him.

"To go get my friend." she snapped.

"Calm down, lil mama. I'm trying to talk to you."

"Okay, I'm listening." she said hurriedly.

"Why didn't you call me today?"

"I didn't know that I should."

"Yeah, you should. Don't be afraid to let a nigga know how you doing. We better than that."

"I didn't know how we were." she shrugged.

"Okay, well now you know." he nodded. He knew that she had an attitude, but it was one that he could work with. "Are you straight?"

"Yeah, I'm good."

"How your pockets looking?"

"I still have all the money you gave me."

"*All* the money?" he asked with a confused look. He just knew that she was going to blow that small amount of cash.

"Yeah, *all* the money." she laughed.

"Did you look for a job on Friday?" he asked. He took her to the room on Thursday, so he wanted to see how serious she was about getting her shit together.

"Yeah, shit I even put an application at the Burger King right by the room."

"That's what's up." he nodded. "But here, I got…" was all he got out before he was interrupted.

"Tino, what the fuck is this?" the chick that rode with him questioned as she and Toya walked out the store.

He turned to Tory then placed his hand up to halt her. "I'm talking." then he refocused on Falen as he dug in his pocket. "I got something for you." he told her as he pulled out a knot and peeled back eight large ones.

Falen couldn't believe that he was doing the game like this. Not only was he blatantly disrespecting his broad, but he was also handing her money in front of a crowd of niggas. Most niggas were too proud to issue out cash in front of the fellows.

"No, I'm good." she told him as she waved the money off.

"Girl, you better take this." he insisted, as he shoved the money in her hand.

"Tino what the fuck?!" the broad yelled.

"Look, mind your business." he said calmly.

"Who is she?"

"None of your business." he shook his head.

"*Tino*, I'm about to burn, okay. I'll holla." Falen announced as she grabbed Toya's hand and they trotted down the street.

Toya was cracking up laughing. "Tino, what the fuck!" she mocked. "Did you see the look on that bitch's face?"

"Yeah, I saw it." Falen grinned. She was floating on cloud nine, because Tino kept it real. He could've played her to the left like so many younger guys would have.

"So, what cha doing with that money?"

"Saving it."

"You aint gon buy yourself nothing?" Toya asked slightly disappointed.

"Toya, I am homeless. I can't depend on Tino or anybody else for that matter. I have to hold on to the money at least until I find a job. Then we can get a place."

"That's what's up." Toya agreed seeing the bigger picture. "At least buy yourself a Cricket cell phone. You need that shit while you're staying in that damn room. In fact, I might start staying there with your ass."

"You're more than welcome to. And I think I will get a phone."

"Yeah bitch, we are going to get out shit together." Toya laughed. "Watch and see."

Chapter 4

The Cost to be the Boss

A week had flown by and Falen was overjoyed. She'd landed a job at Burger King, and she was set to start that day. She was fully prepared. She took one last look at herself in the mirror. She made sure that her uniform was nice and neat. Her hair was pulled up in a ponytail, so that she could wear her BK cap.

She knew that Burger King wasn't a glamorous job, but it would serve as a stepping stone. It would keep her alive, until she found something better. That job meant that she no longer had to worry about sleeping on the streets. She didn't have to worry about going hungry, and she didn't have to rely on a man.

Falen strolled to her new job that was just three blocks away from the motel. She was twenty minutes early but she was so excited that she couldn't sit in that room a minute longer.

As soon as she entered the building the manager spotted her. "Well, well, I see somebody takes their job serious."

"Hello." Falen smiled.

"Hi, Ms. Falen." he spoke back in his flamboyant voice. A blind man could see that he was gay.

"Are you going to show me how to clock in?"

"Yes, ma'am. Right this way." Bill said as he switched over to the time clock.

Just based on her eccentric manager Falen knew that this would be a colorful experience.

Falen's first day on the job was a bit stressful, but she

knew that it was something she could handle. Once she'd gotten off she still had plenty of energy, and decided to head over to Kelly Courts. She could've caught Metro, but she opted to walk down the feta of 59. The walk was only twenty minutes long, and Falen was accustomed to walking.

By the time she reached the complex she had to piss like nobody's business. So, she was speed walking to Toya's. On her way there she saw Joe leaning on his truck. She wanted to speak but couldn't waste time.

"Falen, it's like that?" he opened his arms.

"It's like what?" she stopped, and asked even though she wanted to run like hell.

"Tino got you scared to speak to a nigga?"

"Aw come on, it aint even like that." she shook her head. "In fact, I'll come back out and fuck with you after I take a piss." she promised, as she hurried towards Toya's building.

Joe watched her run all the way to Toya's door. He was glad to see that she'd found a job. He knew how plenty of people treated her but knew that the good hearted ones would always prevail. He also felt that she was looking sexy as hell in that uniform.

Falen knocked hard on Ms. Gloria's front door. She'd called Toya as she walked over so she knew to expect her.

"Who the fuck is knocking like the police?" Janah snapped as she snatched the door open.

"Hey, is Toya here?" Falen said as pleasant as she could muster.

Janah closed the door in her face. Seconds later Toya reopened it. "What's up, bitch? Why didn't you just come in?"

"I didn't want no problems." Falen said as she stepped inside the apartment. "I gotta use it." she said as she made her way to their downstairs bathroom.

"So, how does it feel to have a job?" Toya questioned as Falen remerged from the bathroom.

"Okay. Girl, my manager is this gay man and he keeps me laughing."

"For real? Why didn't you put in an application for me when you did yours?"

"I don't know. That was a spur of the moment type thing. I really just stopped there to buy something to eat and then decided to feel out an application. But I will try to get you in."

"That's what's up." Toya nodded. "I'm going back to the room with you tonight."

Toya had been sleeping at the motel with Falen for the past four days. She'd only gone home because she didn't want to stay there while Falen was at work.

"Okay. And you know that we have to find the time to look for a place to stay sometime this week. I aint trying to give my money to that motel when I could be paying for a permanent spot."

"Cool." Toya nodded. "Falen, I hope that you brought a change of clothes." she laughed.

"Yes, I did." Falen rolled her eyes.

"Well, come on, let's go upstairs so that you can change."

After Falen changed into the metallic black leggings and long tight race back shirt that Toya convinced her to buy, they headed outside. But not before Toya untied her hair, allowing Falen's curly mane to hang free.

"T, you think that you're my personal stylist or something." Falen giggled.

"No, I'm the fashion police." Toya laughed as they walked down the sidewalk. There they saw Joe still leaning on his truck.

"Look at you." he smiled as he saw Falen in her new fit.

"Look at me." Falen replied joking with him.

He licked his lips. "What's up, yall wanna blow one with me?" he asked.

"Hell, yeah." Toya replied.

"Okay, well let's hop in my truck. I aint trying to have too many heads on this shit here."

"You talking like you got some hydro." Falen laughed.

"That's all I smoke." he told her seriously.

With that all three jumped in his ride and rolled the windows up. Joe allowed Toya to fire up the first stick. She took one long drag and felt the effects.

"You look fucked up." Joe teased looking back at her.

"I am." Toya giggled.

"Well, let me hit that shit." Falen said as Toya passed it to her.

Joe sat and watched as Falen took a few drags like a vet. "Falen, you full of surprises. I just knew that you'd be the first to choke."

"What? Nigga, please. I been fucking with 'dro."

"Okay, Ms. Gangstress." he smiled. "Why you sat in the back? You got a nigga feeling like a ole pedophile."

"Who, Toya?" Falen asked.

"No, you." Joe uttered as he eyed her. He could already see the effects of her dealing with his cousin. She was developing her own little swag and it had him more than a little curious. Not to mention since Tino had hit her and claimed that he'd broke her in, he'd been getting a hard-on every time he laid eyes on her.

Boom, Boom. They all heard somebody's car beating down the block. "There go my nigga!" Joe laughed as he honked his horn at the Escalade.

"Oh, that's Tino." Toya giggled as she looked back at the truck.

The mention of his name made Falen's heart skip a beat. She hadn't talked to him since the day he gave her that money, but she thought about him constantly.

Tino parked a few spaces over and hopped out of his truck and strolled over to the driver's window. "Nigga, roll down the window."

"Get in, I'm smoking." Joe told him through the dark glass.

Tino walked around to the passenger's side and slid in. He then took a look at the backseat. Immediately, his antenna went up. "I didn't know that you had people in here with you."

"Yeah, they getting fucked up with me." Joe laughed.

"Falen, you get high?" Tino asked.

"Sometimes." she replied.

"Sometimes, huh?" he gave her a strange look. He wasn't exactly comfortable with her and his cousin hanging. He told Joe everything, so he was aware of him and Falen's friendship. Still, he knew Joe had a thing for her. Probably even more once he found out that she was virtually untouched.

"Yeah, sometimes." Falen giggled as she took another hit.

Tino shook his head, but Joe knew his cousin well enough to know that he wasn't digging the scene.

After Joe took a long pull off the 'dro he tried to hand it to Tino. "No, I'm good." he shook his head.

Joe knew that Tino was mad about something because he never passed up hydro. The only person that seemed to be oblivious to his foul mood was Falen. She kept on giggling despite the fact that Toya elbowed her a few times.

"He he, he." Tino mocked. "What's so funny, Falen?" he snapped.

This completely caught Falen off guard. She'd never seen Tino let anything or anyone affect him. He was always Mr. Calm Cool and Collected.

"W…what are you talking about?" she stuttered.

Tino started to go off on her ass right then and there, but decided to keep others out his business. "Get out and let me holla at you." he told her as he got out the truck.

Falen paused for a second and gave Toya a confused look. "Why is he tripping?" she asked.

"I don't know. Go find out." Toya shrugged.

Just then Tino snatched the door near Falen open. "Get out." he told her.

"Okay." she replied as she stepped down from the truck and followed him.

Joe and Toya just sat in silence for a few seconds before Joe chuckled, "She got that nigga hotter than a bitch." as he choked on the smoke.

"You aint never lied." Toya giggled.

Tino and Falen sat in his truck while he stared her down. He had to think for a minute before finally speaking.

"What you doing aint a good look." he finally told her.

"What are you talking about?"

"Play crazy. I'm talking about the way you conducting yourself. Now, if I didn't care I wouldn't even be discussing this with you. If you want to get fucked up you should do it in private around people you can trust. You was getting higher than Cootie Brown out here. I know that eventually you was gon end up back on foot out here. That aint cool. For one it takes you off your note and some motherfucka can take advantage of that. And it's un-lady like to allow people to see you in that state."

"Okay, I get that. But why didn't you just say that? There was no need for you to get mad."

"I aint mad." he lied. "But that aint my only

problem, either. How the fuck did you end up sitting in Joe's truck?"

"He asked us if we wanted to smoke with him."

"Have he ever asked you that before?"

Falen thought about it for a second. "No, this was his first time."

"Well, look I like you and I think you know that. I know that you're going through some changes right now and I'm willing to help you. I aint tripping on being here for you, but you have to respect me."

"I do respect you." she told him.

"No, what I mean by that is that I won't feel comfortable with you *talking* to other men."

"What you mean by *talking*?" she asked him searching for clarity.

"For one, I aint cool with you fraternizing with any of these Kelly Court niggas. If you need anything just call me. Shit, don't even take anything from my cousin. The same rule applies to him."

"So, you're saying that you don't want me to even talk to them?"

"I mean, is there a reason that you should?"

Falen shook her head no, although her wheels were still spinning.

"Good, I'm glad that we got this understood." Tino smiled. He pulled out a wad of cash and began counting. "Here." he said as he handed her five hundred dollars.

"Thank you." she said as she took the money and placed it in her bra.

"You know that aint a safe place to keep your dough. You gon end up losing that shit."

"When I go get my purse out Toya's crib I'll put it in there."

"You shouldn't leave your purse in nobody's house. Especially not Toya's. I don't think that she would get you, but there are plenty of other people in that bitch that would."

"I know." she agreed.

"So, what you been doing with your money?" he asked her.

"Saving it."

"That's what's up. I heard that you found a job."

"Yeah." she smiled.

"That's cool. It only took you a week. A go getta. I likes that, but you should try to find yourself a real spot. You got enough cash."

"I was already making plans. Me and Toya are going to try to find a place before the week is over."

"You and Toya, huh?" he rubbed his goatee. "That's cool. You don't need to live all by yourself. She's cool peoples."

"I know." Falen nodded.

Tino started eyeing her. She was looking good enough to eat. "What time do you have to be to work tomorrow?"

"At two, why?"

"Okay, cause you gon spend the night with me at my spot." he told her as he started up his engine.

"Well, let me go get my stuff."

"Alright. I'll be waiting right here." he said as she hopped out his ride.

Toya was waiting on the sidewalk with her hands planted on her hips.

"About time, bitch." she rolled her eyes at Falen.

"Shut up. Walk with me so that I can grab my bag." she said as she walked towards Toya's building.

"What, he's about to take us to the room?" Toya questioned.

"No, he can drop you off there if you'd like."

Toya stopped walking. "So, where are you going?"

"With him."

"Get it bitch!" Toya said excited for her girl.

"Shut up." Falen blushed.

"So, what was yall talking about?" Toya pried.

"Girl, the nigga was going on about how I shouldn't get high in the streets. But then he got to what he was really tripping on."

"And?" Toya wanted to know.

"He told me to stop *talking* to the niggas around here. Including Joe."

"You lying? He tripping like that?"

"Yeah. So what should I do?" Falen asked.

"Did he just break you off?"

"Yeah, but what does that have to do with anything?"

"Shit, he's paying the cost to be the boss."

"Whatever." Falen rolled her eyes. "He might start trying to tell me what to do, you know. I aint trying to open the doors to bullshit. He talks to whoever he wants to, so how the hell can he expect for me to do something that he aint willing to do?"

"He's a man. That's how they are. Welcome to the real world." Toya laughed.

"I guess." Falen sighed.

"And he sure can give me a ride to the room. I can have company while he's digging in your guts."

Falen followed Tino into his apartment. She glanced around and was impressed. It was definitely worlds apart from the motel she slept at in Fifth Ward. He had plush couches and a television that damn near covered the entire wall.

"Take a seat, baby." Tino said as he headed for his bedroom.

Falen sat down on the couch and just continued to scope out how Tino was living. The apartment was spotless and barely looked lived in. She figured that he either had someone keeping it up for him or that was just one of the many spots he had.

"Why you sitting there clutching your purse and shit? Sit back and relax, man. You here with me right now." Tino said once he re-entered the living room with some basketball shorts on and no shirt.

"Oh, okay." Falen said in a daze as she stared at his six packs.

Tino flopped down right next to her. He took the time to really look at her. She was one of the purest beauties he'd ever seen. He couldn't get past that. She was all natural and surprisingly breathtaking. He could tell that Falen was clueless to the exquisiteness she possessed.

"Relax, baby." He whispered as he leaned in for a kiss. Her lips were nice and soft. "Put this down." He said as he slid her purse out of her hands and placed it on the coffee table.

Although, Falen had physically been with him before she found it difficult to contain her nerves. Tino could sense this as she fidgeted around.

"What's wrong?" he asked her.

"Nothing." She sighed.

"Don't lie to me, Falen. You scared of me?"

She took a deep breath. "A little."

"Why?"

"Cause, Tino, you make me feel like…you make me feel funny."

"Funny?" he repeated with a raised brow.

"Yeah. I aint never even had a real boyfriend before and here you are. All the girls in Kelly Courts would kill me if they knew that I was here with you. I'm not really with all that." She shook her head.

"With all what?"

"The drama. The flash. The hype, you know?"

"The hype?" Tino chuckled. "So, what you trying to say, lil mama?"

"You know what I mean." She giggled. "All the girls feinding over you because they think you're God or some shit."

Tino got serious. "No, I'm far from thinking that I'm God."

"No, I never said that you think that way. I'm talking about how the girls jockey you."

"Oh, so you don't like all the attention that I draw?"

"Exactly."

"But what does that have to do with you being nervous?"

"Cause, I'm finding myself digging you on a level that I'm not supposed to."

"Who said that it's a certain level that you're supposed to dig me?" he asked as he wrapped his arm around her.

"I did. I mean, I'm not crazy. I know that you aint trying to be with me for real, but my silly ass still wants you."

"That's not true." He whispered as he kissed her. "If I wasn't feeling you, we wouldn't be here right now."

Falen slightly shoved him away. "But for how long?"

"For however long you willing to stay down with a nigga." He growled as he climbed on top of her.

"But Tino." Falen panted as she felt him pull her pants down. "Wait, Tino." She whined as he pulled her shirt over her head.

"Stop that." He whispered as he unsnapped her bra and pulled it off of her.

She arched her back as he slithered his tongue across

her nipples. "Umm." She moaned.

He easily slid his hand inside her panties and ran his finger between the lips, stroking her clit. "You like that?" he asked her.

"Umm hmm." She purred.

"You gonna be a good, girl?"

"Umm hmm."

"Well, hop on this dick like a good girl should." He whispered as he pulled his shorts and boxers down. His piece sprang into action.

Falen sat looking at his dick, almost swearing that it was bigger than the last time she'd seen it.

Tino sat back stroking himself. "Come on, baby. Hop on it." He said as he pulled her onto his lap.

She slowly stroked her clit on his tool. "Why you teasing me?" he asked her as he gazed into her eyes.

She decided not to answer, but lifted slightly so that he could slide inside of her. They both shuttered as their bodies met. Falen took her time sliding up and down his dick as Tino gripped her ass.

"That's what I'm talking about." He moaned as he slapped her ass cheek. "Ride that dick."

"Uh, this feels so good." She panted.

"It feels good, huh? Well, show me what this pussy can do." He gritted as he spread her legs wider and dug in deeper.

"Oww."

"Can you feel that?" Tino asked as he softly bit her bottom lip. "Huh?" he asked as he drilled her making her ass cheeks bounce harder and harder.

"Uhhhh." She moaned as he took a nipple into his mouth. "This is so good."

"Oh yeah? How good, baby?"

"This good." She muttered as she sat completely down on his dick and wound her hips into him.

"Oh, yeah. That's what I'm talking about." He moaned. Just then Falen picked up the pace and was bouncing faster than he could keep up. "Wait, mama. Hold up." He told her.

She ignored him and continued to do her thing. She didn't know until that very moment what she'd been denying herself. Having sex was one of the best feelings on this earth. She loved every inch of meat that Tino slid inside of her.

"Got damn, girl." He gritted. "You trying to put it on a nigga, huh...shit I'm about to blast if you don't quit it." He warned her.

"Well, do what you gotta do then."

Tino gripped her waist and forced her to remain still as he let loose inside of her. "Aw, shit." He moaned. "I told you, didn't I?"

"Yeah you did." She giggled right before she leaned in for a kiss. His tongue was damn near down her throat when his cell phone went off.

"Hold up, baby. Let me get that." He said as he pulled away from their kiss. He reached over and grabbed his cell all while never breaking their connection.

"Hello."

"Where the fuck you at?!" a female's voice shouted over the phone so loudly that Falen could hear her clearly.

"Man, I'm around. What's good?"

"Why are these bitches calling me and saying that they spotted you leaving with some bitch from The Bottoms?"

"What? Man, I don't know what the fuck you talking about." Tino lied and Falen gave him a look as if he'd lost his mind. She attempted to lift up off of him, but he pulled her back down. "Chill out." He told her.

"Who the fuck are you talking to?!"

"Don't worry about that. What did I tell you about

calling me with that he say she say bullshit?"

"And what did I tell you about disrespecting me in these streets?"

"Girl, watch out. Is that the only reason you called me?"

"Pretty much."

"Well, where my daughter at while you sitting your ass around gossiping?"

"She's at your mama house."

"She at my mama's, huh? Well, let me call over there and check on her."

"Oh, so now you concerned about Tia? You can't bullshit me, Tino. Where are you?"

"I'm handling my business. That's all you need to know."

"Well, maybe I need to go handle some *business* too."

"Ha ha ha." He piped sarcastically. "You do that." He said before hanging up his phone.

Once again Falen tried lifting off of his dick. "What you doing?" he asked as he held her waist, preventing her from getting up.

"Let me go." She snapped as she tried to pry his hands off of her.

"What's your problem, man?"

"Nothing. Just let me go."

"You mad at me?" he asked as he hardened inside of her.

"What are you doing, Tino?" she questioned as he started long stroking her.

"What? You don't like how that feel?" he asked her as he grinded his hips into her.

"I don't like what you're doing." She moaned as her eyes rolled in the back of her head.

"That's right, take this dick." He whispered. "I'm

here with you right now. That's all that matters."

Falen was feeling so good to Tino that he couldn't stop himself from standing up with her wrapped around his waist. He found the nearest wall and rested her body against it. Then slammed himself deep inside of her.

"Ow!" she howled. "Umm."

"Yeah. That's what I'm talking about." He moaned as she rolled her hips.

"Oh Tino!" she shouted as he pumped harder. "Oh my God!"

"What are you doing to me?" she asked him.

"I'm making sure that you know that no other nigga can make you feel like this."

She was out of breath. "Tell me something that I don't know."

Chapter 5

Hard times Call for Drastic Measures

"Do you like this one?"

"Not really."

"Dang Tino, you don't seem to like anything that I pick up." Falen whined.

"Man, I told you to get the best of the best. This shit that you picking up is the worse of the worse, girl."

"What's wrong with this Baby Phat outfit?" she asked confused.

"It's *Baby Phat*." He chuckled.

Falen gave him a look. "You know what, fuck you." She snapped with her hands on her hips.

"You mad now?" he asked as he grabbed her by the waist.

"Move." She pouted as she slightly shoved him.

"Don't be like that." He whispered as he knelt down to kiss her.

Falen had Tino feeling like a love sick teenaged boy as he walked through the mall with her. She was rocking the hell out of the Bebe dress he'd bought her. They'd just left the salon where she'd gotten her hair straightened and was now tearing down the stores. Any chick on his arm had to dress to kill and nothing less. Falen had the beauty so now she just needed the style.

He was introducing her to high fashion verses urban wear. He was picking out things that she hadn't even heard of before. He quickly found that anything looked good on Falen's body. Money wasn't a thing, so they racked up a new wardrobe for her in Saks Fifth Avenue.

"Ay, you don't like this dress right here?" he questioned as he held up a Valentino original.

She stepped closer and took it from him. "It's cute

but I never heard of this designer."

He gave her a grin as he shook his head. "Come on. Go try it on." He pulled her to the fitting rooms. The attendant had just stepped away, so he stepped into a room with her.

"You can't be in here." She whispered nervously.

"Why I can't?" he asked as he backed her against the mirror.

"Tino..." she whined as he smothered her mouth. "Umm." She moaned as he kissed her.

He slid his hand underneath her dress and snatched off her thong. Her mouth dropped, enjoying his boldness. He maneuvered his hands between her thighs and cuffed her pussy. His index finger soon found her clit.

"We can't do this here." She continued to whine, knowing that he was going to have his way with her.

"Is this my pussy?" he asked in between kisses.

"Um hmm."

"Well then, I can do whatever I want, whenever I want."

She obediently nodded.

"Now, pull my dick out." He instructed.

She slowly did as she was told. Once his rock hard member was freed she began stroking him. She could feel the pre-cum oozing from the head.

"Yeah, jack that dick off." He whispered.

She continued to stroke him, while he lifted her dress above her perky breasts. He lifted her bra, exposing her. He then leaned his head down and lightly flicked his tongue over her nipple.

"Ooh." She whimpered as her head fell back and she quickened the stroke to his dick.

"Damn, that shit feel good." He told her just before lifting her thighs. She wrapped her legs tightly around his waist, as he easily slid inside of her.

She was saturating his dick with her juices and they could both hear her wetness, bouncing off the walls. Her pussy began farting as he leaned her against the mirror, pounding in and out of her. To anyone in earshot, it was obvious that they were having sex. Things had just gotten so intense that neither of them cared about getting caught.

They were both in heat and were quickly losing control. He bounced her up and down his length, as she scratched his back. "I'm about to cum." He grunted.

"Cum." She urged as she bit his bottom lip. "Leave this pussy dripping wet with your hot cum." She squealed, surprising even herself. She had tapped into her inner freak.

"Ugh." He let out as quietly as he could. His dick was jerking as he busted a fat walnut inside of her.

Falen leaned against the wall as he placed her back on her feet. She was still trying to catch her breath. Tino stood back admiring her beauty. Her body looked almost sculptured. Her tight thick thighs were so enticing. He could see his cum dripping down her thighs. He couldn't resist it. He dropped to his knees and licked her dry. She placed her hands on the walls as he caused her body to quiver.

"Uhhh." She bucked as she came all over his face.

"Damn, that pussy taste so sweet." He told her as he stood up. He leaned in for a kiss making sure that she tasted their conjoined juices.

"You are so nasty." She grinned while wiping his mouth, and he pulled her dress down.

"Nasty is a good thing." He told her as he pulled his jeans up.

She helped him buckle his belt before they left the fitting room, leaving the Valentino dress behind.

By now the fitting room attendant was back at her station and looked at them strangely as he pulled her towards the front of the store.

When it was all said and done Falen had bags filled

with Christian Dior, Prada, Alexander McQueen, Chanel, and Gucci. Until that day she hadn't even heard of some of the designers.

Tino knew that he wanted to upgrade her a bit, but even he didn't go with the intentions of spending the kind of money he'd just shelled out. The fact that she didn't ask for much compelled him to give it all. Besides, the pussy was so good, that he didn't mind spending every penny he had in his pocket.

Falen felt like a celebrity as she walked around with Tino. She was quickly picking up on his style. He was kind of compulsive when it came to him and his appearance. Everything had to be perfect. It was crazy because he had such a thuggish swagger with a pretty boy twist.

She also picked up on how all the women damn near broke their necks as they strolled past. Tino was an extremely handsome man and it was obvious that everyone around agreed.

Tino was noticing how all the men were peeping Falen. That ass she was carrying around was irresistible and he was trying to stop himself from developing another woody.

"Oh, Tino they have the musical hula-hoops!" Falen said excitedly, practically jumping up and down as she stood in front of The Disney store.

"What, you want that for your niece, or something?" Tino questioned as he held her hand.

"Umm, no. I want it for myself." She smiled just like a little school girl.

"You serious?"

"Yeah. Come on, let's go get it." She laughed as she pulled him into the store.

"I see that it don't take much to satisfy you." Tino chuckled.

Since he'd been hanging with Falen he felt like a

new man. He didn't have to go out of his way to impress her. She took joy in the simplest things, which he found sexy as hell. Everything just flowed with her. No complications or expectations.

Falen liked to do corny shit like walking through the mall holding hands. She liked feeding ducks in the pond, playfully wrestling Tino to the ground, and playing on the PlayStation with him. Her high spirit did something to Tino, and he saw himself keeping her around for a long while.

"Okay, ma'am so you'd like extra cheese with that?" Falen asked her last customer for the night.

"Yeah." the fat lady replied.

Falen was beyond exhausted. She'd earned every penny of that seven twenty-five an hour. She damn near ran to that time clock. She wanted to do nothing more than fall into bed and go to sleep. She had her fingers crossed that Toya didn't have one of her many male friends over.

As Falen began her walk to the motel room a wave of nausea hit her like a ton of bricks. She tried to hold it back, but everything that she held in her stomach came up. She hurled on the middle of the sidewalk. She was barely out of the Burger King's parking lot and was sick as a dog.

Falen was attempting to wipe her mouth when she saw a black car pull up at the Burger King's menu as if they were about to place an order. The only problem was that it was closed. Falen was about to chalk that up to stupidity on the driver's part, until she saw a guy get out the car and grab a heavy trash bag that was placed in the bushes right behind the menu. The man then hopped back in the car and the driver sped away.

"What the fuck." she mumbled to herself.

Finally, Falen made it to the motel. She had to knock since Toya had the key card.

"Damn, bitch what's wrong with you?" Toya asked when she opened the door and read the expression on Falen's face.

"I don't feel too good." Falen said as she lay in the bed.

"Well, why didn't you call me? We could've given you a ride. You don't need to walk by yourself this late at night."

Falen didn't respond.

Toya's friend Tony was chilling in the chair, but Falen didn't acknowledge him. Toya gave him the eye saying, "It's time to go, nigga."

"Well, I guess that it's time for me to burn out." he said rising from his seat.

"Alright, I'll fuck with you later." Toya said as she walked him to the door.

"Call me." he said as he left.

"I will." she replied before closing the door. "Falen, what's wrong?" she asked as she sat on the edge of the bed.

"I just threw up."

"Awl, poor baby. You ate too much food?"

"No, I haven't eaten anything."

"Well, don't you think that maybe that's the reason you don't feel good? You can't work all day without eating."

"Shut up. It's some shady shit going on at Burger King." Falen said deciding to change the subject.

"What, people are stealing the buns?" Toya laughed.

Falen sat up. "Bitch, I'm serious. I saw this nigga pull up and get a trash bag out the bushes."

"Oh wow. That's some conspiracy shit right there."

"Toya! I'm for real. You had to be there to see what I mean. The niggas was riding clean in a black Lincoln

Town Car. This dude hopped out and grabbed this heavy ass trash bag, then got back in the car. They sped off real quick. If I would have blinked I would have missed the entire thing."

"Maybe it was some money." Toya said even though she still thought that Falen was reading too deep into the situation.

"I don't know what it was, but I would sure like to find out."

Within two days Toya had found a spot around the corner from the motel that cost only three hundred a month. Rent was always dirt cheap in the hood. Fifth Ward was flooded with poor folks so landlords couldn't ask for too much.

Falen was happy to hear that Toya took the initiative to find them somewhere to live. She didn't want to give her money to a motel anymore. She had a little over fifteen hundred bucks put away so they were more than prepared to cop a place.

Falen knew that Toya often had company in the room so she never left her money in there. She would always safely tuck it in her Gucci backpack when she walked to work. Tino had spent nearly two stacks for it, and she always kept it with her. At night she did the same even though Toya begged her to at least call so that she could meet her halfway.

So, Falen strolled to the room like she'd do on any other night. Tino had crossed her mind so she decided to give him a call. After his voicemail picked up for the third time she realized that he wasn't going to pick up.

"Bitch ass nigga can't answer the phone?" she snapped. She hated how he had her going. She knew that they weren't committed but the more time they spent together, the more it felt like he belonged to her. So, it drove her crazy whenever she couldn't reach him. The very way she was feeling was the thing that she'd been trying to avoid. She was so wrapped into her thoughts that she didn't hear someone approaching on a bike until they were right up on her. Before she could react the man snatched her bag clean off her shoulder.

"Hey!" Falen yelled as she chased after the dude.

He was too quick. Within seconds he was down the street, leaving her in the wind.

"Motherfucka!" she cried. "You bitch ass nigga!" she shouted to his back.

Falen just stood there and cried. She didn't stop until she heard her phone ring.

"Hello." her voice trembled through the phone.

"Falen, what's wrong?" Toya asked her.

"He, he took my money." she sobbed.

"Who took your money? What happened? Where are you?"

"I'm on my way there." Falen said trying to straighten herself out.

"No! Stay right there. Craig is here. We're going to come get you."

"I'm already walking towards there." Falen said.

"And we're already in the car." Toya told her. She and Craig drove down the street until they spotted Falen.

"Get in." Toya told her as Craig pulled in front of her.

As Falen slid in the car Toya could still see the tears in her eyes.

"Now tell me what happened?"

"Some bum ass nigga snatched my bag and fled on a bike."

"You had your money in it?" Toya asked hoping that

it wasn't the case.

"Every penny." Falen broke down.

"Damn, Falen. I told your ass to…" Toya started to preach until she realized that it wouldn't change anything. The worst part was that they were in the same boat. Gloria had grown tired of the constant bickering between her and Janah and had kicked them both out. Janah moved her things to Crystal's and Toya moved hers to the room with Falen.

"You know that I told that man at the motel that we were leaving tomorrow. We can't stay there another night without any money." Falen reminded her.

"Fuck! You don't have no money?"

"All I have is ten dollars in my pocket." Falen sighed.

"And all I have is twenty. That aint enough." Toya shook her head. "Maybe you can try and call T." she said using initials to keep Craig out of their business.

"T?" Craig asked. "If yall talking about Tino, that nigga is out of town. Everybody been looking for his ass. Shit, I can't even rescore."

"Who said that I was talking about him?" Toya snapped.

"Man, everybody in the Bottoms knows that he's knocking Falen down." he laughed.

"What?" that knocked Falen out of her trance.

"Yeah, yall thought that I didn't know, huh?" Craig turned and looked at her. "I see that nigga's leaving his mark and everything." he pointed out referring to the three passion marks on her neck.

"Anyways, Inspector Gadget, when will Tino be back?" Toya asked him.

"I don't know. I heard that the nigga is in Miami. Then again that's what I *heard*. I don't know when he's coming back."

"What are we going to do?" Falen cried.

"Stop all that crying, girl. If yall don't have nowhere else to go yall can come to my crib. I'm sure that my uncle won't mind if yall stay for a couple of days."

"You for real?" Toya asked.

"Straight up."

Falen tried calling Tino for the umpteenth time. Each time she got no answer. She and Toya had been staying at Craig's for two *long* days. They say that you don't truly know a person until you live with them. Falen had to learn this first hand.

The first night there Falen woke up with Craig's uncle on top of her. When she pushed his ass off her he swore that he must've been sleep walking. Craig's hand would magically slip on her ass every time he passed her, and they *accidentally* walked in the bathroom while she was showering.

The second night was even crazier. Some silly broad showed up in the middle of the night beating on the door. She was screaming at the top of her lungs. Apparently, she thought that Craig was her man. Falen and Toya were too through when the nigga actually let the psychotic woman inside.

Craig had the nerve to introduce them to the woman as his cousins. Toya wasn't bothered one bit. She was happy for the focus to be off of her. Craig wouldn't have to sniff up her ass for some pussy.

Falen saw that situation in an entirely different light. What Toya failed to realize was that if she wasn't fucking Craig then there would be no reason to keep them around. They needed to remain in their good graces at least until she got paid. She didn't think they'd make it another week there. Something had to give.

Falen sat and thought about the weird things that she'd noticed around her job. Every day like clockwork this big bulky dude would come and exchange a few short words with the manager. Then once she noticed the big guy pass the manager an envelope which she assumed was cash. Then at twelve midnight someone would drop a bag behind the building. By 12:05 another car would pick up that very same bag.

Falen felt that the people behind the drop were some complete idiots. There was no one staying on the property to insure that everything went down correctly. All it took was for one person to notice the routine and slide in during that small window of opportunity. That person would have to be willing to take a chance, though.

That trash bag stayed on Falen's mind the entire day. She thought about all sorts of ways to get away with that money. She was actually considering doing it on her own. The only problem was that she couldn't pull something like that off without a vehicle. She knew that they made the drop every Monday and Thursday.

"Bitch, why are you so quiet?" Toya pried as they both sat on Craig's bed.

"Cause I'm thinking of a master plan. You in?" Falen asked seriously.

"In on what?"

"I'm gonna get that trash bag." Falen smiled.

"Get that trash bag?" Toya repeated confused. "Oh, your ass is still hung up on that trash bag shit?"

"Hell, yeah! So, you down or what?"

Toya took a second to see if she was serious. "Bitch, you know I'm down."

"Okay, cool. So, call one of your friends with a car."

"Falen, you tripping. I have plenty of niggas with cars but why would we want them in our business? What if we really get something? We can't have them hoe ass niggas in our mix. The whole world would know before the sun comes up."

"We can't do this shit without a car."

"You know that Craig loves handle bars. So, I'll give him my last two bars. His ass will be sleep within the next few hours. And you know that his uncle's old ass goes to sleep at nine. That bitch went home today. So, it's set. We'll just steal the old man's keys."

"Okay, so what will we do after we steal his car? You know that the old man gon put our asses out."

"I mean, do you seriously think that there is some money in those bags?" Toya asked.

"It gotta be."

"Well, let's do this tomorrow night. We have to understand that no matter what we aint staying here again. Shit, he might not realize that we took his car, but we have to be prepared. So, we'll just get our shit out the garage when we burn."

"That's what's up, but I want to do this tonight." Falen admitted.

"Tonight?" Toya asked. She was growing a bit apprehensive. They weren't exactly sure of the risks they were taking. "Why tonight?"

"To be honest, if we wait until tomorrow I might punk out. We have to do this while my mind is made up. And besides the next drop is not until Thursday."

"Fuck it." Toya shrugged. "What do we have to lose?"

Chapter 6

We got That Work

Falen and Toya quietly packed their belongings into Uncle Tim's Buick. Taking his keys was easier than expected. He was so drunk that he gave Toya his keys and as planned Craig was knocked out full of those pills.

Toya had to laugh at herself. She was willing to ride with Falen through whatever. There they were packing their shit with nowhere to go. There was a strong possibility that they might come out of the situation empty handed, but it was a chance that they both were willing to take. Anything was better than relying on other people to provide shelter for them.

"Okay, are you ready to do this?" Falen asked her as she started the car.

"As ready as I'm gonna be." Toya sighed.

They arrived in Burger King's parking lot at ten o'clock as planned. They parked in a spot on the lot where they could see all the comings and goings. At 10:30 the bulky dude had a talk with the gay manager as usual. They watched him exit the lot at 10:38.

"Okay, as soon as those niggas leave the parking lot I'm going to run over and grab the bag." Falen told Toya for the hundredth time.

"I heard you the first million times." Toya rolled her eyes.

"I'm just making sure that you got it."

Their plan was all mapped out. At 11:45 Toya would make a few blocks and wait for the drop while Falen hid in the brush across the street from the lot. After Falen calls she'd head towards Burger King. Falen would be waiting on the curb with the bag.

11:45 was there in no time. Falen hopped out of the

car dressed in all black and floated across the street. She watched the Buick turn a corner. At 11:59 a Cadillac pulled into the lot.

Falen called Toya. "They're here." she said before hanging up.

Falen watched as the car swept the lot before the same bulky man that pays the manager stepped out and made the drop. Only this time instead of a trash bag he left a duffle bag. He then quickly hopped back in the car. She watched intently as the car exited the lot.

Falen's heart was racing as she emerged from the brush and made her way across the street. She was running like her life depended on it. She made it to the bag within ten seconds flat. She grabbed what she thought was cash and headed for the feta, where Toya was already waiting. She snatched the car's door open and slung the heavy bag inside and jumped in.

"Let's go, bitch!" she shouted.

With that Toya put the petal to the metal. She jumped on the freeway and they were home free.

"Falen, are you sure that that is some money, because that bag seemed mighty heavy."

Falen had to catch her breath. She didn't know that she had that much strength. They had never used a duffle bag any of the times she'd witnessed the drop. "I don't know what the fuck is in here." she finally got out. "I damn near broke my back."

Falen decided to take a peek in the bag as Toya drove down the freeway.
"Let's see what we have here." she sighed as she unzipped the bag.

She couldn't believe her eyes. There wasn't any money inside that bag. She just sat there in shock.

"So what do we have, bitch? Spit it out." Toya said as she tried to look at Falen in the rearview mirror.

"I don't know." Falen shook her head.

"You don't know? What it look like?"

"It looks like some...cocaine." Falen said exasperated.

"Cocaine? Are you sure?"

"I aint a hundred percent but I believe that it is."

"So how much is in it?" Toya wanted to know. She didn't understand why Falen wasn't excited. Dope was just as good as money any day.

"It looks like ten."

"Ten keys?" Toya asked getting excited.

"I guess." Falen answered not totally sure.

"Fuck, I gotta see this shit for myself." Toya said.

They drove around for an hour trying to make sure that they weren't being followed. Mainly, it was out of paranoia because at that time of the night there were very few cars on the streets.

"So what do we do now?" Falen asked.

"Okay, I took fifty dollars out of Craig's pockets, so we can get a room. The thing is we need to bring this car back before they realize that it's gone. So we'll drop all our shit at the room, then take the car back. From there we'll figure out a way to get back to the motel."

"Sounds like a plan to me." Falen nodded.

They found a motel off of Highway 45. Toya checked in and then they unloaded their belongings inside their room. Minutes later they were back on the road headed to Craig's house. It was four in the morning, so Falen felt a bit better about bringing the car back. She knew that by the time they dropped the car off Metro would be up and running.

"Aw, shit." Toya sighed as she pulled in front of Craig's house. All the lights were on telling them that someone was wide awake.

"Oh well, fuck it. We'll just say that Tim let us use

this bitch. Shit, they can't prove nothing." Falen spat.

"Yeah, well I aint going in there. Those niggas might try to jump stupid." Toya laughed. "I'll just leave the keys in the seat." she said as she hopped out the car. Falen was right behind her.

Falen slammed the car's door a tad too hard because Craig jumped straight up.

"There them bitches go right there!" he yelled to his Uncle Tim.

By the time he reached the door the girls were long gone.

"Bitch, I haven't ran this much since I was on the track team." Falen huffed as they continued to jog down the street.

About five blocks down they found a bus stop. They really didn't care where it was headed. They needed to get out of dodge. Both girls were relieved when a bus pulled up at the stop and they hopped on.

"We need a scale." Toya told Falen as they rode on the bus.

"Well, I aint got the money for one." Falen sighed.

"Well, that don't change the fact that we need one. We're going to go by Wal-Mart." Toya said.

Falen knew what time it was. They had to do what they had to do.

"I'm glad that I brought my oversized bag." Toya laughed as they got off the bus right in front of Wal-Mart.

They entered the store on a mission. They headed straight to the aisle where the digital scales were kept. After selecting the scale that they wanted Falen took it out of the box insuring that there were no hidden censors. As a decoy they also grabbed three more boxes of different brands.

Then they strolled down various aisles searching for a blind spot.

Although, Falen was in denial about her snatching somebody's bricks she wanted to be prepared for whatever. So, she suggested that they grab some miniature baggies just in case they had the real deal.

By the time they reached the front of the store Toya's bag was filled with anything they thought they needed. Falen giggled as they breezed pass the door's monitor.

"I am so damn tired." Toya complained as they entered their room. They'd done so much shit before the sun had even risen.

"Well, we still have shit to do so brush that shit off." Falen told her as she unloaded the things from Toya's bag. "Test that shit or something. We need some money before the day is over. Check out time is at eleven. It's seven right now."

Toya went over to the duffle bag and removed one of the bricks. She used a razor blade to slice the package open. She dipped her finger in the powder substance and ran it above her teeth. Her gums went numb instantly.

"Oh yeah, this is the real deal." she nodded. She'd learned plenty while fucking with Tony. He dealt on a small time scale and occasionally tooted some as well. He taught her how to test cocaine's purity level.

"It's some fire, bitch?" Falen questioned with a smile.

"Hell, yeah." Toya grinned. "I wonder who this shit belongs to."

"I don't have a clue. That's why we have to be careful about this shit. We could fuck around and try to sell this shit to the people we stole it from."

"But how are we going to move this shit?" Toya asked.

"Well, first we should focus on making some quick cash to get us a place. So, call a few coke heads or some niggas that might want to rescore. Tell them that you know where the wholesale at. They going for half. Tell them that you have to take them to the person and that only you can make the transaction. We can get those stupid niggas to take us around the block somewhere. Then one of us can get out and pretend to cop. We come back with the work and they'll never know where we got it from."

"But why go through all of that?" Toya asked confused.

"How many of those niggas you trust?"

Toya had to think about it. "None." she finally replied.

"Okay then. We are some none threatening females. If those niggas find out that we're holding then we'll become easy targets. Not just that, but shit is hot right now. Somebody just got hit up in the worse way. People talk. We don't want our names in the middle of that shit. We're probably the last people they'd suspect, especially if we play it safe."

"Okay, that's what's up. I'll call Tony right now." Toya said as she grabbed her cell.

The phone rang a few times before he picked up. "Hello."

"Tony, are you up?"

"Hell, yeah. I'm stressing like a motherfucka, right now. Why is *your* ass up so early?"

"I don't know. I just can't sleep. What's wrong with you?"

"Shit, the streets is dry right now and my pockets is hurting." he complained.

"You talking about that flower?" Toya asked. This had to be their lucky day.

"Hell, yeah."

"Well, I know this nigga that's letting them go for half right now." Toya said coolly.

"No shit, Toya? You playing right?" he asked, interest piqued.

"I'm dead serious." she said trying to contain her laugh. She was waving at Falen trying to grab her attention. She mouthed "We got one."

"Okay, well a nigga only got about four to spend."

"Well, this nigga that I fucks with don't do no baking so you definitely can stretch your money."

"Real talk?"

"Real talk."

"Okay, when can you hook something up?" he asked anxiously.

"Shit, we can take you to him right now."

"Who is we?"

"Me and Falen."

"Oh okay." he sighed. "So where yall at?"

"Shit you can just meet us on Tidwell and 45 in about twenty minutes."

"On what side?" he asked.

"On the side by the shopping center."

"I know exactly where you're talking about."

"Alright, just call me when you're exiting the freeway."

"Okay, make sure that you answer, main. Don't be playing no games." he warned.

"I will, nigga." she snapped as she hung up.

"So what the nigga say?" Falen asked.

"He said that he had four to spend, so that means that we have to have eight ready."

"Okay well let's separate this shit." Falen said rubbing her hands together.

They separated the work meant for Tony then a few eight balls just in case. They both stuffed the drugs in their underwear and headed out the door.

When Tony pulled into the shopping center he spotted Toya and Falen. They were both dressed in rather loose fitting clothes. They quickly hopped in his ride.

"What's up?" he asked them.

"Chillin." Falen replied.

Tony could tell that they were both worn out. "Okay, so where am I going?"

"Go down Airline to Crosstimbers." Toya instructed. They were guiding him to some duplexes that were aligned in rows in which would make it difficult from him to figure the supposed trap's location.

When Tony pulled up at the duplexes Falen said that she'd cop the work.

"Where's the money?" she asked him.

He gave them a suspicious look then reached down in his pocket. "Here." he said as he handed her a wad of small bills.

Falen sat and counted every dollar. After she was sure that the money was correct she hopped out of the car. She quickly hit a corner then glanced around. The coast was clear. She pulled the coke out of her pants. She then waited for exactly five minutes before walking back around the corner.

She looked around before getting back in the car.

"Let's go." she told Tony.

He put his car in drive and pulled off.

She reached over and placed the dope in his lap. "There you go."

Tony glanced down at the work. He got so excited that he swerved a little. That was indeed twice the amount he'd spent. He took his hands off the steering wheel to test it. He rubbed it across his teeth and tongue.

"That's what the fuck I'm talking about. This shit is some fire!"

"I told you that I got you." Toya boasted.

"You damn right." he smiled.

Tony was so pleased with the hook up that he gave Toya forty dollars right before he dropped them back off at the shopping center.

"Bitch we did that!" Toya said excited as they watched Tony's vehicle exit the lot.

"Right, right." Falen laughed. "Now our asses can get a few hours of sleep." she yawned.

"Hell yeah." Toya smiled as they walked back to their motel room.

Chapter 7

Money over Everything

I'm boyfriend number two cause the first one don't really seem like he know what to do.

"What the fuck?" Falen spat as she lifted her head.

She and Toya had been sleep for hours. Half of the time that song had been playing.

"Toya, turn that radio off." she said as he head crashed into the pillow.

"What radio?" Toya questioned groggily.

"The one playing that same damn song."

"What song?" Toya asked waking up a bit more.

"You hear that shit."

Toya sat and listened. "That's my cell phone." she yawned as she reached over and got her phone off the charger. "Hello."

"Toya?"

"Yeah, who this?"

"This Tony, girl. Your ass still sleep?"

"Yeah."

"Man, get your ass up."

"For what?" she asked.

"You know Jacob?"

"Yeah, that's your cousin, right?"

"Yeah. Well, he need that same favor."

Toya was fully awake now. "He want the same amount too?"

"Nah, he got seven to spend."

"Seven?"

"Yeah, so can your people do it?"

"Yeah, I know they got it."

"Okay, when can yall take him?"

"Shit, right now."

"Alright. We'll be out there in like thirty minutes." he told her as he hung up.

"Falen, wake your ass up! There's money to be made." Toya said as she shook her girl awake.

"What, bitch!" Falen moaned. She was tired as hell.

"We got another lick!"

Within two days they repeated the same routine seven times. At the end of the second night they were five thousand strong. They both decided to buy a cash car. They spent 3500 on an '02 Impala. Right after they pulled off the lot they drove over to a house that Falen spotted two days ago. She dialed the number on the for rent sign. Within three hours they had the keys to the three bedroom home.

Even though they were damn near broke again they weren't worried. By the end of the day they hit two more licks. Each was worth a G. That was the largest score yet. Tony kept bringing them the customers, so they would give him a little incentive, courtesy of Toya's *friend* of course.

The second day spent in their new house was surrounded around them buying furniture. Falen went to a small furniture company and was able to buy a decent living and dining room set for just 1500. She then found a dude that sold quality beds for a dirt cheap price. Luckily for them he turned out to be a smoker. They walked away with two king sized beds for one eight ball which had a net worth of a hundred twenty-five dollars.
With just one call from Tony they made another 1500 before the day was over.

Once they woke up for the next day they went out and bought a '42 inch flat screen for their living room. Falen was so proud of what they'd put together. She wished that she could just bring Crystal over to see how she'd bounced back within just one month. Deep down, Falen knew that she couldn't go against her own rules. She and Toya agreed that they'd wait awhile before revealing to anyone that they had a little change. They wanted to keep a low profile for as long as possible.

Falen figured that Tony would eventually catch on to them. So, she made sure to keep things short when he'd question them. She even began choosing new meet up spots to keep things fresh. She didn't want anything to become routine. Hell, it had been two weeks and he still hadn't seen what kind of car they drove. They were overly precautious.

"Falen, I think that it's time that we go shopping." Toya said as she turned the radio down.

They were cruising around smoking a blunt. Besides the dro, there was no other drug in the car. Although, they felt that the odds of them getting caught riding dirty were slim to none, they didn't like to chance it. Police rarely searched the cars of women. That was mainly reserved for the young black males in Houston.

Usually, Falen was not concerned with fashions but since she now had money to blow she was like what the hell. "I was thinking the same thing."

Six hours later they were leaving the Galleria with too many bags. Falen had stuck to the high end clothes Tino had introduced her to. They'd shopped so much that it felt as though they'd worked a full shift at work.

"We're going to the beauty shop." Toya said after they were back on the road headed home.

"Bitch, it won't be today." Falen shook her head.

"And why not?" Toya snapped.

"Have you looked at your phone? Tony been blowing us up. Money has to be made."

"Well, say no more."

Toya was pissed as she and Falen walked down the street. They actually caught the bus to the Kelly Courts. It was Gloria's birthday and she demanded that they both attend her party. Falen was cool with it, but still felt that it was too soon to reveal their hand, so they caught a cab downtown. From there they caught the bus.

They even made a pit stop to pick up Falen's first and last check from Burger King. The gay manager wasn't on duty. In fact, there was a new manager in his place. She collected her five hundred dollar check and was on her way.

They'd finally made it to the salon. Falen had her hair bleached blonde and straightened. She seemed to have transformed into a new person. She was rocking the hell out of some True Religion ripped jeans with a red leather bikers' jacket. She was mad at herself for allowing Toya to talk her into wearing some red pumps, though.

Toya was wearing a similar ensemble with the exception of hers being blue. She had a half black half blonde feathered bob. The two friends were nothing less than fierce!

"We finally made it." Falen sighed as they walked up to Gloria's building. The party had already started outside.

"Don't be huffing and puffing when we could've just drove here." Toya rolled her eyes.

They hadn't noticed but all eyes were on them. People were trying to figure out just who those ghetto superstars were. Even Ms. Gloria was trying to figure out who the two girls were that were trying to walk inside her house.

"Uh, can I help you? The party is outside." she said about to check somebody. The entire party stopped and stared.

"Damn mama, it's like that?" Toya asked.

"Toya?" Gloria asked confused. The girl did sound like her daughter, but damn!

"Yeah, Gloria." Toya snapped.

That was when Gloria knew that she was looking at her smart mouthed Toya. "Girl, I didn't even recognize you. Who you got with you?"

"Oh Ms. Gloria, you don't know me either?" Falen asked.

"I know that aint Falen?" she laughed.

"Yes, this Falen."

"Yall look like new money."

They both chuckled a bit, but never acknowledged that last comment.

Janah and Crystal were both sitting at the card table. It seemed that all their words were lodged in their throats. Just the day before they were swearing that both Falen and Toya were in some shelters.

No one could believe Falen's transformation. She seemed out of place in the hood.

"Say nigga, where you get that barbeque from?" Tino asked Joe as they stood in front of the corner store.

"Oh, Janah's mama's having a birthday party. She giving everybody plates." Joe answered with a mouth full of food.

"I know that shit is good the way you chewing on it. I need to go get me a plate."

"Shit, go get one, nigga. You know that bitch Janah will give your ass about ten plates."

"Fuck her. I wonder where Falen nem at. Aint nobody been seeing her around. I haven't talked to her since I lost my phone damn near a month ago."

"Shit, she might be around there. Everybody and they mama over there." Joe chuckled.

"Alright, walk with me over there." Tino said as he headed back to the apartments.

"Nigga, what this is, high school? I'm walking with you to find some young girl." Joe teased.

"Fuck you." Tino laughed.

As they rounded the corner Joe spotted a chick in a red leather jacket.
"Got damn! Nigga, fuck Falen. That little bowlegged stallion right there is the business!" Joe shouted as he grabbed his piece with one hand and held his plate with the other.

Tino took a good look at the chick. She was indeed bad. He studied her walk for a few seconds. He knew that walk from anywhere. "Nigga, that *is* Falen." he said proudly.

"Nah!" Joe shouted before taking a better look. "That is her. She must got a paid nigga."

Tino gave his cousin a look. "Nigga, please." he spat as he briskly walked over to Falen.

He grabbed her and wrapped his arms around her waist. "Long time no see." he whispered into her ear.

This caught every female's attention within a ten block radius.

Falen turned to see Tino. She was so happy to see him that she was beside herself. She jumped into his arms and wrapped her legs around his waist. She didn't care that they were the center of attention. "Where you been, boy?" she asked him.

He walked away from the crowd, while she was still wrapped around his waist. "I should ask you the same thing." he laughed as he leaned in for a kiss. He'd genuinely missed her.

Mouths dropped as everybody watched Tino kiss a broad. Until that very day it was unheard of. This was one for the history books.

Finally, Falen landed on her own two feet. "Tino, all kind of shit has happened since the last time I saw you."

"Like?"

"Too much to tell you right now."

He pulled her closer. "Damn, you're looking sexy, baby."

"You too." She gave him bedroom eyes.

His dick instantly rocked up. "Let's get out of here. Come hang out with me for the rest of the day."

"Okay." she said with no hesitation. "Let me go tell my girl what's up."

"Alright." He gave her a love tap on the ass. "And fix a nigga one of those plates." he told her as she headed back towards the party.

When Falen didn't see Toya outside she went inside Gloria's apartment to find her. She stumbled across Toya and Greg talking.

"Come on, Toya. I'm your brother. Show me some love. I know all about you taking these niggas to this big time nigga. I need some of that love." Greg pleaded.

"Greg, I am not about to introduce you to him, just so you can turn around and rob his ass!" Toya spat.

"I don't want to rob him. I just want to cop."

"Well, we can make that happen for you." Falen interrupted.

Greg turned around. "You'd do that for me, Falen?"

"Yeah. But me or Toya has to be the middle man. We can get you what you need."

"Why can't I meet the nigga?"

"Because that's not how he operates. So, either you go through us or not at all." Falen laid down the law.

Greg thought it over. "Okay, when can we do this?"

"Today." Toya spoke up.

"Nah, tomorrow. I got something to do today." Falen told Toya.

"What?" Toya asked.

"Something, bitch. Let's just leave it at that."

Toya walked over to the screen door and peered around. After surveying the crowd she spotted Tino. "I guess bitch. We putting money on hold for dick?" she spat as she glared at Falen.

"Toya, don't do that. I never say a word when you chill with all those niggas. Can I do me without making any apologies?" Falen snapped.

Toya softened up a bit. "My bad girl. You right. Hell, I should be pushing your ass out the door. If it wasn't for that nigga, you'd probably be a nun."

"Fuck you." Falen laughed, as she gave her the finger. She turned to Greg. "We can do this tomorrow. In fact, if you have any friends that need some love we can help them out too. But you'll have to be their middle man. We can't help them if you're not present."

Greg nodded but his mind was at work. It was beginning to seem like they were more involved in the dope game than he originally thought.

Tino and Falen were hanging at one of his many secret hideaways. He would usually keep one of his main bitches there, but due to a series of unfortunate events he'd fired a majority of his team. He couldn't trust anyone.

Falen was enjoying Tino's company but she couldn't help but think about all the money she was missing. Just in the last hour, her cell had vibrated twenty times. Each time Tino gave her a strange look. By the look on his face she could tell that he assumed that those were men calling.

They sipped on Grey Goose as they hung on his balcony. Falen was impressed with the upscale apartment in the Uptown/Galleria area of Houston. The apartment sat on the fifth floor and overlooked a huge indigo sparkling pool.

After the second glass Falen was feeling herself. So,

she grabbed Tino by his tee and stood on her tip toes to give his soft lips a kiss. That kiss led to several others. Finally, Tino broke away.

"Why you stopped?" Falen asked in a husky voice. She was ready to take things to the next level.

"Who you been giving my pussy to?" Tino questioned out of nowhere.

"Nobody." she whined as she motioned for his belt buckle. He slapped her hand away.

"Stop. Who bought you these clothes?" he said as he tugged at her jacket.

"I did."

Tino was not convinced. "Who have you been staying with?"

"Me and Toya found a house."

"Where?"

"Not too far from 1960." she told him purposely being vague.

"Well, how are you paying your bills? You aint working no more."

"How do you know that I don't have a job?"

He gave her a look that said it all. "Who is this nigga that you're fucking with?"

"I am not fucking with anybody!" she snapped.

Tino grabbed her chin forcefully. "The one thing that I don't tolerate is a liar." he seethed before releasing her.

Falen couldn't believe the way that he was handling her. "I would never do anything like that to you." she cried, as she turned her back to him.

Tino stood in silence for a few minutes. The only thing that could be heard was her sniveling. Finally, he turned her around, knelt down, and kissed her. She wanted to push him away but her body had other plans. His hands were all over. She was so caught up in his rapture that she didn't realize that he was undressing her.

When Falen felt that night's cool air kiss her bare skin she snapped out her reverie. "Tino, let's go in the house and finish this."

"Un uh, we're cool right here." Tino moaned as he continued to undress her.

Falen made a weak attempt at pushing him away. Of course, Tino didn't budge. Seconds, later she was standing on the balcony in just her bra and panties. He didn't stop there, though. The Grey Goose had him not giving a damn.

When she felt him pulling down her panties she thought that he'd lost his mind. "Tino, let's go in the apartment."

Tino ignored her as he dropped her panties to the ground. Within seconds he was out of his jeans and boxers. He then lifted Falen as if she weighed nothing and slid her down on his dick. They leaned against the wall as he drove deep inside of her.

"Umm." she moaned.

"You like that?"

"Uh hmm."

"I said, do you like it?" he asked as he pumped slightly harder.

"Yes!" she yelled. She was trying to hold back, but having sex outside was exhilarating.

To hear her scream was invigorating. He showed the pussy no mercy. With each pump he made her scream louder and louder. They were smacking skins and going crazy, not caring who heard or saw them.

"This my pussy." he growled. "Whose pussy is it?"

"Yours." she moaned.

"It's mine?"

"Yeah, it's yours! Is this my dick?"

"Yeah, this your dick. You can have it anytime you want it."

"Oh my God, I love you!" she blurted out without

thinking.

Tino heard her loud and clear. He'd heard it so many times out of so many mouths that he had trouble separating the real from the fake. "Don't say nothing that you don't mean, Falen."

"I only know how to say what I mean and mean what I say." she spoke seriously.

"Oh, yeah?" he inquired, as he placed his forehead on hers. "So, you love me, huh? We'll see."

Tino pressed her body harder against the wall and pushed her legs further apart. Then he was able to venture deeper. This caused Falen to scream once more.

"Tino! What are you doing to me?!"

He didn't answer but continued to pump. He was on a mission as her juicy walls took him to another planet. "Fuck!" he let out before exploding inside of her.

Falen was sleeping in Tino's arms as he thought about their situation. He found himself having deep feelings for her, but he didn't quite know what to do with them. He was at a point where he could trust no one. Whenever money was a part of any equation there was always betrayal. Still, Falen gave off a harmless vibe. He liked that but knew that it could be misleading.

If Tino was going to allow her to enter his world, she'd have to play by his rules. That would be the only way that he'd be able to stay sane. Being his woman was no easy task. Just the association with him could make her an easy target. This meant that Falen would have to change her entire way of life. She would no longer be able to just hang in the projects, or consort with many from there. In so many ways, she'd become a kept woman. It would be for her own protection, but more so because Tino kept his women on a short leash.

When Falen finally woke up the next morning he sprung his idea on her. "Baby, do you like this apartment?" he asked her as they lied in bed.

"Yeah, this shit is nice as hell." she nodded.

"Well, how would you like living here?"

Falen thought about it. A month ago that would have been music to her ears, but since then things had changed. She was getting her own money and she liked it. She couldn't see herself living with him and hustling too. The two couldn't co-exist. The only way that it might work was if she told him her secret. That wasn't something that she was prepared to do.

"That would be cool, but I signed a lease and I just can't leave Toya on stuck."

"A lease? That's not a big deal. I can pay for you to break a lease. And as far as Toya is concerned she can visit you here."

"But she can't pay all those bills alone."

"As a woman she need to stand on her own two feet. I understand that she's your girl." Tino paused. "I'll give you one better. We'll give her your half of the rent for the rest of the lease agreement."

Tino had her cornered. How could she turn him down after that? How would she be able to justify that? "Tino, let's just give it some time. Can we at least wait until the lease is up?" she asked with apologizing eyes.

It was as if she'd picked up a shotgun and aimed it directly at his ego. No woman had ever denied Tino. He didn't even know how to handle rejection. "That's cool." he forced himself to smile.

Tino climbed out of the bed and walked his naked body to the bathroom. Unconsciously, he slammed the door behind him. Falen knew that he didn't understand her reasons. She wished that she could tell him the complete truth, so that they could be together. In reality, she knew that life just wasn't that simple.

Staying with Tino would mean more than just telling him about the ten keys. It would cause her to choose. She and Toya had put everything on the line together, so she had no right to decide to add another person into their business without Toya's input first.

When Tino dropped Falen off he was beyond pissed.

She wouldn't even allow him to take her home. Instead, she was dropped off at Willowbrook Mall. He didn't even acknowledge her as she vied for attention.

"Bye." Falen attempted to lean over and kiss him.

He quickly jerked his head away, before her lips could reach him.

Her feelings were hurt, as she eased out the car. "Call me." She spoke solemnly.

He never uttered a word, as he pulled off.

Tino was hot. He knew that Falen was lying about something. He figured that she was already living with some other nigga. So, he exited the lot after he dropped her off and re-entered on another street. He drove around to the other side of the mall in which he'd left Falen and saw her hopping in an Impala. He thought about following her, until he came to his senses. If she wanted to play games the next man could have her. He was done.

Chapter 8

A Little Package

Money was flowing like water for Falen and Toya, and getting it was becoming addictive. That was all they did. The craziest part was that they only dealt primarily with four guys. Tony, Greg, Slim, and Do-Do were the only hustlers they'd serve. Slim was Falen's first cousin and Do-Do was Toya's cousin.

The women only dealt with four people, because of safety issues. They needed to deal with people that wouldn't stick a gun in their faces. So, if any newcomer needed some product they'd have to see one of those four men. Even, those four were clueless about the true source of the drugs.

They made sure to always keep the illusion that they had to contact a third party to make things happen. So, when people called for work they'd tell them to call back after they confirmed a few things. Then they'd tell the customer that their people had what they needed. The customer was then required to drop the money off to them, and the girls would come back an hour later with the product.

As far as people knew the girls were just the traffickers. So, the guys never asked to get fronted, because they thought that for the most part Falen and Toya just didn't have that kind of pull. Everyone thought that the girls couldn't get near the product without money in hand. In reality, they continued to do this to decrease the chances of getting robbed.

Falen was constantly changing things up, because she was always paranoid. She'd gotten a state of the art alarm system installed, and surveillance cameras set up outside the house. She even bought two shot guns for an extreme emergency. They had two safes. One sat in Falen's closet and the other they kept in the attic. She was even thinking about getting an apartment just to store their work, because as long as the money and work remained in their home there could be no visitors.

Toya was loving their new lifestyle, but hated that they had to keep such a low profile. She wanted to flash her fortune in the haters' faces. Right then she had to settle for the speculations.

Falen's main concern was stacking her paper. If she wasn't getting money, then she was sitting on her ass at home eating. In the past month, she'd gained ten pounds or more. All she did was eat, sleep, and get money. There wasn't much else to look forward to. Tino hadn't answered her calls in weeks. She knew that he was done with her. It hurt like hell, and she spent plenty of nights crying herself to sleep. The hurt was so deep that she couldn't tell another soul about it.

The bright side of things was that in three weeks Booby would be released from jail. Falen had been filling his commissary to the max and had already bought him a new wardrobe. She was considering letting him in on the action, as well. Still, she would offer limited information, but first she would have to talk things out with Toya.

Falen decided that she'd bring up the Booby thing after she took a nap. For the past few weeks she'd been extremely tired.

"Falen. Falen!" Toya screamed as she entered her room.

"What!" she jumped up.

"Your ass is paranoid, girl." Toya laughed.

"Fuck you. What did you want?" she snapped.

"You got some pads or tampons?"

"No. Now leave me alone."

"Well, get up and ride with me to the store."

"Toya, I'm tired." she whined.

"Get up bitch, cause we have to meet Greg in an

hour, anyway."

"Fuck!" Falen yawned as she threw the covers aside, and sat up in bed.

Toya stood and studied her for a second. "Falen, you sure have been sleeping a lot lately, and you're getting fat."

"Shit, I be tired." Falen yawned, completely ignoring the fat comment.

"Why don't you have any pads or tampons? When was the last time you had a period?"

"I don't know." Falen shrugged.

Toya gave her a disgusted look. "You don't know?"

"No, I don't know." Falen said, growing agitated.

"Shit, we need to go pick up some tampons for me, and a pregnancy test for you." Toya giggled.

"That aint even funny."

"I'm serious, Falen. You need to find out what's going on. What if you've been getting high all this time and you're really pregnant? You never watched 'I didn't Know that I was Pregnant?"

"Toya, stop trying to make this sound so crucial. I aint pregnant." Falen rolled her eyes.

"Whatever. My friend got a little Tino in her belly." Toya cooed.

Falen gave her the finger as she walked over to her closet. After selecting a Juicy Couture sweat suit she headed to brush her teeth. Once she unwrapped her hair and got fully dressed they headed out the door.

Toya ran into Walgreens, while Falen sat in their truck. She grabbed herself some tampons and purchased an EPT for Falen. As she headed back to the truck she wore a huge smile.

"Bitch, what you smiling at?" Falen asked, as Toya climbed back into the Navigator.

"Here you go." Toya laughed, as she slung the test into Falen's lap.

Falen picked up the box and stared at it. So many things had been going on that she hadn't thought about getting pregnant. Nor had she done anything to prevent it. She knew that there was a possibility of her being pregnant, and it scared the living shit out of her.

"Okay, I'll use this after we handle our business." Falen sighed.

"What business?" Toya faked confusion.

Falen lifted a perfectly arched brow. "I thought that you said that we had to meet your brother?"

"Oh, I forgot. That's tomorrow."

"So, you bamboozled me?"

"Not at all." Toya cheesed, as she backed out of the lot.

"Falen, open the door!"

"No!" Falen cried as she sat on the toilet, with her pants still at her ankles.

"Come on, girl. It can't be that bad." Toya said through the restroom's door.

Falen had been in the bathroom for thirty minutes, crying. She refused to unlock the door for Toya. She just wanted to be alone and wallow in her own misery.

Toya was tired of trying to get through to Falen. The girl was so damn stubborn. She knew that deep down Falen was tripping, because Tino wouldn't even talk to her. Toya didn't know the reason behind their fall out, but she was sure that it was all Tino's fault.

After another thirty minutes of crying, Falen finally got off the toilet. She wiped away her tears and decided to face the world. Well, if not the world at least Toya. So, she opened the door to find her standing there.

"Are you done, cry baby?"

"Yeah." Falen sighed, as she headed for the living room.

"So, I guess we're expecting."

"Yeah."

"So, are we about to hunt Tino's ass down to let him know that he has a baby on the way?"

"No. I'll let him know whenever I see him." Falen sighed, as she flopped down on their suede and leather sectional.

Toya knew that it was a good time as any to get more information about her and Tino. "So, Falen why did yall stop talking?"

Falen thought about changing the subject, but realized that it was an issue that wasn't going anywhere. "He wanted me to move in his apartment. I knew that it wouldn't work while we're doing our thing. He's probably thinking that it's about another nigga. Then he really got pissed off when I wouldn't let him take me home." she admitted.

Toya shook her head, disappointingly. She thought for sure that it was something that Tino had done. "Falen, you could have handled that better. Why didn't you just let him take you home? It aint like he gon knock us over the head. He has his own money."

"But I would've had to explain too much. He would have took one look at this house and knew that something was fishy. He still would have thought that I was fucking with some nigga. The only way that he would have understood was for me to tell him the truth."

"Falen, you could have told him the same shit that we tell these niggas. Tell him that we're the middle people and that we get paid to do that."

"I think that he is too deep in the game to buy that. He would have wanted to know who we're working for. Besides, I didn't have much time to think, so I did what I felt was best. I thought that you might get mad if I let him see shit that nobody else could. I didn't want you thinking that I wasn't practicing what I was preaching."

"Well, when you do see him you're going to have to be more open."

"I know."

"I can't believe that you walked around all this time without even knowing."

"I know." Falen sighed as she sat on the passenger side of the Navigator.

Toya and Falen had just left the doctor's office. They were blown away when the doctor told them that Falen was four months pregnant. In fact, the doctor was able to tell her that she was going to have a bouncing baby boy. So, that meant that Tino had gotten her pregnant on their first encounter.

"Falen, you need to tell that nigga, Tino." Toya repeated for the tenth time, within the last five minutes.

"And I keep telling you that I will."

"Whatever." Toya rolled her eyes.

"Valet park cause I aint trying to do unnecessary walking." Falen yawned, as they pulled up in front of the Galleria.

Toya cut her eyes at her friend. "Let me find out Tino got you all high maintenance and shit."

Falen smiled at the thought. Hanging with Tino had definitely broadened her horizon.

The two primarily focused on shopping for Falen, because her clothes were a bit tight. Toya swore that Falen was squeezing her godson with her snug jeans. Falen reminded her that she was the culprit that coerced her to wear tight fitting clothing in the first place.

They both turned heads as they strolled through the mall. Falen wore her straightened hair down with a part in the middle. The black off the shoulders shirt and leggings that she had on were hugging her ass and thighs. Her silver Chanel sandals and oversized Gucci bag brought flare to the ensemble. Toya was ultra-sexy in her Seven jeans and white halter. As always she rocked a feathered bob.

"So, how do you think Tino will react?" Toya asked.

"What? I don't know." Falen shrugged. She was tired of hearing Tino's name, because every time she heard it her heart seemed to ache.

"How do you want him to react?"

Falen cut her eyes. "What the hell? You know that I want the nigga to stand up."

"What if he don't?"

Falen thought for a second. "I don't know."

"Well, I know. If that nigga stunt on you, I'ma kick his fine ass." Toya blurted.

Falen rolled her eyes. "Whatever, Toya."

"Real talk, I ought to kick his ass on GP. Got my friend sniveling, all through the night."

"What?" Falen smiled. "Fuck you, bitch. I do not snivel over anybody at night."

"Sure Falen and I only fucked two niggas in my lifetime."

Falen gave her the finger.

"Don't be mad because you got it bad, girl."

Falen shook her head, hating how well her girl knew her. She would give anything in the world just to see Tino's face. He'd somehow changed her, and nothing seemed right without him around.

As they were leaving the Juicy Couture store Falen spotted a tall slim guy, walking out of Foot Action. She squinted to get a better look. Had they talked that nigga up? "Aint that Tino?"

Toya squinted too. "Yeah, that's him. Let's catch up with him."

They both hurried in that direction. "Tino!" Falen shouted, trying to capture his attention.

He turned around and saw Falen and Toya headed in his direction. He decided to continue walking.

"Did that nigga just keep walking?" Toya snaked her neck. "Oh, hell no!"

"Tino, I know you heard me." Falen gritted, as she caught up with him.

"What you want?" he snapped, as he spun around.

"Damn, it's like that?" she asked in shock.

"You already know that. So, what's up?" he questioned, with a frown.

She sighed not appreciating the way he was handling her. "We need to talk."

"About what?"

"Umm." was all Falen had a chance to say, before she was interrupted.

"Daddy, mommy got me a new dress." a little girl said as she walked up to Tino and held his leg.

"Oh, she did?" Tino smiled down at his daughter.

"Yeah, I got her three." a Halle Berry dead ringer said as she walked up. "Who's your friends, baby?" she asked gesturing towards Falen and Toya.

"I know them from the hood." Tino told her.

"Oh, you more than know my friend!" Toya fumed.

"Come on, Toya. Let's go." Falen sighed, attempting to pull her away.

"No, Falen. You need to read this nigga his rights."

"Fuck him. I don't need him." Falen waved Tino off.

"It's just the principle, cause we don't need nobody! But he aint just gon stand there and diss you!"

"Tino, who is this?" his baby mama asked him.

"Man, let's go." Tino said, picking his daughter up.

"Naw Tino, tell your woman who she is." Toya teased.

"Falen, get your friend." Tino warned.

"No, no, no. I aint gon get shit! Fuck you, you bitch ass nigga, and don't ever put my name in your mouth again!" Falen yelped, as tears streamed down her cheeks.

"Falen, are you fucking Tino?" the baby mama questioned. "I mean, what's the problem?"

"Jamie, I know you see our daughter right here. Let's go!" Tino barked, losing his cool.

"Fuck this." Falen tried her best to keep it together. "You know what, Tino, you aint shit! I should've known better than to fuck with a nigga like you. But you know what? Never again!" she shrieked, before storming off. Toya ran after her.

Jamie just stood in that same spot, until Toya and Falen were out of plain view. Finally, she had a face for the name Falen. She'd seen the number in Tino's phone. She'd also discovered that at one point they talked quite often. That was the same name that her friends had been slinging around. Falen was supposed to be his new tender that he was tricking on.

Jamie was actually hoping for less attractive competition. Ms. Falen was a brick house with a Cover Girl face. She should've known that her daughter's father would have nothing less; hell, he had her.

"I see that you keep your bitches fresh. I'm still trying to get that Gucci bag." Jamie snarled.

"Jamie, don't start this shit. We're supposed to be having a peaceful day. You know a *family* day. Aint that what you wanted?"

"Fuck you, Tino. That's why I aint with your sorry ass right now. You and all these bitches. All I know is that you better not have my child around that little bitch!"

"Lower your fuckin voice." he gritted. "Like you just

said, we aint together. So, your ass was out of line for asking that girl if we were fucking. That is none of your business."

"Whatever." Jamie rolled her eyes. "I see they're getting younger and younger. She looks like she's fresh out of high school. And you doing some major tricking. How many girls her age are walking around with 1500 dollar bags?"

He shrugged, knowing that at least he didn't buy that one. "Shit, I was wondering the same thing."

Chapter 9

Putting Him On

"Bitch, pass me the flat one. No, not the jack."

"Here. Falen, you need to hurry up, before somebody comes." Toya whispered, as she passed her the tool. She couldn't believe that she'd allowed her girl to talk her into stealing Tino's Escalade.

They had sat outside of his aunt's house for hours, watching everybody come and go. Whenever Tino was kicking it in the hood on his bike he'd park his main ride of the day at Joe's mama's house. Falen thought that it was her lucky day when she found out that the Escalade was going to be the vehicle that Tino would never have again.

"I got it." Falen said as she popped the lock. The alarm system was blaring. "Pass me the wire cutters."

"Here." Toya handed her the tool.

Falen quickly disarmed the alarm and hopped in the truck. "Get in, bitch." she whispered.

Toya scurried to the other side of the truck and hopped in, right before Falen backed out of the driveway.

"I can't believe that you stealing that nigga's shit. And where in the hell did you learn how to steal cars, anyway?"

Falen gave her a look.

"Well, I guess that Booby is good for something, after all."

Falen wickedly smiled. "I know, right."

"So, are we about to park this bitch somewhere and do some damage?"

"Hell no. Why waste all that energy and money? I'm taking this bitch to the chop shop."

"The chop shop? Falen, what the hell do you know about the chop shop?"

Falen twisted her lips. "You would be amazed at what I know about."

"I see. I just wish that I could be there to see that look on that nigga Tino's face when he realizes that he ride is gone."

"Tino, where you at?"

"I'm still in the hood. Why what's up?"

"Where you put the bike?" Joe asked.

"Where I put the bike? What chu talking 'bout? My bike right here, nigga."

"So, where the Escalade at?"

"At your mama house, nigga. Where else? Are you high?"

"Hell, naw. Well, maybe a little, but that truck aint at my mama's."

"How you know?"

"Cause I'm at her house as we speak."

"What? Nigga, stop playing so damn much."

"This the one time that I wish that I was playing. Your truck is gone, my nigga."

"What?!"

"Yeah, I'm telling you. Mama said that the alarm went off about two hours ago, but she assumed that it was you outside, because it only sounded for a few seconds."

"So, she didn't bother to look and see what was going on?"

"Man, you know how my mama is. She be in bed no later than eight thirty. That shit happened at twelve something, so you know that she didn't want to get her ass out of bed."

"Fuck!"

Joe allowed his cousin to vent for a minute, before

speaking. "Don't even trip. You know the streets talk, so we'll hear about this shit from somebody. Then we can handle whoever these motherfuckas is."

Falen waited anxiously outside of Keagan's State Jail. She'd given one of the C.O.'s Booby's clothes. She knew that he'd be surprised when the officer's handed him his Louie fit, with ice white Forces. She wanted to see her friend leaving that bitch in style.

She was kind of nervous about what he'd say. She hadn't told him about her pregnancy. In just three weeks she'd begun showing. Maybe she'd been showing for a while, and had just noticed. Her belly was still relatively small, but also round and hard.

"What the hell is taking these niggas so long?" Toya complained.

Just then a line of former inmates emerged from the building. They were still inside an electrical gate, waiting for the C.O. to decide to open it. All the guys were skimming through the crowd that had gathered outside the gate, in search of their loved ones. Booby spotted Falen and Toya decked out in Coogi dresses and thigh high boots.

The November air was cool, but not freezing. Still, Toya swore that if they didn't open that gate within the next minute she was going to walk back to their truck. Finally, the gates were open and the guys all filed out and into their loves ones' arms. Booby all but ran over to Falen and lifted her in the air, as he hugged her. He could feel her hard stomach pressing against his body.

He put her back on her feet. "You're pregnant?" he asked with a frown.

"Yeah." Falen smiled uncomfortably.

Falen hadn't visited Booby in two months. She'd

been too busy. She barely dropped him two lines in her letters. She'd write just enough to inform him about the cash she'd sent him. So, Booby had no idea about her extracurricular activities or her unborn child.

"Why are you looking at her all crazy? Yeah, she pregnant. So, what?" Toya interrupted. "If you don't like it your ass can walk home."

"And hello to you too, Toya."

"Whatever." Toya rolled her eyes. "You ready, Falen?"

"Yeah, come on, Booby." Falen said as she pulled his hand. She led him to the Navigator.

Booby was definitely not expecting them to be riding that clean. An all-black and silver Navigator with twenty-four inch rims symbolized money. "Who truck yall driving?"

"Ours." Falen told him as she hopped in on the driver's side.

Toya rode shotgun, as Booby sat in the back fiddling with the screens sitting in the headrests. He was trying to figure out how Falen and Toya could afford those things.

"Did that nigga Tino give you this truck?" he finally asked.

"Fuck, Tino!" Toya exclaimed. "Mentioning that name in this truck will get you shot."

Booby was glad to hear that Falen and Tino weren't cool like that anymore. "So, Falen who are you pregnant for?"

Falen took a while to answer him. She didn't know if she wanted to open the door to that conversation, especially since she swore to him that she wasn't fucking with Tino. "Well, the sperm donor is Tino Wiltz." she let out.

"So, you *was* fucking with that hoe ass nigga?"

"I did. I aint gon lie, but we're done."

"That's just like a nigga. Since you carrying his

baby, he aint trying to fuck with you, huh?"

"Well, I aint gon lie on him. He actually doesn't know that I'm pregnant."

"What? So, when are you going to tell him?"

"I don't know. Maybe one day, but it won't be anytime soon. We don't need his ass, anyway." Falen spat.

Booby had mixed feelings about the situation. He was glad that Falen and Tino were done, but he'd been around long enough to know that things could change. He also knew that Tino was a stand-up type of dude that would provide for his seed. He was the nigga that threw annual block parties and fed the entire hood. Shit, he'd buy half of the projects their school shoes. So, there was always the chance of Tino re-entering the picture, especially if he knew he had a baby with her. Then Booby didn't like the idea of her carrying that nigga's child. That should've been their seed that she was carrying.

Falen had a long discussion about bringing Booby into their quiet operation. Toya still had her reservations about him, but agreed that they needed muscle. Therefore, they agreed to let him in. Of course, he'd be told what he needed to know, and nothing more.

Booby was the first guest to enter their home. He couldn't believe his eyes as he entered the large brick home. The place resembled something out of Home Décor. There was a huge plasma television mounted on the wall, a plush white sectional, all glass and marble tables, a huge fish tank, and ice white carpet.

"Man, yall have to put me down with whatever scam yall got going on."

"It aint no scam, but we can help you get your weight up." Falen told him.

"And how is that?" Booby questioned intrigued.

"We know somebody that can front you some work. They only deal with us, but we can make it happen for you."

"I don't know. I aint trying to work for some nigga. I can cop when I get my money right because I don't like owing people a damn thing."

"Well, you won't be working for some nigga. We're going to show you some love and in return you just have to watch our backs. Let's just say that we're going to *give* you some start up work and let you do your thing. And when you've flipped your money you can just cop the work yourself."

"Who's going to *give* me some work?" Booby asked thinking that it had to be too good to be true.

"Me and Toya are going to work some magic and get you some work at no cost to you. You see, we do business with some people and they pay us to bring them customers. They only deal directly with us so we're the ones that handle the transactions. The thing is that we can never step foot in their spot without the cash first. So, we always take the customer's money first and then come back with the product. We would love to cop some work for ourselves that maybe we can move, but we wouldn't get far without somebody here to hold shit down for us."

"You serious?" Booby asked with a raised brow.

"Yeah." Falen nodded.

Booby couldn't believe his luck. He was fresh out and was already about to get his feet wet. He thought that he'd have to kick a few doors in before he could even think about coping something.

"Okay, I'm down." Booby nodded.

"Girl, Booby got out of jail looking cute." Toya told Falen as they drove to Overnight Storage.

"Toya, shut up. You're just trying to set my ass up. I keep telling you that I don't like him."

"Em hmm." Toya cut her eyes at Falen. She was trying to find out if Falen was trying to fuck with Booby. She personally felt that it would be a bad move, but she meant it when she said that Booby looked good.

Jaylen James aka Booby was 5'11, slim, light brown, and sexy ass hell. He carried a strong resemblance to the singer Trey Songz. His features could be considered pretty, but his gangster persona spelled trouble. He was known to creep in a back door, pull out the four four, and take a nigga for everything they owned. He didn't hesitate to pull out his pistol and let a few rounds off. Many around the way felt that he was a dirty individual, yet they kept their opinions to themselves. Booby didn't take shit from nobody, and that's why Falen felt that he'd be a valuable asset to their small operation.

"Just grab a quarter." Falen told Toya as she hopped out the truck. They were at the storage picking up the work for Booby. They made the decision to store the cocaine at the storage when Falen volunteered Booby a place to stay.

Two minutes later Toya was locking the storage and back in the truck. She hid the powder in a hidden panel near the glove compartment as Falen pulled out of the lot.

"Oh, my goodness." Falen shrieked.

"What?" Toya asked on full alert.

"I think this little nigga just kicked me."

"Aw. My godson moving around?" Toya smiled as she tried to touch Falen's belly.

"Move, bitch." Falen smiled as she pushed her hand away. "You know I've been thinking and I want to name the baby Tez."

Toya was happy to hear her friend talk about the baby. For weeks Falen barely acknowledged that she was with child. Toya saw the situation as a blessing, and until just then she thought that Falen saw it as a burden.

"That's a cute name. You're trying to give him that *T*

like as in *Tino.*" she teased.

"No, it's *T* as in *Toya.*" Falen corrected her.

"Oh, that would be so sweet if it was the truth."

"Whatever." Falen smiled.

Booby wasn't having any trouble in adjusting to his new crib. Everything was so luxurious and comfortable. He was loving his plush king sized bed and plasma TV. Falen had gone all out for him. She'd recently bought a pool table and he was the first to test it out. He played for hours by himself.

He was waiting on Falen and Toya to return. They'd told him that they had several errands to run. He was sipping on the Grey Goose that they had left on the bar and was feeling lovely. He couldn't wait for Falen to return, because little did she know, he was about to dig in those guts. He'd been fantasizing about her for seven months, and was planning to release that anxiety.

When Falen and Toya entered the living room Booby was sleeping on the couch, shirtless. Falen had never noticed just how defined his body was. He was a slim guy, but was ripped. His abs and wash board stomach looked good enough to eat.

"Booby, wake up." Falen said as she stood over him.

"What's up?" he asked groggily as he opened his eyes.

"We got something for you." she sat next to him.

"What's that Pretty Girl?" he flirted, as he stroked her cheek.

Toya saw Falen melting from his touched. She needed her to stay focused. "We got the issue." she interrupted.

Booby realized that he wasn't getting anywhere with

Falen, while Toya's around. "So, how much is it?" he asked, getting down to business.

"A quarter." Toya sassed.

"A twenty five piece?" Booby asked, offensively.

"Oh my God. Small minded ass niggas." Toya rolled her eyes.

"We're talking about a quarter of a key." Falen cleared things up for him.

His eyes grew three sizes larger. He wasn't expecting that much product. "No, shit?"

Falen reached in her bag and pulled out a package and tossed it in his lap. "Can you make this work?"

He picked up his future and said, "Hell, yeah. I'ma show yall what to do with it."

Chapter 10

Speculators

"Damn baby, slow down. I aint trying to cum just yet." Booby moaned.

"Shut up and take this pussy anyway that I give it to you."

"Falen, stop playing with me, girl." he growled, as he smacked her ass.

Falen ignored him and continued to do her thang. She was in a zone as she rode Booby's dick. She was surprising herself at how good she was. She loved being able to make him climax over and over. He was like her little sex toy and she'd work him until he had no more to give.

Booby was enjoying the sight of his dick sliding in and out of her hot and wet pregnant pussy. He'd discovered that Falen was a pure freak and loved to fuck all day. He didn't know if it was the pregnancy or that she was coming out of her shell, but whatever it was kept her going. She'd wake him in the middle of the night in desperate need of a dick down.

"Girl, you lucky that your ass is already pregnant, otherwise I'd have you carrying some triplets with this one." Booby panted breathlessly, as he released inside of her.

"Uh, shit I'm good." she sighed, completely out of breath as she lay on his chest.

"I'm tired as hell."

"Me too. So, go get in your bed so that I can get some rest." Falen ordered, as she rolled off of him and gave him her back.

He pulled her so that she was now on her back again. "Let me get a kiss good night." He said as he leaned in for a kiss. He went for her lips, but she slightly turned her head.

Therefore, his lips landed on her cheek.

"Oh, it's like that?"

"What? I know you aint bothered by that. I aint the kissing type." She said as she turned her back on him again.

Booby just sat and stared at her back for a few minutes. He was starting to feel like her bitch. She'd fuck his brains out then refuse to share a bed with him. He now knew how women felt. Used. There was no need to argue with her, because she'd swear that she just didn't want any confusion between her and Toya. He knew that was bullshit, but what could he do about it? So, he reluctantly gathered his clothes and headed for his bedroom.

Wayne, Joe, Trent, Kay-Al, and Junebug were all hanging on Joe's baby mama's porch in the Kelly Courts.

"Say, aint that Falen?" Wayne asked.

"Who are you talking about?" Joe asked.

"That broad that used to live in the back, you know, Crystal's sister."

"No, I'm not asking *who* Falen is. I'm asking which chick do you think is her, because I don't see her." Joe explained.

"The pregnant one." Wayne pointed out the chick who was with about three other females.

Joe narrowed his eyes trying to get a better view. "That looks like her ass."

"Man, who is that bitch pregnant for?" Junebug asked.

"Shit, hell if I know." Joe shrugged.

"You sure that it aint Tino's baby?" Wayne pried.

"Not that I know of, but you never know."

"Yall seen that Navigator she rolling in? That bitch is nasty." Kay-Al added.

"Man, that's probably some nigga's truck." Joe spat.

"I don't know, main. The only people that I see pushing that bitch is Falen or Toya." Junebug said. "Oh, and that nigga Booby, but I know that it aint his shit."

"Booby?" Joe asked confused. "He fucks with one of them?"

"I don't know. All I know is that the nigga been out for just two months and already mashing. He even got a trap out in Studewood. That nigga done came up."

"That bitch ass nigga must've got straight out and took some lame for their shit. You know that nigga was always a tennis shoe hustler, so he had to do something grimy." Joe fussed. He never did like Booby, because he was the type to come through the spot, blow on your weed, and then leave your windows unlocked. He loved to catch niggas slipping.

"Well, somebody getting money over there. My gal's mama lives out there close to 1960. The last time I went out there I saw Falen pulling up to this nice ass house. She fucked my head up when she used a key to go in. Now, just a few months ago that chick was broke like these other broads and now they're living good. I was thinking that maybe Falen was laid up with some nigga, until my mother-in-law told me that those hoes live there by they self." Junebug explained.

"When was this?" Joe asked, stroking his goatee.

"Shit, that was about three months ago."

"On the cool, I heard that they be having those thangs, but I didn't believe it." Kay-Al interjected.

"Get the fuck out of here! Man, those broads aint doing it like that. If anything one of them probably fucking with a nigga with some cash, but that's about it. I know those girls and they don't have it in them." Joe laughed.

"Shit, I don't put nothing pass nobody. I know that somebody been looking out for Greg's ass. He got two trap houses now. Niggas, is saying that he can get you work for a real good price." Kay-Al told them.

"Who told you that?" Joe asked seriously.

"Shit, a few people. I just haven't fucked with him, because I don't trust the nigga. But my people been telling me that it's been all love."

"How long they say he's been having some work?"

"For about two or three months, if that long. But like I said, he can *get* you work for a real good price, but he aint the one that's holding."

"Maybe those bitches got the connect." Junebug laughed.

The streets had really dried up since the main suppliers had taken a huge loss. Since then niggas have been cracking under pressure. It seemed that no one could be trusted and the hood had become a war zone. People had to cop from outsiders who weren't showing any love, which resulted in many taking more drastic measures to get their paper. Doors were getting kicked in left and right, people were dying, and affidavits were being signed.

Things were getting so rough that not even Joe and Tino were excluded. Joe was out on a hundred thousand dollar bond, because niggas were taking major chances for minimum gain. It seemed that somebody couldn't do their time, so they mentioned Joe's name in a sworn affidavit. With that Joe couldn't make a move without being watched, which meant that he couldn't make money. Things were so hot in Houston that Tino had left to try to make things happen in Atlanta.

"Naw, yall niggas are tripping." He shook his head in disbelief. "Man, those broads are just some prime examples of what good pussy can get you." Joe chuckled, refusing to believe that Falen was capable of pulling the wool over his eyes.

Crystal sat outside on her stoop, watching her kids have the time of their lives. Falen had just bought them all brand new bikes and Nikes. As much as she wanted to appreciate what her sister had done for her, she still felt that Falen did it all just to put it in her face. So, now her children were looking at her little sister like she was their hero.

Everywhere she went everybody had Falen's name in their mouths. She was the talk of the town. Bitches in the Ward were superficial, so having a banging wardrobe and nice ride meant that you were a somebody. Crystal was having trouble wrapping her mind around the fact that her little sister had more going on than she did.

No matter how things went down, it seemed like there was somebody watching after Falen. Even though, she and Crystal came from the same environment, Crystal felt that she'd always had it harder. Doors seemed to always open for her ratty sister.

At the end of the day Crystal felt that she had been dealt the worse hand. She was the one that was more deserving of a better life. Falen was feeding her and her kids table scraps, so why in the hell should she appreciate that?

"Falen, you should let me cut your hair into layers." Shan, Falen's beautician told her as she placed a perm on her hair.

"I don't care what you do to it." Falen shrugged.

"Falen, how many months are you?" Janah asked, as if she gave a damn.

"Did somebody say something?" Falen rolled her eyes.

"You a trip." Shan grinned, as she continued to work

on her hair.

Janah hated the fact that she, Falen, and Toya all visited the same beauty shop. Bitches were sniffing so far up their asses that one was bound to have a skid mark left on their face. People were acting like Falen was the best thing since sliced bread. Everybody wanted to know where she bought this from and where she got that from. Since when was Falen Bright the fashion guru?

Falen could smell the hate oozing from Janah's pores. She wore a snide look as she glanced her way every few seconds. Little did the bitch know, her attitude was the reason that she wasn't getting money with her. She was a firm believer in karma, so she knew that Janah's day would come. Falen didn't hold grudges, but she didn't forget, either. So, she just looked over Janah and Crystal when they gave her those plastic smiles. Although, Crystal fucked her every chance she could get, Falen spoiled all of her nieces and nephews rotten. She knew that the kids had nothing to do with their ignorant mother.

"So, Falen when is your baby shower?" Shan questioned.

"Umm, next week."

"What you having?"

"A boy." Toya interrupted as she sat under the dryer.

"You stay your ass under that dryer." Toya's beautician Shanice told her.

"When are you due?" Shan continued to pry.

"March." Falen yawned.

"Okay, so I'm invited to the shower right?" Shan asked.

"Of course."

"And me too." Shanice added.

"And me." Danielle raised her hand.

"And me." Joisha said.

"Okay, damn all yall can come. As long as you

bearing gifts."

"Them bitches just want some free food." Toya said from the dryer.

"Hey, what I told you." Shanice joked.

Toya laughed as she gave her the finger.

"Shan, how many customers you have?" Jamie asked as she entered the shop.

"Just two." Shan told her.

"Okay, cool." she said as she took a seat. As always she was dressed to the nines in her Cavauli jeans and blouse with Gucci sandals. She looked around the shop at all the faces. Some were familiar yet a lot she had never seen. She took a second glance at the chick sitting in Shan's chair. She'd recognize Falen anywhere.

Falen had immediately recognized Tino's baby's mama. Her high pitched voice was very distinctive. "Sliced apples." Falen called out she and Toya's safe words.

Toya looked up and saw Jamie. "Sliced apples." she repeated.

"Apple pie. What the hell are yall talking about?" Shanice asked confused.

"That's their code word for when they're talking about somebody." Janah blasted.

"She always knows when we're talking about her ass." Toya shot right back flipping the script.

Janah knew all too well who Jamie was. They had a few run-ins back in the day. Although, Jamie was three years older than her they both attended Wheatley High together. Janah had a reputation for fucking anything with a pulse while Jamie was one of the most popular girls in school. Obviously, Janah was jealous of Jamie and her beauty, so they always bumped heads. Once it even escalated into a fight in which Jamie lost, but to most she was still the victorious one. Janah almost died when Jamie had Tino's first and only child.

"Jamie, where is Tia?" Shanice asked.

"With Tino's mama." those words caused Falen's heart to drop to her stomach.

"Oh, okay. How is Mrs. Wiltz doing, anyway?"

"Girl, missing her big head ass son."

"So, Tino is still in Atlanta, huh?" Shanice questioned.

"Yeah." Jamie sighed. "Aint no telling when that nigga coming back. Shit, he probably got a bitch out there knowing him." she said strictly for Falen's benefit.

"Okay Falen, let's go wash this perm out your hair." Shan told her.

Falen stood up and her belly protruded through the plastic shawl. Jamie couldn't believe her eyes. There was one of her baby daddy's bitches standing there pregnant. The ironic part was that Mrs. Wiltz superstitious ass had been asking her if she was expecting for the past few months. Mrs. Wiltz had been dreaming of fish and when those dreams came to her that always meant that someone close to her was having a baby. Then once Tino started complaining about being nauseated and tired it confirmed things for his mama. Mrs. Wiltz swore that men could experience sympathy pains from their baby's mother.

Jamie was never into the old folk tales, but Tino's mom's predictions always came true. Hell, Mrs. Wiltz was the first person to tell her that she was pregnant with Tia, and she hadn't even missed her period by that time. So, something deep in Jamie's soul told her that Falen was carrying her daughter's sibling, and she was praying that it just wasn't so.

Chapter 11

The New Arrival

"Bitch, come outside! You bad! Bring your bitch ass out here!" Shaquita shouted while parading up and down the sidewalk barefooted with a scarf wrapped around her hair.

Falen stood there and watched that clown do her thing. The girl's in Kelly Court loved to talk shit and cause a scene. Any other time she would have ended that conversation with just one mean slug, but the circumstances had changed. She couldn't get out there when her due date was just two weeks away.

"Bitch, I know one motherfuckin thang, you better get your bitch ass from in front of my mama house!" Toya spat.

"Now, this yellow bitch got something to say. Toya, you know that I will drag your skinny ass down this sidewalk!"

Shaquita was Booby's baby's mama and wanted to fuck up anybody close to Falen. She was a short dark skinned chick with a round ass. She knew that Booby lived with Falen and she was pissed. The crazy girl actually thought that Booby was Falen's baby's father even though he was clearly locked up when the baby was conceived.

The thing that got Shaquita going was that Booby never bothered to deny the baby. In fact, he purposely allowed people to assume that he was the father. He was more comfortable with that versus telling anyone that Falen was carrying Tino's child. So, in Shaquita's eyes Falen had taken her man, although he never belonged to her from the beginning.

Janah was enjoying the scene but she didn't appreciate Shaquita putting on a show in front of her mama's apartment, either. "Say Quita, I suggest that you move around!"

"Janah, I aint got nothing against you, but I'm going to hurt these two bitches."

For some reason people took one look at Falen and Toya and assumed that a light wind could come through and knock them down. Toya was never the type to run from a fight but she never went there unless it was absolutely necessary. She could have easily called a few of the local goons to handle Shaquita, but she needed to send the haters a message. So, she stepped off of her mama's porch and laid dead in Quita's ass.

"Get that bitch, Toya!" Janah yelled.

Falen was surprised to see her rooting for her little sister. Maybe Janah was actually growing up.

Toya had Quita in a headlock as she battered her face. It seemed as though the entire projects had made their way outside. Little high yellow Toya was fucking Quita's black ass up. Eventually, Booby made his way over and found his baby mama in the center of a brawl. A slight smile invaded his face as he watched Toya handle her.

"Toya stop!" Falen screamed. This caught everyone's attention because her voice dripped with pain.

"What's wrong?" Booby ran to her side.

"I think that my water just broke." she let out as she held her belly.

"Oh, shit!" Booby panicked.

By that time Junebug had finally had the good sense to pull Toya and Shaquita apart. "Man, yall chill out, Toya, Go see about ya patnah."

Toya turned to see Falen holding her belly. She ran over to her, "What's wrong, Falen?" she asked as she attempted to wipe Quita's blood off of her.

"Her water broke." Booby spoke up.

"Well, let's take her to the hospital, then." Toya said excitedly.

"Bitch, you aint going nowhere with me with that blood on your clothes." Falen cringed.

"Shut up." Toya smiled. "Yall need to go to the truck while I change." she said as she ran into her mama's apartment.

"You okay, Falen?" Gloria's neighbor, Tasha, asked her.

People were still standing around being nosy even though Shaquita had taken her ass around the corner. So every step to the Navigator people asked Falen if she was okay. She nodded and kept it moving.

Booby aided her as she climbed in the truck as another contraction hit her. "Toya need to come on! Tez is not trying to wait on her ass!"

On February 14, 2009 Tez Jaylen Wiltz was introduced into the world. The moment Falen laid eyes on her son any doubts she had vanished into thin air. He was now her reason to live. She never thought that she was capable of loving her child the way that she loved him.

Booby and Toya stood by Falen's side the entire time. Initially, Booby felt indifferent about Falen having another man's child, but once he held Tez all of those thoughts left his mind. He could feel the love blooming in his chest.

Toya adored her godson and was planning to spoil him rotten.

"Hey, Tez." Toya cooed as she held him in her arms. "You are so handsome. Looking like a baby Tino. Yes you do."

Falen shook her head as she listened to Toya. Booby had gone to the cafeteria so they were in the room alone. "He really does look just like that man." she laughed.

"Yeah, man. Every time I look at him all I see is his daddy." Toya nodded. "So, does Booby know that you're giving the baby Tino's last name?"

"No, but it doesn't matter. I don't have to tell him anything. He aint my man."

Toya gave her a look. "Falen."

"Falen what? He is not my man, Toya."

"Well, you could've fooled me. I guess that I thought that yall was together since you fuck him every night and wanted him at every doctor's appointment. That sounds like couple shit to me. But hey, that's just me." Toya said sarcastically.

"Whatever."

Toya rolled her eyes at Falen as she answered her ringing phone. "Yeah."

"Toya, where Falen at?" Tony asked her.

"Why, what you need?" Toya asked keeping it strictly business. Since the day they started doing business with him she'd kept it platonic. She was dead serious about not mixing business with pleasure. Besides, who wanted to be with a man while you're his supplier?

"She told me that she was going to front me something." Tony said. Since Booby had been home they'd let it be known that they had the work, but only he could serve them. So, everyone knew that Falen and Toya made most of the decisions, but mainly Falen.

"Well, Falen just had the baby and is doped up on all types of medication, so you gon have to call in a couple of days."

"Toya, don't do it like that. I need the issue right now." Tony pleaded. She could hear the desperation in his voice. He was sounding like a washed up junkie. It was obvious that he was using too much of his own product.

"Okay, well call me back in a few." she told him before hanging up. She didn't even bother to ask Falen about any promises to Tony. She knew that Tony was full of shit. He was a master manipulator. She'd just spoken to Tony's cousin Jacob and told him about Falen giving birth. Tony must've seen that as the perfect opportunity to claim that Falen promised him a front. He knew that she was probably heavily sedated. The thing was that Falen didn't front anybody. It was all or nothing with her.

Booby walked back inside the room with three brown paper bags. "Man, why Tony just called me saying that Falen promised him a front?"

"He did? He called me with the same shit." Toya replied.

"Yeah, that powder head is up to no good."

"He damn sure is cause I didn't tell him shit." Falen added. "You got those from Grammys?"

"Yeah." Booby nodded.

"Grammys?" Toya asked confused. "That place is on the other side of town."

"Yeah, I got one of my little niggas to get it for me."

"Booby, you need to stop catering to that bitch." Toya knew that Booby sometimes went out of his way to please Falen. She was a picky person and would sometimes have some of the silliest demands. Like a dumb ass Booby would break his neck to make it happen for her.

"Whatever, you hater. So, Booby did you order the burger the way I like it?"

"A burger with lettuce, tomato, red onions, Swiss cheese, American cheese, double meat, bacon, and honey mustard, right?" Booby asked Falen.

"That's right." she smiled as she rubbed her hands together.

Booby sat her bag in her lap then took all of its contents out. He unwrapped her burger and placed her seasoned fries next to it. After that he drizzled ketchup all over the fries just the way she liked it.

"Are you serious? Why don't you just chew her food for her too while you're at it." Toya teased.

Falen gave her the finger as she stuffed her face. Her hair was all over her head but Booby just sat back and lovingly gazed at her. It was clear to see that he was head over hills in love with her. It was too bad that she didn't feel the same way about him.

It was two in the morning and three week old Tez had just awakened screaming at the top of his tiny lungs.

"Booby, can you grab Tez for me?" Falen whined.

Booby was half sleep. "Okay, where his bottle at?"

"In the kitchen." Falen yawned as she fell back into her pillow.

Booby slowly rose to his feet and headed for the kitchen. Since Falen had given birth to Tez she allowed Booby to sleep in her bed. That way she could call on him when Tez decided to have those late night feedings.

As Booby fed Tez Falen had her back to them; snoring her ass off. Oddly, he didn't mind doing those things for the baby. He actually loved Tez like his own son, and as far as he was concerned he was his father.

Chapter 12

Stick to the Script

A sudden wave of depression had hit Falen like a ton of bricks. She couldn't stop the crying. All she did was lay around and stare at her son. He was so beautiful and a huge part of her wished that Tino could be there to see their wonderful creation. In fact, since she had finally gotten the chance to sit still she realized just how much she missed him. Staring at the hoopla-hoop he'd bought her made her bawl every time.

Although, Falen had only dealt with Tino for a short while she felt that it would take a lifetime to get over him. He was the closest thing that she'd ever had to a boyfriend. Booby was cool, but he just didn't do it for her. It was something about Tino's touch and the way he looked at her that had her going. It wasn't about his money or his street fame; he just had a mean ass swagger that turned her inside out. She didn't know any other man in Houston that could fuck with him.

Despite the fact that Falen missed Tino, she just couldn't see herself reaching out to him. She was entirely too vulnerable when dealing with him. She didn't like that side of her and only he could bring it out. She loved being in control and Tino was a man that ran things, so she didn't see them getting together. Still, she was haunted by the memories of his sweet kisses.

Tez squirmed around a little bit before opening his eyes. "Mommy's baby is awake." Falen cooed as she cuddled her son.

Tez was still so small and fragile but he'd learned the sound of his mother's voice, so as she cooed a slight smile crossed his face. That smile brightened up Falen's day. Every time she looked her baby, she saw Tino.

"Falen, look at what I got for Tez." Booby said as he entered her bedroom with a Kids' Footlocker bag.

"What's that?"

"Some Jordans for Tez."

"Oh, let me see them." she smiled as she reached for the bag. She opened the bag and pulled out the small box. "These are so cute." she laughed as she examined the shoe. Every time Bobby copped himself some shoes he also bought his daughter Kyah and Tez a pair.

"My little nigga gotta stay fly." Booby smiled as he joined Falen and Tez in bed. "What's up Jaylen?" he said as he took the baby from her.

Booby loved calling Tez by his middle name. He was so proud when Falen named the baby after him, but didn't understand why she gave him Tino's last name. If he had it his way, that would soon change.

"Oh, my God, Falen. Please hurry the hell up." Toya yelled.

"Bitch, shut up! You cannot rush beauty." Falen said as she modeled in front of her full length mirror. Her pregnancy had left her slightly thicker in all the right places. She was amazed at how she filled out her short black slinky off the shoulder Gucci dress. Her strong legs were on center showcase and the black Gucci heels just gave them a finish touch. Her ears were adorned with black chandelier earrings. Shan had done her lashes perfectly. Her long hair was done up in huge curls falling to the left side of her head.

"Yeah, you a bad bitch. Come on if you a bad bitch. I got a bad bitch. I got a bad bitch!" Toya teased rapping Webbie's *Bad Bitch.*

Falen giggled. "Come on, let's go."

"About time." Toya laughed as she followed her to

Falen's '02 Lexus. The car was not brand new but you couldn't tell Falen that. The original owner kept the car in mint condition and it barely had forty thousand miles on it. After she threw some twenty inch chrome wheels on it you couldn't tell her nothing.

"You got Booby's gift?" Falen asked Toya as they pulled up at club Pampe.
Booby was having a huge twenty-eighth birthday bash that night. He wanted to show everybody that he was getting money.

"Yes, Falen." Toya rolled her eyes. She was decked out in a white race back dress by Prada. Her silver stilettos were by Jimmy Choo and her round ass was by Gloria and Mike.

"I hope Booby aint fucked up already." Falen laughed as she pulled in front of the valet.

As they entered the club the deejay was playing *Blame it* by Jamie Foxx and T-Pain. The crowd was thick and all the faces were unfamiliar. They knew that Booby and his friends would be in VIP, so they headed in that direction. Neither could get far without some guy stopping them trying to get a number. Each time Falen turned them down, while Toya had taken at least three of the numbers.

Booby was enjoying his night; still he was looking out the corner of his eye searching the crowd for Falen. It was a little past twelve and she still hadn't made it. Right when he was about to call her cell for the third time he saw her and Toya walking towards him.

"What took yall so long?" he questioned over the loud music.

"You already know that this slow poke was taking forever and a day." Toya yelled.

"Whatever." Falen waved her off. "Happy birthday, Jaylen." she laughed as she gave him a warm hug. He took that opportunity to grab her ass.

"This dress is sexy, but a little too short." he whispered in her ear. His breath smelled like Winter Fresh bubble gum.

"Don't hate." she playfully pushed him.

"I aint hating. You better have on some panties." he said as he slid his hand under her dress. She tried to remove his hand.

"Booby, people can see you." she whined.

"So, this my pussy." he told her seriously. Right then Falen knew that he'd been drinking.

"Give me some of whatever you drinking on." she said attempting to change the subject.

"Come on." he said as he grabbed her hand and pulled her towards the table where all the liquor was set up. She knew then that he was making a statement. They were there together.

Plenty of chicks were glaring at Falen. She was the best dressed in the room and had one of the sexiest niggas by her side. There were hundreds of other women in the room but he only had eyes for her. Booby was killing them in his black V-neck shirt, denim jeans, Gucci belt, sneakers, and backpack.

After three cups of the Incredible Hulk Falen was fucked up. She was dancing to every song the deejay played. The VIP section wasn't jumping enough for her so she ventured out to the main dance floor. The minute she started rocking her body to the beat someone joined her wrapping his arms around her waist. She turned and saw a cutie standing there and continued to do her thing.

Men were gathering to watch Falen make those sensual moves. She loved to wind her hips like a girl fresh from Jamaica. R. Kelly's *Seems like you're ready* was spinning and she was killing it. When she dropped down to the floor niggas were breaking their necks to see what she wore underneath that short dress. The men couldn't believe that they were witnessing a show like that for free.

Booby was turning a whole bottle of Grey Goose up. He was beyond high. All he could think about was going home and blowing Falen's back out. That's when he realized that he hadn't seen her for the past thirty minutes.

"Toya, where your girl at?" he asked her as she sat on some nigga's lap.

"I don't know." she shrugged.

After searching the crowd again he headed for the main dance floor.

I don't want your man cause I got it like that. And it aint even gotta be like that ha ha ha. Your man he be calling me back he say I'm fine as a matter a fact... blared through the speakers. That was Falen's song and she was hyped as she screamed the words. She was so into the words that she was actually singing to some random dude that just so happened to be in her face. "If he aint gon treat you the way he should then let him go-oo!"

As Booby spotted Falen he saw some nigga place his hand on her hip as she swayed in front of him. Instantly, he became infuriated. He stormed over and pulled her by her forearm.

"What the fuck are you doing?!" he shouted.

He caught Falen completely by surprise. "I was dancing."

"Why was you in that nigga's face?" he asked as he dragged her through the crowd.

"Booby, let me go!" she yelled as she tried to pull away.

"Don't make me act a fool in this bitch." he gritted as he pulled her closer.

She was so embarrassed as he dragged her along. He was fuming. Luckily, the time was two and the crowd was dispersing. Their friends helped them with Booby's gifts as they continued to argue. Even once outside they went at it.

"You know what, fuck you Jaylen!" Falen shouted as she waited for the valet to bring her car.

"Fuck you!" he yelled as he big faced her causing her to lose her balance.

Falen stumbled to the ground. "Bitch, I will kill your ass if you touch me again!" she seethed as she struggled to her feet.

"Booby, chill out, dog." Kay-Al said as he tried to pull him away.

"Fuck that!" Booby lashed as he yanked away from him. "Come here." he gritted as he grabbed Falen's hair.

"Un uh, let her go!" Toya ran up out of nowhere. She tried to wedge herself between the two. "Move, Booby! This aint cool. Stop!"

"Get out my way, Toya!" he shouted refusing to release Falen.

"One of yall niggas grab him!" Toya yelled at the niggas that worked for them.

"Booby, come on, my nigga." Junebug pleaded as he pulled Booby off of Falen.

"Bitch, you dead!" Falen screamed as she charged at him. Toya grabbed her by the waist.

"Stop, Falen. Let's go!" Toya yelled. Just then the valet pulled up with Falen's Lexus.

"Fuck that bitch!" Booby barked as he kicked her car.

"Keep playing and I'm a pop the truck on that ass." Falen threatened.

"Do it then." Booby fumed getting in her face.

"Come on, dog." Junebug said as he pulled him away again. "Falen, yall burn off, main. Go while I got this nigga."

Falen and Toya hopped in her car and jotted out of the lot.

As they drove home Falen vented. She screamed and

shouted about how she was going to fuck Booby up. Toya sat quietly and listened. Usually she'd be just as vocal as Falen but not that night. Falen picked up on this.

"Toya, why are you so quiet?"

Toya just shrugged.

"What that mean?"

Toya took a deep breath. "I saw this shit coming. I told you not to fuck with him. But noo, you got this, remember?"

"Whatever."

"No for real. Falen, you know that I never liked Booby, but he aint that bad. He's still a grimy motherfucka but the boy got a soft spot for you. It's obvious that you don't want him like that. You're doing what's convenient for you. You can't expect him to do all tha shit he does for you without him taking it personal. You want him to play daddy to Tez. Give you back rubs. Have a shoulder for you to lean on. Fuck you when you feel like it. All so you can turn around and say that yall are just friends. That shit aint cool. You're playing with fire. Put yourself in his position. Would you like it if he did that shit to you? There's a thin line between love and hate."

"I know." Falen admitted. "But his ass was still wrong for putting his hands on me."

"He was." Toya nodded.

"But to end this drama I'm a have a long talk with him. I'll let him know that we're going to have to stop this. We're going to remain friends and get this money together."

"This been one hellova night." Falen sighed as they pulled into their driveway.

"You aint lying. You motherfuckas blew my high with all that damn drama."

"Shut up, bitch." Falen sighed as she climbed out the car. She hated to know that Toya had been right all along. She should have never gotten involved with Booby.

Business and pleasure just didn't mix.

"Come on Toy…" Falen was about to say before she felt cold steel pressed against her temple.

"Don't move, bitch." a masked man gritted.

"What the fuck?" Toya spat as she hopped out the car.

The masked man grabbed Falen by the neck and aimed his gun at Toya. "Where the money at, bitch?"

Toya unconsciously lifted her hands. "Whatever you want, take it."

"Take off that ring." he demanded.

Toya did as she was told.

"Take off those shoes too. My bitch will like those."

Toya stepped out of her seven hundred dollar heels while realizing that robber's voice was awfully familiar.

"Take off those earrings." he demanded. "Matter of fact, take off everything."

"What?" Toya asked exasperated as her hands shook.

"Bitch you heard me!" he lashed as he gripped Falen's neck tighter.

It was then that Toya realized exactly who was pointing a gun at her. She decided to keep quiet about that, because he might be inclined to kill them if he knew that they could come back for him or turn him into the police.

Toya proceeded to undress until they heard tires screeching loudly. They all turned to see four niggas jump out of a ride.

Everything was happening too fast for the masked gunmen and he didn't know who to point his pistol at. By the time he made a rash decision to focus on the dudes it was too late. Once he turned his head he was cold cocked in the head with the butt of a gun. Falen was able to pull away from him as Booby and his boys commenced to kicking his ass.

"Get the bitch ass nigga!" Toya seethed as she joined in stomping him. "You want to try to humiliate me after I put you on!"

"Fuck you, bitch!" he lashed even while taking blows.

"Take this nigga to the car. Put him in the trunk." Booby demanded as his boys dragged him away.

"You okay, baby?" He asked Falen.

She nodded.

"Thank God, I followed yall home or else I would have never saw that nigga waiting at the gas station up the street and followed yall home."

Toya nodded. "That's what's up. I knew that Tony's bitch ass was going to be a problem, but I never saw this shit coming."

"Friends?! You want us to be just friends?" Booby roared. He couldn't believe that even after everything had gone down she was still on some other shit.

"Yeah. I want us to continue to do our thing but I just can't deal with a relationship right now." Falen sighed.

"So, that's really what you want?"

"Yes, Jaylen. I love you but just not the way that you want me to. I would be wrong if I continued to lead you on."

"Whatever, Falen. I'll be back." Booby huffed as he stormed out the front door and hopped in his Cadillac.

Falen took a deep breath as she took a seat on the couch. She looked at Tez in his swing. "I got your Booby mad at me."

Tez stared at his mama with a huge grin.

Chapter 13

He's Baaack

"Ay, bitch ass nigga!" Tino shouted from his G-Wagon.

"Say, Tino come holla at me." Junebug shouted.

Tino felt good flossing through his hood. He'd been gone for close to ten months. Atlanta was cool, but there was nothing like home. He'd definitely gotten his weight up, while in Georgia. His cousin had a Colombian connection that had raw uncut cocaine. So, in just ten months Tino had made himself a very rich man. He'd left determined to get his money right. After taking a ten key lost he had to make shit happen.

Big Jeff, Tino's old supplier swore that they'd made the drop behind the Burger King as usual. The thing is that Tino's workers claimed that the drop was never made. Personally, Tino didn't know who to believe so he laid down every person that was ever involved in the transactions including the gay ass manager of the Burger King. Even if they truly didn't know anything he felt that they all were at fault.

For months Big Jeff's worker Tim and one of Tino's workers named Shun had been beefing. Shun was the person that Tim had to deal with while making the drops. Many times they'd drawn over a few words exchanged, so Shun had the bright idea of just leaving the work or money behind Burger King instead dealing directly with each other. Initially, Tim would stay on the scene until Shun and his boy made the pick-up, but when Shun cussed him out for being late he stopped. So, eventually that became their routine. One wouldn't pull up until the other was gone. That way they didn't have to kill each other. It worked for an entire year until that one night the ten kilos came up missing. Tino was livid because he was never told about the drop changes. So, he handled every person involved.

After the ten kilo loss things changed amongst his crew. Niggas felt that if he could so easily kill damn near ten people that any one of them could be next. So, a few of Tino buyers backed out. He thought that it was out of guilt and started doing niggas dirty. Fifth Ward started living up to its old name *Tha Bloody Nickel* again. Tino had his people kicking in doors and laying down any nigga that they thought had something to do with stealing their dope. Eventually, the snitching began which landed Joe in jail on some attempted murder charges. He was able to get them lowered to aggravated assault and then was given ten years' probation. That alone cost them one hundred thousand, then even more if you count all the money they missed while he fought his case.

Tino made a U-turn and pulled up in front of Junebug, while he was standing in front of the corner store. "What's good, nigga?" he asked as he hopped out his ride.

"Shit chillin." Junebug stated, as he gave Tino one of those half hugs where they gave each other dap and a snap. "How long have you been back, nigga?"

"Not even a week."

"Oh, yeah? So, how was Atlanta?"

"It's cool down there. It's a lot of money out there, nigga."

"No shit? So, what, you moving down there?"

"Hell nah. You know I'm a Fifth Ward nigga to the death of me. I can't stay away for too long."

"Bottom Boy can't leave it alone, huh?" Junebug laughed.

"Already." Tino nodded. He was back in his element and there was no better feeling. "So, who have these niggas been fucking with for the past few months?" he asked, because he and Joe had completely shut down their operation in Houston. They were waiting for the heat to die down, but now Tino was ready to get it popping again.

"A lot of people just recently started fucking with Falen." Junebug replied.

"Falen?" Tino asked confused.

"Yeah, Falen. The broad that you was knocking down. Don't act like you don't know who I'm talking about, nigga."

"How…I mean where did she get some work from?" Tino asked, as he scratched his head.

"Nigga, I don't know. Shit, don't nobody know. She just really started letting everybody cop from her. At first she would only fuck with certain people. She's real secretive. She don't even deal directly with people, either. We can only pay her, but Booby serves everybody. In fact, they got a few trap houses around here."

"Booby? *Jaylen James* Booby?" Tino questioned.

"Yeah." Junebug nodded.

"He fuckin with Falen?" Tino asked, feeling a surge of jealousy. In the back of his mind, he'd been thinking that he was going to run into Fallen, and slay her at least one good time. She'd been on his mind heavily, while he was away. Now, with a clearer head he was ready to chop it up with her.

"Man, I don't know what them crazy motherfuckas do. Two months ago they had a fight at his party. I had to pull that nigga off of her. Then when I asked her if she fuck with him she told me no. She swears that they are just friends. And that shit is just crazy, cause he swear that her little boy is his."

"She got a baby?" Tino asked in shock. *Got damn, I aint been gone that fucking long for her to get pregnant, and have a baby by another nigga.* He thought to himself. That just didn't make a lick of sense to him.

"Yeah, she got a little boy. Booby be taking care of

that little nigga. The only thing that don't make no sense is that Booby had to be locked up when she got pregnant. Aint no way in hell that lil' boy is for that nigga. Falen had that baby like four months after he got out, and he was in jail for seven months before then. You do the math."

Tino was a math genius so he'd figured that out before Junebug was done talking. So, he knew that it was impossible for Booby to be the baby's daddy. He then tried to figure out if he was fucking her during that time. Yeah, of course her was…but he shrugged it off, figuring that Falen must've fucked with another nigga during that time, because what chick would have *his* baby and not want him to be a part of that?

"Nigga, your ass is the hood reporter." Tino laughed.

"Whatever, nigga. Lil Tez got the same color eyes as your ass. You sure that he aint your son?" Junebug joked.

Tino's smile faded. Did he have a son out there that he'd never met? No, Falen wouldn't do the game dirty like that, or would she?

"Falen, I think Tez just shitted." Shan said as she held her nose.

Falen walked over to her son and took a peep inside of his diaper. "No, he didn't. He probably just passed gas."

"You a little disrespectful something, huh?" Shan asked Tez as she held him. "How you gon just do that to me, Tez. Huh?"

"Girl, leave my baby alone." Toya giggled.

They were all shopping at SharpsTown's Mall. For the past few months Shan and Falen had grown closer. So, she had a new hanging buddy when Toya was away with one of her many boyfriends. Shan was Junebug's sister and had grown up in the Kelly Courts all of her life. So, the three women went way back.

"Aw, this would be just too cute for Tez." Toya gasped, as she picked up a Roca Wear outfit inside of the Macy's department store.

"Let me see it." Falen moved in for a closer look.

"This baby don't need no more clothes." Shan shook her head.

"Girl, Tez is growing every day. So, he always needs new clothes." Falen mumbled, as she skimmed through the racks of clothing.

Shan was beginning to hate going shopping with Falen and Toya. Those chicks could spend three hours in one store. A day of shopping was from sun up to sun down with them. "Look, I can see that yall aint gon be done no time soon, so me and Tez gon go grab something to eat."

"Okay." Falen nodded, never bothering to take her eyes off the rack of clothing.

"You taking his stroller with you?" Toya asked.

"No, that's too much trouble. I got him." Shan said as she strolled away, with Tez on her hip.

Tino and Joe strolled through the mall in search of some new shoes. The new Jordans had just come out, and Tino had some reserved at Footlocker. They'd mainly come to pick up the shoes, but Tino had decided to get his hair cut, while he was there.

Right after the barber finished up Tino's tapered fade, they headed back to Footlocker. As they were leaving out the barber's salon Joe bumped into Shan, literally.

Shan was about to go off, until she realized who'd run into her. "Joe your ass was about to get cussed out." she laughed.

"Oh, my bad, Shan." Joe apologized.

"That's alright. You lucky you my nigga. And hello to you too, Tino."

"Oh, don't even act like that, Shan. You know that I

was about to speak." Tino chuckled, as they strolled alongside her.

"Boy, you looking good." Shan complimented Tino. He always did look nice, but on the block he mainly wore white tees and jeans. That day he was sporting a brown and black Louis Vuitton shirt, Louie belt, jeans, and sneakers. His thick platinum chain was eye catching, and his pull out top and bottom grill were blinding. He was looking and smelling like money.

"Thank you, you looking good yourself." he told her, as he stared at the little boy she was holding. It was crazy. He couldn't take his eyes off the baby. He looked just like his daughter Tia when she was that size. The baby had the same curly hair, light eyes, and complexion. His smile was even reminiscent of Tia's.

"Don't I know it." Shan blushed. She'd always had a crush on Tino, but felt that he was out of her league. She was a plain Jane, even with her hair all done up. She knew that he went for the long hair Pocahontas types. Something like Falen or somebody.

"I aint know you had a baby that small." Tino laughed.

"That aint her baby." Joe shook his head.

"No, he's not my baby. You remember, Falen? Well, this is her son."

Tino stopped dead in his tracks. "This is Falen's baby?"

"Yeah." Shan nodded.

He stood there and studied the baby. He felt something brewing at the pit of his stomach. "What's his daddy's name?" he finally asked.

Shan really didn't know. She'd heard Falen say that Booby was not her baby's daddy, so she didn't know who Tez's father was. She had no clue that Tino and Falen used to fuck around. "To be honest, I don't know. His mama aint never told me, and that aint something that you just ask a person if they never bring it up."

"Let me hold him." Tino demanded, as he held out his arms. Shan handed him the baby.

"Nigga, that baby look just like you." Joe realized for the first time. He'd only seen Tez once, and that was from afar.

Tino rose Tez eye level. "He do, don't he?" he smiled. Just then Tez smiled back and Tino felt this powerful connection.

Shan stood by with a perplexed expression. She'd never known Tino to be the baby loving type. Usually, he'd give the kids in the hood a few dollars, and keep it moving.

"Where his mama at, Shan?" Joe asked.

"She's in Macy's. Why?"

Tino turned around and headed towards Macy's. "Tino, where you going with that girl's baby?" Shan opened her arms.

"To Macy's." he answered, never bothering to face her, or stop walking with Tez.

Falen was trying on a pair of House of Derion jeans, as Toya talked on her cell. They had clothes piled up to the ceiling, outside the fitting room, and planned on buying every single item.

"Toya, how do these look?" Falen asked, as she stepped out of the fitting room.

"Good, bitch. Now hurry up. We got some shit to handle." Toya said, trying to hurry her girl.

"Is that Toya?" floated over her shoulder.

Toya turned to see who knew her. She spotted Tino, holding Tez, while Shan and Joe trailed behind him. "What the fuck?" Toya mumbled to herself.

Falen stood frozen. Where the hell did he come from, and how did he end up with her baby?

"What's up, Falen?" Tino spoke as he approached

her. The spooked expression on her face couldn't be missed.

She put out her hands. "Give me my baby." she frowned.

Tino didn't move or bother to hand her Tez. "Don't you think that we need to talk?"

Falen peered around him. "Shan, why did you give this nigga my baby?"

"I didn't know that it was a problem." Shan offered, in an apologizing tone.

"How many months is Tez, Falen?" Tino interrogated.

She couldn't believe that he was there questioning her. "Why Tino?"

"You know damn well why I'm asking you." he gritted.

"Give me my baby!" Falen snapped, trying to take Tez out of Tino's arms.

"Falen, you causing a scene. Calm down." Toya told her, as she pulled her back.

"How can you say that when this hoe ass nigga won't give me my baby?"

"Falen, you know that I got your back no matter what, but I aint gon uphold you when you wrong. It's too many kids out here that wish that they knew their father. You aint gon do Tez like that."

"Is this my baby?" Tino asked, getting aggravated.

"What the fuck you think, Tino?" she sassed

Tino bit his bottom lip. "Falen, don't make me do some shit that we both gon regret. Are you going to talk to me like a real woman or what?"

She took a deep breath. "Yeah. Let me go change. Don't go nowhere with my baby." she spat, as she went back inside the dressing room.

"Give him here, Tino." Toya said as she reached for Tez. To her surprise he turned his small shoulder away from her.

"He don't want you." Shan laughed. She reached out for him and he did the same thing to her. "So, Tez you don't know me now?"

He smiled, as he held on tightly to Tino's shirt.

"That's you, kinfolk." Joe nodded, with a smile as he stared at Tez. "He look just like Tia did when she was his size. Got your eyes and everything."

Falen had changed back into her clothes, and was just sitting in the fitting room. She sat and listened to Tino interact with his son, as she tried to calm her nerves. She didn't know what to expect from him. Maybe he was upset with her. Then again he could just be grateful to finally meet his son. Then Booby crossed her mind. How would Tino being around affect him?

"What's taking Falen so long?" Tino asked.

"I don't know." Toya shrugged. "She gotta come out, eventually. Come on yall, let's go the food court." she told Joe and Shan, trying to give Tino and Falen some privacy.

All three made a beeline out of the store. Finally, Falen stepped out of the fitting room. "Let me pay for Tez's stuff." she uttered nervously, as she tried to gather all of the clothes she intended to buy, avoiding eye contact.

"What's his whole name?"

"Tez Wiltz." she replied, purposely leaving out his middle name.

"You gave him my last name?"

"Yeah." she nodded, never bothering to look up.

"But you couldn't tell me that you was pregnant or that you had him?" he snapped.

Falen's head shot up. "Oh, don't try to act like I did you so dirty. I tried to tell you that day I saw you with your *family*. I mean, what the fuck was I to do? You wouldn't answer my calls. I wasn't about to put my business out there by telling your people, so I said fuck it."

"Girl, that's some bullshit if I ever heard it. We know too many of the same people. You know damn well I would've got the message."

"Well, if it took me telling a million people for you to know that you had a son it wasn't going to ever happen." she rolled her eyes.

"I don't like your attitude. You have a whole lot of nerve having an attitude. I been the one missing out on my first son's life. That was some selfish shit you did, you know that?"

"Whatever." she sighed as she piled the clothes on the checkout counter.

"How are you about to pay for all this shit?" he asked her with a raised brow. She easily had over two grand worth of clothes on the counter.

"With my money." she gritted.

"Two thousand two hundred thirty dollars and thirty three cent." the cashier called out the total, as she finished ringing up the last item.

Tino skimmed over all the clothes and noted that most of it was for Tez. "I got it." he said, as he pulled out a knot wrapped with a rubber band.

"No, I got my own shit." Falen spewed, as she motioned for her purse. She soon figured out that she didn't have it. "Oh shit, where is my purse?!" she panicked.

"Well, since Toya only need one bag, I guess that one of them had to be yours." Tino stated, as he counted twenty three hundred dollars, and handed it to the cashier.

"Can I have my baby?" Falen asked, as the cashier bagged the clothes.

"He's good."

Falen had never saw Tez so comfortable with a stranger. Not once had he even tried to reach for her. "Tez, you don't love mommy no more." she pouted.

Tez gave her a toothless grin. Tino just stared at the baby, as he continued to hold him. When he got out of bed that morning he never thought that before the day was over he'd have a son.

Falen couldn't stop fidgeting. She knew that the day would come, but not that soon. She wasn't prepared emotionally. Her feelings were still in the rawest form, and she didn't want to get swept up in Tino's world. She knew that he wasn't good for her. Although, she was a hustler her views hadn't changed about relationships. She knew that Tino loved to play the field, and she didn't want her and her baby to become some little sideline venture. She knew that they could never completely have him, because he belonged to too many other people.

"Here's your receipt." the cashier said, as Falen loaded all the bags in Tez's stroller.

"Thank you." Falen smiled, as she took the receipt and placed it in her pocket.

"Let's go sit down and talk." Tino commanded, as he led the way out of the store. Falen had no choice but to follow him.

She took her time as Tino walked ahead of her. Eventually, there was so much distance between them that there was no way to tell that they were together. So, as a few chickens that Tino and his friends used to pluck walked by, they all stopped to speak.

"Tino?" asked a light brown skinned girl.

"Yeah." Tino nodded.

"You don't remember me?" she asked with her hand on her hip.

"Angela, right?" he guessed.

"Yeah, that's me. How have you been?"

"Good." he smiled.

"Where is your cousin?" asked Angela's light skinned friend.

"Oh, Joe is somewhere in here." he told her.

"Is that your little boy, because he looks just like you?" asked another light skinned chick that he didn't recognize.

Tino beamed with pride, as he nodded his head.

Falen finally caught up with him and took a good look at the women surrounding Tino and her son. This was the very thing that she hated about him. Bitches were always on dick. She didn't want to compete with that.

She was dressed plainly in just denim skinny jeans by True Religion and a race back white muscle shirt. Her long hair was pulled up into a ponytail, yet she still had all of those girls beat.

"Hello." Falen waved at everyone.

Angela saw the stroller filled with Macy's bags, and then realized that Falen had to be with Tino. "Hey." she spoke dryly.

Tino turned to look at Falen. "Well, it was nice seeing yall again." he told Angela and her crew. "Come on." he told Falen as he continued walking.

Falen just shook her head, as she followed behind them.

Finally, they made it to the food court. Tino found a table and took a seat with Tez in his lap. Falen enjoyed the sight as she sat across from them.

"So, tell me why I didn't know about him" Tino demanded to know.

Falen sighed. "I thought that we just had this discussion?"

"No, you gave me this bullshit excuse. You never gave me a real reason why."

"Okay, Tino let's be real for a minute. I tried to tell you after I found out, but you weren't speaking to me by then. I didn't want to leave that type of info on your voicemail so I decided to tell you face to face. So, when I saw you in the Galleria that's why I tried to talk to you." Falen explained.

"At the Galleria?" Tino asked confused. "By that time you had to have known for a while."

"No, I didn't. I had just found out. I didn't find out that I was pregnant until I was almost five months. Shit, by the time I made it to the doctor he was able to tell me that I was having a boy."

"How the hell did you walk around and not realize that you was pregnant? Or was it that you just didn't tell me?" Tino questioned, not fully believing her.

"Tino, I had a lot of stuff going on. Sometimes I would get sick but I thought that it was because I wasn't eating right. Shit, I was living out of a motel and you know that. Then right when I thought that shit was about to get better it got worse. I saved all the money you gave me just for some bum as nigga to come snatch it. So then I couldn't move or pay for the room. I just had so much shit on my plate that I hadn't stopped to think about a period *or* a baby."

"So, why didn't you call me?"

"I did but you wouldn't answer. Somebody told me that you was in Miami."

Tino thought back on the trip he took with Tory to Miami. He was doing business and she made it all pleasure. "Oh yeah, I did go out of town, but why didn't you go to Joe or somebody? They could have gotten in touch with me."

"I needed help right then and there. I didn't have time to go searching for your cousin, besides you was tripping on me talking to him, anyway. So, we ended up staying with Craig from 2c's. That didn't last but two days because him and his uncle couldn't keep their hands to their selves. So, I had to do what I had to do. Me and Toya hustled up money to pay for a room. Then we just did whatever we had to do to survive."

"So if you was really struggling why didn't you take me up on my offer?"

"Because Tino, by then me and Toya had our own thing going. We were trying to get shit together for ourselves so that we wouldn't have to rely on other people. What you was offering required me to put my life in your hands and I wasn't down with that. I know what it's like to need people and it's not a good feeling. When I was little I needed my mama and she never came through for me. When I got older I needed my sister and she turned her back on me. So, I knew that it would be a matter of time before you did the same, and I was right."

"I didn't turn my back on you." he frowned.

"Oh you didn't? Well, what do you call it when you stop talking to somebody? Or when you stop answering their calls?"

"Come on, lil mama. Don't play me like that. You pushed me away. I came at you, remember? You turned me down and gave me a bogus ass excuse, so I figured that you wanted to be down with some other nigga."

"Tino, I did not turn you down. I just told you that I wanted to keep living where I was at. I knew that you just wanted to run shit and have me living where you could know about every move I made. Not once did I tell you that I didn't want to fuck with you anymore. You just didn't like being told no, so you said fuck it."

"If that was the case why didn't you want me to know where you stayed?"

"I don't know, Tino. I was doing a whole lot of shit that I wasn't prepared to talk about so I decided to keep shit from you. I knew that one question would have led to a million more. At the time I didn't think that you would stop talking to me because of that."

"What was you doing, Falen?" he asked, even though he already had a good idea.

"Stuff, Tino." she sighed.

"*Stuff* can get you in trouble."

"You do *stuff* all the time." she sassed, as she folded her arms.

"And I'm a man that can handle myself out here. I'm willing to do whatever. Can you handle whatever? Can you handle a nigga sticking a pistol in your face because he want what you got? Can you fight a nigga off if he strong arm you into a back room? What can you do to somebody if they decide to keep your money?"

"I handle mines."

"No, you have somebody else handling shit for you and if that nigga decided to fuck you tomorrow there wouldn't be shit that you can do about it."

"You take those same chances and you're still here." She knew that he'd really have something to say if he'd known that she'd been held at gunpoint a little while ago.

"That's because I'm that same nigga that you have to worry about. I'm the nigga that will do anything to stay on top. I'm the nigga that follows you home and learn your habits. I'm the nigga that will be waiting in your house ready to duct tape your mouth, and torture you until you take me to that safe. You aint built for this game, and you're walking around naked. You aint gon be around to see Tez growing up; living like that."

"Look who's talking.'"

"Whatever lil girl." he glared at her.

"Okay, are we done with this talk?" she snapped.

"No, so calm your ass down."

"Talk then." she frowned.

"What are you going to do to fix this?" Tino questioned as he bounced Tez on his knee.

"Fix what?"

"Falen, don't play crazy. Here is this little person that I don't even know. It's real fucked up of you, but I can't change that. And you know that I'm a man that takes care of mines, so I need to be a part of his life."

"I never said that you couldn't be." She shrugged.

"Okay well, give me your number so that we can stay in touch." he said as he handed her his T-Mobile G-Three.

"Anything else?" she asked as she entered her number in his phone.

"Where are you going to be tomorrow?"

"I don't know, why?"

"You need to meet me somewhere with him."

"Is that a request or a demand?"

"Call it whatever you like. Just make it happen."

Chapter 14

Avoiding the Inevitable

Booby was relaxing on the sectional watching BET. He was blowing on some hydro, laughing at Lil' Wayne on 106 and Park. He'd been ripping and running so much that he was happy just being able to chill on the couch. Right when he was thinking about taking a nap Falen's cell vibrated on the glass table. She was inside her bedroom so he reached for it.

"Hello."

There was a pause before, "Hello, where Falen at?"

"Who is this?" Booby asked, thinking that it was somebody calling to rescore.

"Who is this?" the guy asked back.

"What? Nigga you called this phone!"

"Where the fuck is Falen?!" the man on the other end of the phone shouted.

"Ay, my nigga, if you can't tell me who you is, then you can't talk to nobody!"

"Booby, who are you arguing with?" Falen asked, as she came out of her room in a short robe.

"Some bitch ass nigga questioning me and shit." Booby huffed.

"Give me the phone." she said, as she took the phone from his ear. "Hello."

"Who is that hoe ass nigga questioning me and shit?" Tino fumed.

"Umm." Falen moaned as she tried to head back to her room. She didn't want Booby to hear her conversation. "That was Booby." she answered once she made it to her room.

"Yall fucking or something?" Tino wasted no time asking.

"No, not that it's any of your business."

"So, why the nigga answering your phone?"

"I guess cause I left it in the living room."

"He live with you?" Tino asked, in disbelief.

"Not really. Kind of."

"What you mean? Either he live there or he don't." Tino snapped, growing aggravated.

"Well, he was staying here but he recently got his own apartment. Sometimes he comes by here to see Tez, and just chill out. He still got a key, so he comes through whenever he wants to."

"You talking like Tez is a reason for the nigga to come and go as he pleases. That aint his son, so why you allowing him to run shit?"

"He don't run nothing over here. He just has been here for Tez since the day I had him, so he's attached. And besides what I do in my house is my business."

"Falen who is that?" Booby questioned, standing in her doorway.

"That nigga still questioning you?" Tino asked, listening to Booby in the background.

"He aint questioning me." Falen sighed, feeling overwhelmed.

"You explaining to some nigga, Falen?" Booby asked as he moved in on her.

"Booby, get out of my room. I'm talking."

"And I'm talking to you!" Booby yelled, so loud that it frightened Tez, who then started wailing at the top of his lungs.

Falen walked over to his crib and picked him up. "Let me call you back." she spoke into the phone.

"No, why you trying to get off the phone? That nigga is scaring the baby. What time are you meeting me with Tez?" Tino ranted.

"I'll let you know when I call you back." she said

before hanging up.

Booby stood there pissed. He'd been trying to give Falen space for her to see that they were meant to be together. He wasn't tripping, because up until that point he knew that there were no other men in the picture. As far as he was concerned Falen belonged to him, and him only.

"Who was that, Falen?"

"Booby, get out of my room." she snarled, as she tried to rock Tez back to sleep.

"Was that your boyfriend?"

"Booby get out of my room." she replied robotically.

"You fucking that nigga?"

"Booby, get out of my room." she sat on her bed with Tez.

"Answer my question!" he demanded.

"Don't you live with a bitch?! Go bother her." she snapped.

"I don't live with nobody. That girl just got that apartment in her name for me. That's it. I stay by myself."

"I don't care." Falen waved him off.

"That's the problem. You only care about yourself!"

"Save the drama for your mama." she gave him the hand. "I keep telling you that we're not together. I don't owe you any kind of explanation. This is the exact reason why I don't fuck with you now. I can't deal with this bullshit. I tell you all the time how I feel, so this is nothing new to you. If I didn't care about you, you wouldn't be here. But you aint my man."

"You know what, fuck you. I'm the nigga that's here for you and Tez. What you searching for is right here in your face. I love you and I love your son. No, fuck that that's *our* son, I'm his daddy and you want to break up our family? For what, Falen?"

"Booby, I appreciate everything that you do for me. God knows I do, but we're just not meant for each other.

And I know that you love Tez, but he has a daddy."

"Since when? His daddy don't do shit for him! I'm that baby's daddy!" he barked.

"You and I both know that his daddy hadn't done anything because he didn't know about him."

"What you mean he *didn't*? He still don't, right?"

"He met Tez yesterday." she admitted.

Booby placed his hands on the top of his head and paced the room. "How did that happen?"

"We ran into each other at the mall."

"So, you stopped and told the nigga that Tez was his?"

"No. As soon as he laid eyes on Tez he knew that he was his, Booby."

"So, now the nigga want to play daddy?"

"What you mean *play* daddy? He is Tez's daddy, and I can't keep him away from his son."

"Fuck that nigga! He aint worried about Tez. He just want some pussy and your stupid ass is gon fall for it."

"So what if I do fuck him?"

Booby bucked and she flinched. "Yeah, bitch I should've knocked your ass out. But I aint gon touch you while you got my lil nigga in your arms." he gritted.

Falen mean mugged him as he left the room. He had her heart pounding. She mumbled, "You aint crazy."

Tino called Falen's phone for the fifth time. Each time his call went to the voicemail. He knew that she had to be avoiding him. Three days had gone by since she was supposed to meet him with Tez and he couldn't get her or the baby out his mind. So, he went to the woman that helped him through all of his women problems; Mrs. Wiltz.

"Mama, where are you?" Tino shouted as he entered his mama's home. She lived in Jersey Village, in a nice subdivision that his money afforded her.

"In the kitchen." his mom shouted back.

Tino walked into the kitchen to find his tall and slim mama throwing down. She was the best cook and he was right on time to taste some of her homemade cooking. "Mama, what you cooking for me?"

"Some smothered chicken, rice, gravy, corn, broccoli with cheese, and cornbread." she answered as she continued to tend to her food.

"That's what I'm talking about." he smiled, as he rubbed his hands together and took a seat at the kitchen's table.

"So, what brings you by so soon? Your ass was just here two days ago." Mrs. Wiltz got right down to it. She knew her only son like a book.

"I can't just stop by to visit my favorite mama?" he chuckled.

"I'm your only mama, nigga." she shot right back. Although, she now lived in the burbs Fifth Ward was embedded in her. She never allowed her change in address to change her.

"You something else, lady." he shook his head.

"Um hmm. So, tell me what's on your mind."

He took a deep breath. "Okay. So, me and Joe was walking through the mall the other day."

"Okay." she nodded, letting him know that she was all ears.

"And we run into Shan, from the Bottoms. Well, she was holding this little boy. I was staring at him because I saw a lot of my features in his little face."

"You fucked Shan?" his mama questioned confused.

"No, mama. Listen. She told me that she was holding Falen's baby."

"Falen? I heard that name before. Aint that the chick that Jamie was tripping over?"

"Yeah, that's her. But anyway, I asked Shan if she knew the baby's daddy. She told me that she didn't know. So, I went and found Falen and asked her the deal."

"Wait. That baby looked that much like you for you to go and ask her that?" Mrs. Wiltz asked with a raised brow. She knew that her son wasn't in a hurry to add another headache to his roster. Jamie was more than enough for the both of them.

"Mama, you know that I wouldn't do some shit like that, unless I really felt like the baby was mine. I mean, he looks just like Tia did when she was his size. You gotta see him. He looks just like us."

"Okay, so what did the girl say?"

"At first she was acting like she wasn't going to tell me shit. I had to pull it out of her. Finally, she admitted that he was my baby. Then she promised that she would meet me with him a few days ago. But now she aint answering her phone."

"Why do you think she's avoiding you?"

"I don't know. I'm thinking that it's because of Booby."

"Booby, who?" Mrs. Wiltz asked confused.

"Jaylen, Ms. Rose's son."

"Oh, that Booby. That girl is fucking with his broke ass?"

Tino had to laugh for a few seconds before replying. "He aint broke no more, mama. But that's not here nor there. The thing is that she has been letting this nigga play daddy, so I think that she's letting the nigga keep the baby away."

"Well, why is it that you're just finding out about this baby?"

"She claimed that she tried to tell me that day I was with Jamie at the mall. And you know right after that I left for Atlanta."

"Oooh, so that's who my dreams were about. She was pregnant during the time that I kept putting that charge on Jamie." Mrs. Wiltz nodded.

"Anyway." Tino shook his head at her supposed psychic abilities. "I'm trying to figure out a way to handle this. I really want to just find her ass and slap the shit out of her, but I'm trying to stay calm. I'm losing my patience." he admitted.

"Don't do nothing stupid, boy. Now try to talk to her with some sense. And when she let you see him, bring him by here. I need to see this baby."

"You know that I'm going to do that whenever this broad stop playing." Tino agreed. Men always had to have their mother's stamp of approval when a chick claimed to have their child. For the most part mothers just knew.

"Well, try to be understanding. I know how you want things your way but that's not life."

"Hurry up, bitch." Falen shouted at Toya. They were in the Kelly Courts for a few minutes too long for her comfort. She'd been avoiding Tino and she knew that if they stuck around too long that she'd have a run in with him.

Falen just wasn't prepared to deal with Tino, so her resolution was to just stay away from him. She needed Booby to keep things running smoothly so she figured that her best interest would be to make him happy. She'd damn near retracted her entire argument about Tino being a part of Tez's life. She just couldn't see Tino allowing her to handle her business the way she wanted. She also knew that a huge amount of her customers were once his, so she didn't want to consort with her future competition. Mainly, she stayed away because she knew that she still held a soft spot for him. She didn't want him to play on her weakness.

"Look, I'm about to go up the street because I have to use the restroom." Falen interrupted Toya's conversation with her new man Tyrin. They were wrapped in each other's embrace while standing on the sidewalk.

"Falen, chill out. If you have to use it, then go to my mama's." Toya giggled, never looking up. She was too into Tyrin to pay Falen much attention. Tyrin was a hustler from the Bottoms who had just been released from prison. He'd been doing big things since the mid 90's while in and out of prison. So, naturally he had long paper and had taken an interest in Toya when she showed up to his welcome home party. Toya felt as though she'd snagged a true life celebrity.

"Some friend you are." Falen teased, as she switched Tez from one hip to the other.

Finally, Tyrin released Toya. "What it do lil nigga?" he asked as he smiled at Tez.

"Say, I'm just chilling." Falen did her best impression of a baby.

"Where his daddy at?" Tyrin questioned.

"I don't know." Falen shrugged.

"Girl, come on. You know where that nigga Booby at." he laughed.

She rolled her eyes. "Booby is not his daddy."

"What? That nigga told me out of his own mouth that this was his baby."

"Yeah, he tells everybody that." Falen sighed, as she watched Joe watch her as he spoke on his cell. "Toya, let's go. These motherfuckas is plotting."

Toya turned and glanced at Joe. "Oh, I know what the deal is." she laughed.

"Do I amuse you?" Falen asked seriously.

"Actually you do." Toya snapped.

Tyrin stood confused. "What the hell are yall tripping on?"

"Nothing, baby." Toya said as she wrapped her arms

around his waist.

Seconds later the roar of a sports bike approached them. "There go my nigga, Tino!" Tyrin greeted Tino as he pulled up and parked right in front of Falen.

He turned off his engine and smiled. "What's good, T-Money?" he laughed, calling Tyrin by his street name.

"Shit, chilling with my baby." he said as he palmed Toya's ass.

"That's what's up." Tino nodded before turning to Falen. "So, this is how I have to do shit? I have to chase you down?"

"Whatever, Tino. I just been busy."

Tino hopped off of his bike "Busy, huh? You playing games." he snarled, as he pointed his finger in her face.

"I don't have time to play." she snapped as she pushed his hand away.

Tez started bouncing on her hip. "You excited to see me?" Tino asked as he took Tez into his arms. "Hey man. You wanna come with me?"

"We're about to go in a few minutes."

"Where we going?" Toya asked.

"Tez is going with me." Tino said.

"Says who?" Falen asked with her hands on her hips.

"I did." he gritted.

Falen reached over and used Tez's bib to wipe his mouth. Tino took this time to take a look at Falen. She'd gained a few pounds since having Tez, but it was in all the right places. She was looking better than ever, but her attitude was worse than ever before. Still, he was having a hard time stopping himself from kissing those succulent lips of hers.

Falen tried backing away to her car, but he grabbed her hand. "Where you going?" he asked, while gazing at her the way he once did when he was about to fuck her senseless.

That look sent chills down her spine. "I'm going to my car."

He closed the gap between them. "Can I spend some time with you and my son?"

Tyrin and Toya stood there the entire time, pretending to be engrossed into each other, but both were eaves dropping. Tyrin had no clue that Tino had ever fucked with Falen. He saw nothing but drama coming out of that situation. He knew that his cousin Booby was in love with her, but he could tell by the way she was eyeing Tino that the feeling was not mutual.

Tino knew that T-Money and Booby were cousins, but he didn't give a damn. In fact, he wanted him to repeat everything. Booby needed to know that the sheriff was back in town. "You coming with us?" he asked Falen again as he stroked her hand.

"What, we're supposed to ride on your bike or something?" she asked saying the first thing that came to mind.

"Nah, I'm a park this bitch at my people's spot and then pick up my Wagon." he told her never breaking their connection.

Falen found herself gripping his hand but she was still caught off guard when he knelt down a placed a wet kiss on her lips. After their lips touched his tongue slipped inside of her mouth. She unconsciously grabbed the back of his head. The only thing that brought her back to reality was Tez wrapping his hand in her hair and yanking her head away.

"Tez, why you hating, man?" Tino chuckled.

"Maybe he know something that we don't."

"Nah, you just had your hair in his face." Tino smiled as he brushed her hair out of her face.

"Umm hmm."

Tino pulled out his cell and called Joe. "Say kinfolk, come do me a favor."

"What's up?" Joe asked.

"Take my bike to the spot and bring back the Wagon."

"A'ight, I was just about to go over there anyway." Joe said before hanging up.

"You could've taken your bike to your spot. Me and Tez could have waited for you." Falen told him.

Tino looked at her with a raised brow. "Yeah, right. I'm good. Joe gonna do it. I can't chance you running off again."

"You gon get in trouble if you keep playing with a nigga like this."

As Tez napped in Tino's king sized bed Falen and Tino hung in the living room. She'd straddled him as he sat on his couch. She could feel him growing inside of his pants. She was enjoying teasing him. Tino was realizing that she wasn't the same inexperienced girl anymore. A huge part of him was jealous, realizing that she'd developed those skills while dealing with other niggas.

"You know you want this." she taunted him, as she stroked her bare pussy on his jeans.

Tino had to laugh. She'd become much more aggressive since that last time they'd made love. "Your ass is nasty. How you gon walk around with a sundress with no panties?"

"Shut up." she moaned as she silenced him with a kiss.

Falen had been sitting on him for over thirty minutes driving him insane. He was tired of playing with her, so in one quick move he lifted her ass, unzipped his jeans, and whipped out his pipe. She sat back down placing his piece between her second lips. She swayed her hips causing him to brush against her clit. She was becoming lost within the feeling.

"You trying to get you one?"

Falen didn't answer as she continued on with a determined look on her face. Tino lifted her ass again and slid inside of her.

"You can get one now." he told her as he kissed her.

She knew that he was packing, but had somehow forgotten how he'd stretch her to the limit. She was quickly reminded as he pulled her dress above her ass and hammered into her wet pussy.

"Oww." she cried out.

"You still can't handle this dick." he laughed, as he continued to pump deep inside of her.

"You wanna bet." she panted as she repositioned herself, so that she was now squatting on him.

"Oh shit!" he gritted as he held her waist. "Damn, F...F...Falen." he stuttered as he bit his bottom lip.

"You like how I'm fucking you?"

"Hell, yeah." he moaned.

"This pussy wet enough for you?"

"Y...Y...Yeah."

She dropped down on him so hard that she felt as if she'd stabbed herself in the stomach. "Shit." she panted.

Throughout the room all that could be heard was their heavy breathing and his pole sliding in and out of her wetness.

"Umm." Tino moaned. "Cum for daddy."

Falen tried to fight it, but she was about to explode. "Oh God!"

"No, don't fight it. Cum for daddy!" he demanded as he smacked her ass.

"I don't wanna cum yet." she panted as her body lost

control.

"Um hmm. That's what I'm talking about." he gritted as he rammed himself deeper. "You gon start listening to me! This still my pussy. You understand?"

"Umm hmm."

"No, I wanna hear you say it. Do you understand me?"

"Yes." she moaned.

"Now, what's my name?"

"Tino!"

"Who this pussy belong to?"

"Tino!"

"Yeah, that's right and don't you forget it." he growled as he used his index finger to stroke her clit, taking her orgasm to another level.

"Umm."

"You like that?" he asked her as he flipped her over and entered her from behind.

"Too much." she moaned as she looked back at him.

"Well, you're about to love this." he growled as he deep stroked her. The harder he pumped the more she clawed his couch. In one quick motion he stepped completely out of his boxers.

Tino was pulling her hair as she threw her ass back at him. He smacked it every so often to encourage her. "Damn, baby. What you trying to do to a nigga?"

"Ugh!" she roared as she released another gut wrenching orgasm.

He gripped her hips tight as he climaxed right after her, and then they both fell into the couch.

"Aahhh!" Tez cried from the bedroom.

"Oh, shit. Let me go get him." Falen said as she struggled to her feet.

"Nah, I got him." Tino said as he placed on his boxers.

Falen made her way to the bathroom as Tino picked up a crying Tez. The crying stopped instantly. "What's wrong lil man? You thought that we forgot about you?"

Tez laid his head on his father's shoulder and fell back asleep.

"He's sleep again?" Falen asked as she entered the room.

"Yeah, but he needs to be changed. He got this room humming." he chuckled softly.

"He sure does." she frowned as she tried to wave away the funk.

"Bring me his diaper bag." Tino said as he laid Tez on the bed.

"Okay." Falen said with no hesitation. She was more than happy to let him change that shitty diaper. As she made it to the living room she heard her cell phone go off. The call was coming from her house. "Hello." she spoke into the phone.

"Where the fuck you at?" Booby questioned angrily.

"Why, something wrong?" Falen whispered as she took a seat.

"What the fuck you whispering for?!"

"Booby, what do you want?" she gritted.

"Tell me where you at!"

"Around."

"You with that hoe ass nigga, huh?"

"Why?"

"Are you with him?!"

"If this call is not about money I don't have time." Falen snapped as she hung up.

"Who was that?" Tino asked as he walked over with Tez in his arms. He could see that somebody had said something to piss her off.

"Nobody."

"Well, *nobody* got you pissed. It was that nigga

Booby, huh?"

She nodded.

"What I'm trying to figure out is what do yall have going on. I know yall hustle together, but it's more to it than that."

"So, what you trying to figure out?"

"Are you fucking him?"

"No." she shook her head and then sighed. "Not anymore."

"But you was, huh?"

She nodded again.

"When was the last time?"

"Tino, I don't think that…"

He cut her off. "No, answer the question."

"A little before you came back into the picture."

"You was fucking him while you was pregnant?" Tino asked, feeling sick to his stomach. He didn't like the idea of her lying with anybody else while carrying his seed.

She looked into his eyes. "Yeah."

He bit his bottom lip. He wanted to call her every bitch and hoe known to man, but deep down he knew that he'd played a hand in how things went down. "Say, I aint gon tell you this but once. Tez aint got but one daddy, main. *Fuck* that nigga from here on out. If you deal with him on a business level then that's on you, but I don't want him dealing with my son. You at least owe me that much."

Is he for real? Falen asked herself. *The same ole bossy, controlling ass Tino.* A part of her wanted to cuss his ass out, but she had to keep it real with herself. Tino had never walked away from their baby. Yeah, he walked away from her, but never Tez. What man wanted some other man being a father figure to their son if they were right there willing to be there themselves? "Alright, Tino." she nodded reluctantly.

"So, what happened to the diapers?" he asked,

moving right along.

"Oh, here they are." Falen sighed as she handed him the bag.

"Yall staying here tonight?" he asked as he took a seat next to her.

"I don't know about that. I have some things that I might need to handle."

"Fuck that shit. I just need yall tonight. Can you give me that?"

After taking a look into his eyes, "Yes." just rolled off her tongue.

Chapter 15

Conflict of Interest

"Toya, I know you know where your girl at."

"Man, I keep telling you that I don't know where she is." Toya snapped. She was so tired of Booby giving her the third degree. Falen and Tez had been gone for the past three days and he was about to lose his mind. Falen had never stayed anywhere overnight with Tez.

"Well, let me use your phone."

"Nah, Booby. She'll call you if she wants to talk to you." she shook her head. She knew exactly where Falen was and that she didn't want to hear from him.

"You wrong, Toya."

"Wrong for what?"

"You going right along with her while she's fucking with that nigga."

"First of all, I don't know where she's at. And if she is with Tino, so what?! He is Tez's daddy. That's not going to change just because you have a problem with it."

"But I'm the nigga that's been there for that baby!"

"So what, Booby? You knew the deal since day one. The only reason Tino hadn't been involved was because he didn't know about Tez. That's not his fault. If anything Falen is at fault for that, but that's over. Tino knows that he has a son now. You and I both know that he aint gon just let you play daddy to his baby. It's not happening. Now, you and Falen is something else. If she don't want to fuck with you then you can't make her. What you're doing is only going to make them closer."

"Man, fuck that bitch!" Booby bellowed as he threw his cell phone across the room smashing one of their lamps.

"Nigga, what the fuck is wrong with you?!"

"Fuck yall bitches!" he roared as he stormed out of

the house.

"This crazy motherfucka." Toya mumbled as she dialed Falen's number.

"What's up bitch?" Falen answered in an upbeat tone.

"Where you at?"

"I'm still at Tino's spot. Why what's up?"

"That nigga Booby just broke a lamp."

"How?" Falen's voice rose.

"He threw his cell phone and smashed it into the lamp. The nigga was on some trip shit, for real."

"Oh, his bitch ass gon pay for that." she seethed. "What makes him think that he can throw a fucking tantrum is somebody's house?"

"Who, baby?" Tino questioned in the background.

"Baby? Did he just call you *baby*?" Toya teased.

"Shut up, bitch." Falen giggled.

Toya hadn't heard that kind of laughter from her in while. She was happy for her girl. "Well, I was just calling to let you know the deal. I think that we should change the locks on his ass."

"That might not be a bad idea." Falen laughed. "I'll call you later so that we can talk about it."

"Okay, girl. Get a nut for me, while you're at."

"Fuck you." Falen grinned as she hung up. Those past three days with Tino had been glorious. She hadn't smiled that much in her entire life. She was actually dreading going back home and dealing with her reality.

"Who was yall taking about?" Tino pried.

"Nobody." Falen sighed.

"You can't bullshit a bullshitter. That nigga tripping?"

"It aint nothing that I can't handle."

"Let you tell it. You and Tez can just live here with me. You aint gotta go back home and deal with that nigga."

"Wow. How did we go from me handling something to us moving here?"

"I gotta be real. I just don't like the idea of Booby coming and going to your house. So, to avoid confusion you just stay here with me, so that I can bond with my son. And he needs to meet his big sister."

"Yall can bond and he can meet his sister, while I continue to live in my own house."

"Why, so you can fuck that nigga?" he asked growing angry.

Falen rolled her eyes to the ceiling. "Tino, this is not about him. I have a home that I'm buying. I'm not leaving something that I put blood, sweat, and tears into. You haven't even seen my crib, so you don't understand how much I grinded to get it."

"Oh, I seen it." he nodded casually. "You the third house to the right in a cul-de-sac."

Falen took a better look at him. "What, you know where I live?"

"Yeah." he hunched his shoulders as if it was nothing.

"Okay." Falen waved her hands. "So, how do you know?"

"Falen, you know me, right?"

"Yeah."

"So, you know that I'm a nigga that has to pay close attention to everything and person in my life. So, with that you should know that I would have to know where my seed lays his head. Especially, after I heard that bitch ass nigga throwing a temper tantrum in the background."

"Well, if you knew where I lived why did you have to catch up with me in the Bottoms?"

"Cause if I would've had to show up on your doorstep I knew that shit wasn't going to be pretty. That was going to be a last resort. Booby is there way more than you claimed."

"So, you was spying on me?" she grew indignant.

"No. I was making sure my seed was straight."

"Boy." she blew out some air. "You's a motherfucka."

"Say what you want. You just remember that there aint shit that you can get past me."

"Who said that I wanted to get anything past you?"

"I'm just letting you know. As long as you got my lil man your business is my business." he said as he lifted Tez up and kissed his cheek. "Say daddy, Tez."

Falen sat and stared at Tino as he took care of their son. He changed his diaper just like a seasoned father. He was even able to keep Tez smiling the entire time.

My mama used to tell me 'bout these broke ass bitches in these streets... Tino's cell phone rang out. By the ringtone he knew that it was Joe.

"What's the bidness?" Tino answered.

"Tee, where you at, nigga?" Joe asked.

"At tha crib, why what's up?"

"Oh, okay. I was just asking. You coming out to tha hood today?"

"Umm...I don't know yet."

"Is Falen still over there?"

"Yeah, why?"

"Let me find out you ova there playing house, nigga."

Tino chuckled. "Fuck you."

"Yeah, a'ight. Jamie been lookin' fo you."

"Man, the fuck she want?"

"I don't know. Why don't you ask her?"

"Man, I don't feel like hearing all that bitching and moaning."

"You cold on these hoes, main."

"Nah, man. You gotta feel me. I get tired of her

calling to argue about what bitch she heard that I was fucking. That shit is getting old."

"Well, stop leading tha broad on, then maybe she'll let go." Joe suggested.

"What?" Tino said as he glanced at his screen. "Man, this her worrisome ass calling right now. Let me see what she want."

"Alright. Just hit me later." Joe said just before Tino clicked over.

Falen sat back and studied Tino. She wasn't that same damn chick that allowed him to blatantly disrespect her. She wanted to see just how far he was going to take the conversation while in front of her.

"What, main?" Tino spoke into his cell.

"When are you going to spend some time with your daughter?" Jamie badgered.

"I'ma come get her in a few."

"That's the same thing you said last time, Tino."

"Okay, and I already told you that I got caught up."

"Yeah, right. You just too busy chasing these hoes. I heard you back out in the Bottoms digging at the bottom of the barrel."

"What?"

"You heard what the fuck I said. You and that bitch *Falen* aint kicking it?"

"Man...I know you aint call me for this shit. Why you worried about it?"

"Why wouldn't I be? You don't even have the decency to go find you a bitch far removed from my world. No. You go and get a bitch that everybody and they mama know, knowing that it will get back to me. How disrespectful could you be?"

"Look, Jamie, man. I don already told you that I don't fuck with you like that. So, whoever I choose to fuck with is my business."

"Oh, yeah?"

"Oh, yeah." Falen interjected.

"Who the fuck is that?!" Jamie shouted as she heard a female in the background.

"Don't worry about it."

"Uh Tino, I think it's time that you bring this little convo to an end." Falen said loud and clear.

Tino shook his head as he ended his call with Jamie. He was seeing firsthand that Falen wasn't that old shy girl anymore. She was letting him know that she wasn't the one. He liked that.

"What the hell you grinning for?" she snapped as he gave her a wide fiendish grin.

"You. Now you gon have this girl blowing my phone up."

"Well, that's her business. All I know is that I'm not about to sit here while you entertain her."

He nodded before deciding to change the subject. "I'm taking him to visit my mama tomorrow."

"Tomorrow? I told you that we're going home *today*."

He sucked his teeth. "Me *and* Tez are going to see his grandma tomorrow. You can come if you'd like."

"I know that it's some shit that you need to handle in these streets. So, let me and my baby go home."

"What I told you about that *your* baby shit. This is *our* son. Now, if you gotta handle some shit then you go and do what you got to do. But Tez is chilling right here."

While Falen showered Tino and Tez chilled out on the couch. She claimed that she needed to handle some business, so she was freshening up before heading out. He really didn't know what to believe. For once in his life, he knew how most women felt. He wasn't as secure as he'd like. Falen was in the streets getting her own money and really didn't need him. Then besides that, he didn't know if she was really about to go chase money or hook-up with that bitch ass Booby. His jealousy was about to drive him insane.

His thoughts were interrupted by Falen's cell. It was vibrating on his glass table. Usually, he wouldn't even play himself by answering a broad's cell, but the phone was calling him. Taunting him. He had to know who was calling.

"Hello." he answered the phone.

There was a slight pause, then, "Where Falen at?"

"Who dis?"

"Who da fuck is this?" the caller shot right back.

"Is dis Booby's bitch ass." Tino asked, never the one to mince his words.

"Say what, hoe ass nigga?"

"Bitch made nigga, you heard me. What the fuck you want?"

"Say muthafucka, where Falen at!" Booby shouted about to give himself a heart attack.

"She in the shower washing that pussy…Or should I say *my* pussy. You know I just wore that ass out, huh? Probably put another baby up in her." Tino teased.

Booby was steaming hot. "Yeah, okay. I'ma raise dat one too. Sorry deadbeat ass nigga."

Tino chuckled never losing his cool. "Nah, you got me confused with that fuck up you see in the mirror every day. I got mines. You need to get yours."

"Nigga, you fucking wit mines now! She probably still got my dick on her breath."

Now, that ticked Tino off just a little. He just knew that his dick was the only one to ever grace Falen's lips. "She sucked ya dick, huh? Was it before or after she found the tweezers?"

Tino could hear Booby breathing but there was no

response. Tez began to whine.

"Say, dis convo was cool, but my son getting tired of ya bitching. Go call some otha bitch and forget dis number. Then I might think about letting you live."

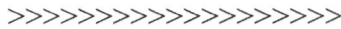

"So, what do you think that we should do, because I aint comfortable with putting too much in this nigga's hands right now."

"Well, we have to do something because we don't even know all the people that he deals with. And I'm just not comfortable with distributing ourselves." Falen told Toya as they drove in her Lexus.

"Really, I think that it's time that we handle this shit alone. These niggas already know that we're holding. We can just continue to pick up the money first and deliver the work to the traps." Toya suggested.

"And what will we do if one of those niggas decide to fuck us?"

"Falen, I thought that we were playing for keeps?"

"We are."

"Okay then, we can't do scared business. We'll just protect ourselves and get dirty if necessary. But we can't put all our faith in Booby. Anything could happen to him tomorrow. Then what? Business still has to be handled. The nigga is already salty so aint no telling what he'll do. Why chance it?"

"I don't know, man. I need to think about this." Falen sighed.

"Oh, don't tell me that you're on some housewife shit. You trying to be Tino's kept bitch?"

"Toya, please don't patronize me. This is not about Tino. I have a son to live for so I don't want to put him or myself in any immediate danger. So, I want to take the route with minimum risks."

"Risks?!" Toya shouted in disbelief. "We've been taking major risks since the day we snatched that shit! We became targets that very same night. So, don't tell me about no risks. Either you with it and be all the way with it or leave it the fuck alone!"

"Bitch, I don't know who the fuck you screaming at but you need to calm the fuck down! You been watching too many gangsta movies. Talk to me with some fuckin sense!" Falen roared.

That took Toya by complete surprise. Falen was usually a passive aggressive person that avoided confrontation. She was always down to scrap, but never really entertained arguing.

"Maybe we both need to calm down." Toya said in a lower voice.

"Yeah, maybe the fuck we should. This whole way of life is getting on my motherfuckin nerves! I wanna just get rid of this shit and wash my hands with dope. Cause I aint built for this and Tez didn't ask for this."

"So, now you saying that you don't want to re-up with those Mexicans again?" Toya questioned. They had slowly but surely gotten rid of the ten kilos and had stumbled upon a connect who'd been supplying them with more bricks. So, both women had agreed to set aside money to re-up when they got down to the last two keys.

"I really don't know." Falen said as she tried to focus on the road.

Toya shook her head and mumbled to herself. "You are so fucking selfish."

Falen turned and stared at her. "No, you the selfish and greedy, bitch. I have to be here for Tez. That work was supposed to help us out of a hole, not dig us a deeper one. We got some change put away. Now, we can sell the house after we finish paying for it and take the money we have saved and live comfortably for a few years. Then you can figure out what it is that you wanna do with yourself. I aint trying to be some D Girl. That aint the life for me. But if you want to be this neighborhood superstar, go ahead cause I aint beat for it."

"Yeah fuckin right. You're just trading one vice for another. You don't want to be a D Girl, but you want to be the D Boy's wife, right? That's the coward's way out. Why get henpecked when you can get your own money? Stop selling yourself short."

"This is not about me being with a hustler. I don't want no parts of the life period. But I'd rather have my own money put up and let that nigga put his self on the front line. Taking the lead aint worth my life."

"That's just like a dizzy head ass bitch to hide behind some nigga that's going to drop her ass once another homeless teenager has his baby." Toya seethed.

"Bitch!" Falen spat as she slapped the fire out of Toya's mouth while never losing control of the wheel.

Toya was in a state of shock. She never saw the hard slug coming. Finally, she was able to focus and slap Falen just as hard. "Don't ever put your fuckin hands on me again!" she roared.

Without any hesitation Falen pulled over on the side of the road and climbed over to Toya's side of the car. She placed all of her weight on her as she threw vicious blows.

"Talk that shit now, bitch. I'm a homeless piece of trash, right?! I got you bitch!"

At the moment Toya couldn't do anything but take the hits. Falen had taken her by surprise and she was pinned to the seat which provided little movement. Eventually, Falen realized how far she'd taken things and decided to return to her side of the vehicle.

They both sat breathless. A few of Toya's tracks were hanging by a few strands of hair and her shirt was ripped, exposing her breasts.

"Take me home." Toya fumed as she fought back the tears.

"I sure will." Falen rolled her eyes as she pulled back into the busy traffic.

For the remainder of the ride there was complete silence. Neither woman knew what to say and both were too pigged headed to be the first to speak. Falen felt guilty about attacking Toya, but she also felt hurt that she'd thrown such a low blow. For years people talked about her crack addicted mother and the way she and her sister lived. There were plenty of nights that she'd cried on Toya's shoulder about the constant taunting from their peers. So, she never thought that her best friend would use that as ammunition to hurt her.

Once Falen pulled in their driveway Toya hopped out. Falen continued to sit in the car contemplating her next move. She didn't want to face the drama between her and Toya right then. So, she decided to call Tino and check on Tez.

"Hello." Tino spoke into the phone.

"Hey, what my baby doing?"

"Your baby? What I told you about that? And anyway why you sounding like that? What happened?"

"Everything." Falen burst into tears.

Tino sat and listened to her whimper into the phone. He wanted to be there to wrap his arms around her and comfort her. "Falen, what's wrong, baby?"

"Me and Toya just had a fight. I'm just tired, Tino. I really am." she sniffled.

"Why were yall fighting?" he asked.

"She got pissed off because I'm not feeling our situation anymore."

"Yall situation?" Tino asked confused. "She's your lover or something?"

Falen had to laugh at his silliness. "No. I'm having doubts about us continuing to get money."

"Oh, okay." Tino nodded. He was glad to hear that she was rethinking things. "So, when are you going to meet up with us?"

"I don't know." she sighed.

"Okay well, come now. Come meet me by my mama's. She wanna meet you."

She took a deep breath. "Okay."

She placed her car in gear and backed out of the driveway. She continued to talk to Tino so that he could direct her to Jersey Village. As they talked she was actually able to take her mind off her problems.

Falen became a little nervous as she finally pulled into Tino's mother's driveway. She didn't know what to expect. Tino was already standing in the driveway waiting to greet her. So, she threw her ride in park and slowly exited the vehicle.

"You don't look like you just had a fight." Tino said as he looked her over.

"It really wasn't much of a fight. She hit me once." she shrugged.

He shook his head. "You something else. Come on." he motioned with his head as he turned and headed inside of his mama's crib.

Falen decided to follow behind him. She entered the home and was impressed. It was laid. Everything from the drapes to the plush couches spoke quality.

Mrs. Wiltz was sitting on the couch with Tez in her lap. She witnessed Falen float inside of her home. She knew that her son dealt with beautiful women but still she was actually surprised at Falen's stunning features. When he'd told her that she was from Kelly Courts she was imagining someone a little rougher around the edges.

"Hello." she spoke in a sing song voice.

"Hello." Falen smiled revealing her dimples.

"So, you're Ms. Falen, huh?"

"Yes, ma'am." Falen replied bashfully.

"Now, I have a bone to pick with you. Cause see, the moment I saw this little boy I knew that he was ours. Why didn't you tell us that we had a baby?" Mrs. Wiltz asked wasting no time.

Falen began fidgeting. Tino had set her up. "Umm, I couldn't get Tino to talk to me. So, I decided to leave it alone."

"Leave it alone? That's a first. You didn't need any help?"

"I mean, yeah I did but I wasn't about to swallow my pride chasing after him, either."

"Chase after him?"

"Yeah. He was mad at me and refused to take my calls. So, when I finally ran into him he basically spat in my face. That was when I decided to do it on my own." Falen explained while relaxing a bit.

Mrs. Wiltz nodded. She knew first-hand how bullheaded her son could get. "Well, I can relate. I know that Tino can be difficult. I just want to let you know that we aint going nowhere, honey. This right here is blood." she said as she patted Tez's small thigh. "So, he's going to be a forever part of our lives and that means that you will be too. So, get used to me and my son, baby."

Falen was cool with that. "Okay." she nodded with a smile.

"And take a seat. Don't be shy."

"Okay." Falen laughed as she took a seat in a recliner.

"So, tell me baby, who is your people? Tino said that you from 5th Ward." Mrs. Wiltz questioned as she rocked back and forth with Tez as he fell asleep.

Falen didn't really want to discuss her family but she

didn't see a way out of the conversation. "Umm, my mama's name is Yolanda." she finally said.

"Yolanda? Is she light skinned with long hair?"

"Yeah." Falen nodded.

"Girl, that used to be my bitch!" Mrs. Wiltz said excitedly.

"For real?" Falen asked surprised.

"Girl, yeah. We used to run Wheatley together. All the girls used to be jealous of us. We had all the guys. Matter of fact, she had the most popular nigga in school. Fredrick Bright."

A smile invaded Falen's face at the mention of her father's name. He'd been in the penitentiary since she was seven years old but the memories of him were still fresh in her mind. "Fredrick is my daddy."

"What? No! Oh my God. You do look just like him. Is he still locked up?"

"Yeah. He don't get out until 2020."

"That's messed up. So, how's Yolanda doing?"

"To be honest, I really don't know. The last I heard she was in state jail. She stopped coming around a while ago."

"Oh. Is she still you know?" Mrs. Wiltz tried to ask in a polite way.

"Yeah, she is still on that stuff." Falen sighed.

"Oh my goodness. I would have never thought that she'd take that route. I guess her head must've been fucked up when Fredrick got locked up."

"I don't know. I can't really remember when she decided to mess her life up. I was too busy trying to keep mines once she got like that."

"I can imagine, baby. I ran into her a few times." Mrs. Wiltz nodded. Her heart went out to any child that had to grow up parentless.

"Yeah, things had gotten too crazy. Me and my sister

floated from house to house until I was like sixteen."

Tino sat and listened to Falen talk about her struggles. He knew that things weren't always beautiful in her life yet he was surprised at how hard she had it. She'd been denied a childhood and the only family she had didn't seem to care two shits about her. That wasn't a life that any child should live and for damn sure his kids weren't going through those same kind of changes as long as he had breath in his body.

"Give him here. I'm a put him in the bed." Tino told his mama as he held his hands out for Tez.

"Here you go." Tina Wiltz said as she handed him her grandbaby. "Put him in my room."

"A'ight." Tino nodded as he headed for the bedroom with his son.

Just as Tino was exiting the room someone rang the doorbell.

"Who the hell is that?" Tina asked.

Falen realized that Tino's mom was a fireball. She was enjoying that. "I don't know." she hunched her shoulders.

"It better not be one of my knucklehead ass nephews." Tina spat as she rose to her feet. "I'm about to cuss somebody out for just showing up here unannounced." she shook her head as she made her way to the door.

Due to the door being made partially with glass Tina could clearly see Jamie standing on the other side. "Hey, what's up?" she asked as she opened the door.

"Tia said that she wanted to see her granny." Jamie said as she entered the house along with Tia.

"Oh. Hey, granny's baby." Tina said as she gave her granddaughter a loving hug.
Jamie was all smiles until she spotted Falen sitting in the recliner that she sat in every time she visited. "Oh, you got company, mama?"

"Yeah." Tina said as she made her way to the couch. She wanted to see where this was going.

"Granny, where's my daddy?" Tia questioned.

"He's in the backroom." Tina answered.

"Daddy!" Tia shouted.

Falen was observing Tino's daughter. She was very pretty and looked exactly like him and her baby. Although Jamie was an attractive woman her daughter had absolutely none of her features.

"Girl, what I told you about that? Go to him. Don't scream." Tina reminded Tia.

"Okay." she said as she skipped towards the backroom.

Jamie stood not knowing what move to make next. She hadn't expected to find Falen there. In the eight years that she'd dealt with Tino she had never found another chick at his mama's. Knowing his immediate family was something that she always felt was exclusively for her. She was the only woman to bear his child and have a relationship with his mom, even if it was rocky at times. They went through changes due to her and Tino's shaky relationship. They were always off and on, and during the off periods she sometimes took her frustrations out on his mom. Still, she felt betrayed as she watched Falen sit in her favorite seat.

"Jamie, take a seat or something. Don't just stand there." Tia said as she flipped through the channels on her plasma television.

Jamie did as she was told, but it was obvious that she was uncomfortable. You could cut the tension in the room with a knife.

From Tina's bedroom Tez's cries could be heard. Moments later Tino emerged with him in tow and Tia was right behind them. Jamie's eyes grew two sizes larger as she saw him hold the little baby. She could not stop the jealousy from invading her heart.   "Who baby you got?" she questioned although she knew the answer.

"That's my baby." Falen spoke up.

"Oh, this your baby? He's cute." Tia smiled as she gazed up at Tez.

"The baby cute to you, mama?" Tino asked his daughter.

"Yeah." she nodded. "What's his name?"

"His name is Tez and he is your little brother."

"He's my brother?" Tia repeated confused. "How is he my brother, daddy?"

Tino didn't quite know how to explain that. Luckily, for him his mama spoke up. "He just is, little girl."

Tia looked at her grandma then at the baby, taking him in. After she took a closer look she could actually see the resemblances to herself on her own. "Well, can I hold him?" she asked.

Jamie wanted to jump up and drag her away from that child but she knew Tino well enough to know that he'd kick her ass if she tried something like that. She felt helpless as the man she loved introduced their daughter to a child that he made with another woman.

"Take a seat on the couch and I'll let you hold him." Tino instructed.

Jamie had had enough. The nigga wasn't going to even try to explain the situation to her before allowing their daughter to get acquainted with this supposed sibling. "Tino, what the fuck? How are you going to just tell our child that you have another baby?" she snapped.

Tino glared at her. "Jamie don't start this right now. She needs to know her little brother and we are not gonna hold this conversation right now."

"You know what, you shoul right." Jamie sassed as she stood up. "Come on Tia, let's go."

Tia wore a disappointed expression on her face.

"Why, mama?" she whined as she poked out her bottom lip.

"Let's go!"

"No, she aint going nowhere." Tino seethed.

"Fuck you, nigga! I'm so tired of your shit! All the shit I put up with and you have the nerve to stand there and try to tell my daughter that you have another baby?! Where's the fuckin respect?" Jamie shouted. She was so tired of Tino. For years she'd allowed him to do as he pleased, because he was her provider. He came to their home when he wanted and left when he wanted. She couldn't see other men while he philandered around town. She'd learned to deal with it over time, but she never had to deal with an outside child. Her worse nightmare had come true.

"Fuck this! Come on, Tia!" Jamie yelled.

Tino handed Tez to Falen and walked over to Jamie. "You need to calm the fuck down." he fumed as he stood in her face.

"Come on, Tia!" Jamie shouted totally ignoring him.

Usually, Jamie knew how far to take things, but she was letting her emotions get the best of her. Tino was a no nonsense type of person, so it wasn't long before he was ready to break her neck. "Shut the fuck up!" he gritted as he grabbed her neck.

"Tino, stop. If she wanna go, then let her go." Tina demanded.

Tino released Jamie and backed away from her. "Mama, you're right. I shouldn't even be doing this. Jamie, if you don't like the scene then remove yourself from it, but my daughter aint going nowhere. So, do what you wanna do." he said as he turned to walk away.

Something in Jamie exploded. "You dirty motherfucka!" she roared as she rained punches all over his back.

Tino quickly reacted as he turned around and

grabbed her wrist. "Calm down!" he demanded. He knew that he'd hurt her deeply. She almost never lost her cool in front of other chicks. The main woman's objective was to never let the competition see her sweating.

Falen sat and watched. She really didn't know how to feel. That could have easily been her in Jamie's shoes. In fact, a year ago that was her. It always hurt to witness your heart crumble into pieces. So, she was beginning to think that loving Tino could become a permanent introduction into a cold cruel world. That was something that she could do without.

"Jamie, stop all that in my house. Show me some respect." Tina spat as she walked over to Jamie and Tino as they continued to scuffle.

Jamie's head shot up. "Fuck you, Tina! I'm tired of you upholding him. You lie for him and now you're allowing his other sluts into your house!"

"Is this bitch serious?" Tina questioned out loud. "I uphold him, huh? No, I think you have shit twisted. I tell him to do right by you and everybody else, but at the end of the day he's a grown ass man. He will do what he wants. Now, it's up to you to tolerate his behavior. He can only take your through what you allow him to. If you wasn't so damn money hungry and lazy, you'd get off your ass and get a job, so that he couldn't use his money to control you. You made your bed, so you need to lay in it."

"Whatever! You got his bitch over here like he aint still fucking me!"

"You's a idiot. You know that? He aint your man. You aint his wife. You are his child's mother. He takes care of you because you have his child. He don't even live under the same roof with you. So, if he wanna bring Joe the hobo here it's his prerogative. And for the record, that girl there is just as welcome as you are, and maybe even more." Tina spat as she pointed at Falen.

"Fuck that low budget bitch!" Jamie barked.

Falen had been trying to remain cool, but Jamie was pushing it. "You don't even know me to know how my budget is." Falen said in normal tone.

"Oh, I know your budget bitch. I guarantee you that you aint seeing the same shit I'm seeing. You post up in the jects while I sit on a lake, bitch. I guess that this little bastard is going to be your meal ticket."

Falen was infuriated, but she never had a chance to reply because as soon as the words spewed from her mouth Tino reached back and smacked the taste out of it.

"Wait, Tino, now." Tina said as she stood between him and Jamie. "Tino, back up! You know that I didn't raise you to put your hands on a woman."

"She aint gonna stand there and disrespect my son like that!" Tino bellowed.

"Are you kidding me?!" Jamie sobbed. "Your fuckin son? What about me, Tino? What about all the promises you made to me? This is me! The woman that you swore that you wanted to spend the rest of your life with! How could you do this to me?!"

Tia stood and watched her daddy make her mommy cry for the umpteenth time. She was use to the show. She knew the drill. Stay out of their way.

"Tia, go to the room." Tina said as she ushered her towards the guestroom.

"Tia, come on!" Jamie shouted feeling like a complete fool.

"Look, I'm about to go." Falen said as she rose to her feet.

"No, you chill out." Tino told her.

"No, you handle this. I got something to do."

"Falen." Tino said sternly. He gave her a look that could kill and with that she sat back down.

"What you trying to keep this bitch here for?" Jamie

asked as the tears streamed down her face.

"Jamie, just go. I'll bring Tia home later on."

"I don't want my daughter around this hood rat. I aint leaving without my child."

"Hood rat? I keep telling you that you don't know me." Falen fumed as she stood and placed Tez on the couch. "You know what? I once thought that you had it made, but now I see what's up. You are here looking and acting a fool over something that has been over. A real woman knows when to let go. It's obvious that he's over you and the fact that you keep clinging on is only going to give him the green light to step all over you. A nigga don't want a bitch chasing after him. You knew about me, so I don't know why you're trying to act like this shit is new to you. We've had quite a few conversations when you called my phone, so save the dramatics."

"Bi..." was all that Jamie got in before Tino cut her off.

"Wait a minute. When did she call you?" he asked Falen.

"She called my phone plenty of times asking me about my baby and who his daddy is. I kept telling her that it was none of her business. Then she told me that I aint the first person to claim to have your baby and I won't be the last. At the end of the day the only child that you will ever take care of is hers. I didn't even entertain her, because I don't need you or any other nigga to survive." Falen told Tino.

"Man, you tripping." he shook his head then turned to Jamie. "I don't know what the fuck your problem is. What part you don't understand when I tell you that it's over between us?"

"Over? You don't say that when you come through and fuck me! Tino, I know that you still love me, baby." she cried. "Why, you keep doing me like this, huh? Is it because you still believe that I sent my cousin to take your shit? Is that it?"

"Shut the fuck up, Jamie." he gritted.

"No, don't tell me to shut up! Tell me why is it that you don't want me no more? I love you. That's all that I have ever done. My cousin fucked up, not me! He lost your ten keys, Tino! Why would I take from us, baby?" Jamie cried as she tugged on his shirt feeling desperate.

The mention of ten keys sped Falen's heart rate up.

"Bitch, shut the fuck up! Just put everybody in my fucking business!" Tino shouted.

"Shut up for what? Everybody know that you blame me for Shun's mistakes! I told you about the Burger King set up. You was just too busy chasing pussy to make sure that your business was straight."

At the very moment, Falen could have fallen out. She'd come up at her son's father's expense.

"Didn't I tell you to shut your fuckin mouth?" Tino yelled as he shoved Jamie to the floor.

Falen felt as though her guilt was written all over her face. She had to get out of there before Tino realized that he'd been targeting the wrong people. So, she grabbed her son and left his belongings behind. She didn't look back as she made a dash for the door.

Once Falen and Tez were securely in her car she attempted to back out of the driveway. She soon realized that Jamie had her blocked in. She was desperate to leave so she maneuvered onto Tina's lawn and backed out into the street. She didn't blink as her bumper scraped the curb. She put the pedal to the metal and skirted down the street.

Chapter 16

When it Rains it Pours

Falen tried to clear her mind as she drove around the city aimlessly. Every other minute her cell was ringing. She couldn't talk to anyone. She didn't know what to do. The only reason Tino probably had any interest in her was because he couldn't trust Jamie; based on some shit that she really did. What if he figured everything out? Would her life be in jeopardy? Would Tino believe that she was clueless when it came to stealing from him? Would he ever be able to look at her the same?

Those questions were all too much for her. She had fucked up in the worse way and it was definitely too late to correct things now. She was wishing like hell that she could call Toya and ask her for some much needed advice. Still, Falen's pride wouldn't allow her to call her best friend.

She needed some time alone, so she checked into a hotel for the night. She put Tez to sleep while she stayed up all night trying to think of her next move.

"You going to the club with us tonight?"

"I don't know." Booby shrugged.

"Nigga, you looking like you just lost your best friend." Kay-Al said as took a drag from his 'dro stick.

"Huh? Naw, nigga you tripping." Booby sighed. "So, who all supposed to be hitting up the club tonight?"

"Shit, everybody, basically. Me, Junebug, DeDe, James, Joe, and that nigga Tino. It's too many niggas for me to even remember."

"Tino, huh?" Booby said cryptically.

"You and that nigga got beef or something? Oh,

wait…You tripping over him and Falen, huh?"

"Nigga, what?"

"Aw come on, dog. You aint got to front for me. I know that you had a thing for Falen. And now they saying that her baby is for that nigga. I know that you love that little boy like your own. You probably feel like that nigga's moving in on what's yours."

"You reading too deep into shit, now." Booby chuckled.

"Yeah, okay. But on the real, my nigga, I think that you should come out to the club. You know them niggas Tino and Joe gon be doing some serious bottle poppin' since they about to get it really on in the hood again."

"That's what I been meaning to ask you about. Why did they really close down shop in the first place? I don heard so many different stories."

"Oh, you aint know? Somebody stole some keys from them niggas. That nigga Tino went on a rampage and niggas was getting wet. Everything got hot after that and them niggas had to shut shit down before they'd end up locked up." Kay-Al explained.

"Yeah?" Booby said as he stroked his chin. Some shit was starting to make perfect sense to him. Perfect sense.

Booby made small talk with Kay for a little while longer before telling him that he had to go. He hopped in his Lac and headed to the crib. He had to gather all his thoughts. As he was thinking he came to the realization that Falen was much grimier than he ever thought. She and Toya were sitting on the next nigga's work. But as slick as they thought that they were they were dealing with a nigga that was a twice as slimy. He was about to show them just how cold the game could be.

Booby sat outside Falen and Toya's home for a few hours. He was thinking of a move that would take everybody off of their marks. After contemplating for over an hour he drove around the corner from their house and got out of his car.

Falen was in a deep sleep until her cell phone jolted her awake. "Falen!" someone screamed into the phone.

"Yeah, who is this?" she asked groggily.

"This is Gloria." She cried into the phone.

Falen sat up in bed. "What's wrong?"

"Somebody shot my baby." Gloria sobbed.

Falen's heart sank. "Who, Ms. Gloria?"

"Toya."

"What?! When?!"

"A couple of hours ago. They doing surgery on her right now. It aint looking too good, Falen."

Falen felt like the room was spinning. This couldn't be happening. Not her Toya. Who would do this? Why would they do this? "Ms. Gloria what hospital is she in?"

Falen quickly grabbed her purse and Tez and headed out the hotel's door. As she walked it seemed like she was in some kind of bad dream. Her best friend had been shot. She never saw this coming.

The ride to the hospital was all a blur as her mind stayed on Toya and her condition. She parked her car and grabbed Tez and ran into the hospital. As soon as she entered she spotted Janah with a tear stained face. Without thinking they both embraced each other.

"What happened?" Falen asked her.

"They said that yall neighbors called the ambulance when they found her crawling out the house."

"Oh my God!" Falen sobbed.

"Give me the baby." Janah said to a distraught Falen as she grabbed Tez.

Falen fell to the floor. "Nooo!" she cried out.

Janah knelt down to caress her back. "It's going to be okay. She gon make it. She gotta make it."

"What am I going to do, if she don't make it, Janah? What am I going to do?" she whimpered.

"We can't think like that, Falen. She's going to make it. That's my little sister. She gotta make it." Janah said as the silent tears rolled down her cheeks.

Eventually, Falen was able to pull herself off the floor and they all took a seat waiting for the word from the doctors who were operating on Toya. Her entire family was there from her mama, brother, cousins, and grandma. It seemed like hours were passing without anyone knowing her condition.

Right when everyone was on the brink of insanity a doctor approached the family. "We've done everything that was within our power to save LaToya's life. We removed four bullets from her body and she lost a tremendous amount of blood. We did a blood transfusion and the operation was a success. Unfortunately, while on the operating table LaToya slipped into a coma."

"What are you saying, sir?" Janah asked.

"What I'm saying is that LaToya may wake up tomorrow or maybe even never."

"Oh hell, naw!" Greg snapped. He'd been maintaining his cool until the doctor said that his little sister may never wake up again. "Yall motherfuckas need to do something to save my sister, main!" he lashed at the doctor as the tears flooded his eyes.

"Calm down, Greg." Gloria told her son. "These doctors are doing all that they can to save Toya."

"Well, I'll leave you guys alone. LaToya will be transported to ICU and you guys will be able to visit her there." The Indian doctor said before walking away.

"I'ma kill the motherfucka who did this!" Gregg shouted.

"Nigga, chill out." Their cousin Do-Do said trying to calm him down.

"Fuck chilling out, nigga! That's my little sister in there!" Gregg bawled breaking down.

Falen felt like ripping her hair out as she watched the devastated looks on everybody's faces. She couldn't help but feel responsible. She knew deep in her gut that Toya was shot over the drugs they stole. Maybe somebody tried to rob them or something but none of that would have happened if Falen had left Tino's shit alone that night.

"Joe, where you at, nigga?"

"I'm in the hood, nigga. Where you at?"

"Shit, I'm at the spot." Tino replied.

"Oh, have you heard about what happened?"

"Nu unh? What's up?"

"You know Falen's friend, Toya right?" Joe asked.

"Yeah."

"Well, somebody shot her ass like five times."

"What?! You lying nigga." Tino said in shock.

"No, I wish that I was lying, main. I'm surprised that you haven't heard about it already. It was all over the news. They was saying that she crawled out of their house after somebody left her ass for dead."

Tino's mind began racing. "Where, where was Falen?" he stuttered.

"I don't know. I don't think that she was at home." Joe told him. He could sense the worry in his cousin's voice. "I heard that her and the baby are okay."

Tino felt a huge sense of relief. "Oh okay. So, is Toya still alive?"

"Man, they're saying that she's in a coma."

"Damn, that's fucked up." Tino sighed.

"I know, dog. She was a little cool something. But it's some shit being said out here, man."

"Like what?" Tino wanted to know.

"Like Toya and your girl is the ones that got us."

"What?! Where you get that shit from?"

"The nigga Kay-Al claimed that Booby told him a couple of hours ago."

"Booby? I wouldn't trust nothing that nigga say." Tino snapped.

"I mean, Tino, the shit make a lot of sense. They have been holding. Where you think they got that kind of issue from? And your girl did work at Burger King during the time."

Tino let it all sink in. "Fuck!"

"That's the same shit I said."

Tino had to laugh at himself. "She got me good, dog."

"Yeah, she did. But do you think that she knew who the work belonged to?" Joe asked.

"Man, I don't know what to think. This whole time she might've been playing innocent with a nigga. Aint no telling what was going through her mind."

"Well, we got to get to the bottom of this shit."

"Oh, most definitely."

Tino sat back and thought about everything. He couldn't believe that he'd been blaming and targeting the wrong people. He'd been looking at everybody in his circle while all along it was Falen. He'd laid down quite a few soldiers because of that incident and had completely broken things off with Jamie. Everything was all coming back to Falen. She had to pay if what he was hearing had any truth in it.

Falen sat at Toya's bedside praying that her girl would open her eyes. Toya damn near looked unrecognizable as she lay in the hospital's bed with all the tubes attached to her keeping her alive.

Everybody was at a wits end. The police had come through and questioned Falen and Toya's family. There wasn't much they could tell the police without incriminating themselves, but Falen did tell them about the surveillance cameras she had positioned outside their house. The thing was when the police searched the home for the recordings they came up empty. Someone had taken every single tape.

"Bitch, you need to wake up. I know that your ass is doing this on purpose. You just trying to get me back for getting the best of you in that fight, huh? Well, how about I let you win the next time? Yeah, I know that you'd like that." Falen told Toya.

"Tez is going to be mad if his antie doesn't wake up. You can't disappoint your little nigga, can you?" she asked as she cried softly and held Toya's hand.

"Toya, please don't do this to me. You know that I can't do this without you." She sobbed.

Her cell phone rung just as she was about to continue with her one sided conversation. "Hello." She answered as she dried her tears.

"Falen, I just heard about what happened." Booby said frantically.

"Where have you been?"

"I was at the crib. Man, I can't believe that this shit happened. I knew that I should've went over there."

"Don't blame yourself, Booby."

"No, I should've went over there. Especially after she told me that Tino and Joe knew about yall stealing their work."

"What?! When did she say that?" Falen wanted to know.

"She told me that last night. She told me that word had got back that Tino had found about yall taking his shit."

"Fuck, man. I can't believe this shit. You think that Tino got somebody to do this?" Falen asked.

"I think so. It was just too much of a coincidence that she was shot right after the word had got out." Booby said. "Have he tried calling you since the shooting?"

"No." Falen realized for the first time. She knew that Tino had to have heard about it by then.

"You see what I'm saying? That nigga knows. He might be coming for us next."

"I don't know." Falen shook her head. "I don't know if Tino would do some shit like that."

"Girl, you better wake up! That nigga killed niggas that he grew up with and knew way longer than he knew you; over that dope. So, what do you think he's going to do to you?" Booby snapped.

"Naw, something just aint right. Let me call him." Falen said.

"Falen, are you crazy?! What are you going to call him and say? *Tino, did you shoot Toya?* or *Did you find out about us stealing all your work?* Come on now. Use your head."

"So, what do you suggest that I do, then?"

"What we can do is get that nigga back. We can get him to meet us and handle his ass."

"You want me to set him up?" Falen asked in disbelief.

"Yeah." Booby said easily.

"Booby, we're talking about my child's father here. I can't do some shit like that to him."

"What?! Are you fucking serious? These niggas killed your best friend, Falen! You need to wake the fuck up!"

"She aint dead, yet. Don't go digging her no early

grave and we don't know for sure who shot her."

"Okay, so walk around here blind then!" Booby shouted before hanging up on her.

Falen sat speechless. She didn't know what to believe or who to trust. She didn't want to believe Booby but at the same time she didn't want to let her guards down underestimating Tino. But then again Booby had all the reasons in the world to point the finger at Tino. It was a known fact that nobody hated Tino's reappearance more than him. She had to use her head to figure this all out and pray that she didn't lose her life before she could get to the bottom of things.

Chapter 17

I Always Feel like Somebody's Watching Me

"Falen, do you need anything before I go to bed?" Shan questioned.

"No, I'm good." Falen replied with a weak smile.

"Okay, well the covers are in the hallway's closet. Make yourself comfortable."

Falen took a deep breath. "Okay."

"Alright, girl. I'm about to take my ass to sleep." Shan said as she headed for her bedroom.

Falen sat on Shan's couch rocking Tez to sleep. She wanted to be right at Toya's bedside but the nurses kicked her out once visiting hours were over. Her home was still a crime scene so she couldn't return there. Shan stepped in and asked her to stay at her place for a couple of nights and after plenty of pleading she decided to stay.

As more time passed the likelihood of Tino knowing about the shooting was more than possible, yet he still hadn't made any attempts to contact her. She was really starting to feel like he may have been involved in Toya's shooting in one way or another. What other reason would he have for not reaching out to her in such a trying time?

The thought of Tino being that brutal was frightening to her. She hated to even think about the father of her child having so little regards for human life. He had to know how much hurting Toya would affect her. But then again maybe those bullets were meant for the both of them. Maybe the only reason she was still breathing was because she decided not to go home that night. Knowing that she could have easily been in a hospital bed or even dead at that moment sent a chill down her spine.

The entire situation was a wakeup call like no other. If she'd listened to her gut they would've walked away from the game months ago. She'd suggested to Toya that they should sell all the work they had left in one setting, and leave the game alone unscathed. Toya convinced her that it would be much more profitable to sell their product stone for stone verses the wholesale route. They had stopped selling their product at wholesale prices once Booby came home and had assembled their little team. So, they kept the workers in the trap houses selling their product and issued out money as if they had a legitimate payroll system. The way things were being handled Falen was seeing the window of opportunity of getting out become smaller by the day. Now, them getting out of the game just didn't affect their lives but everyone that ate with them. They had definitely dug a deep hole for themselves.

Falen knew that a few people were counting on her to make things happen but that was the furthest thing from her mind. If she could, she would give Tino back all ten kilos to get things back to the way that they were. It just wasn't worth it.

Her conscience was weighing heavily on her. Her get rich scheme had come back on her in the worse way. And now her best friend was on her death bed and her son may never have his father in his life. At that very moment all the money that she'd made didn't mean a damn thing.

It took her several hours to finally close her eyes. Every time she drifted off to sleep her head was filled with images of a masked man knocking her over her head with a gun. Each time the masked man took off his disguise there was a different familiar face behind it. One time it was Crystal, and then it was Yolanda. Then it was Gregg, Janah, and Ms. Gloria. The world was out to get her.

Falen woke up in a cold sweat. Her dreams were terrifying. She felt much safer while wide awake. She checked on her son and he was sleeping peacefully. She was wishing that she could go back to his age because his short life seemed worry free. She couldn't live like this. Something had to give. She made a decision to face her problems head on before they consumed her.

The following morning Shan agreed to keep Tez while Falen ran a few errands. She went out and bought her and her baby some clothes, diapers, and food. She wanted to go to their stash spot but was too afraid that someone might follow her so she rode around hours hoping not to find somebody in her rearview mirror. After making a sudden turn her worse nightmare was coming true. She noticed that there was a black Acura tailing her. She could tell that the car was trying to be inconspicuous judging by the distance the car was keeping between them. That still did nothing for the panic she felt in her chest.

She didn't want to alert them to the fact that she knew that they were following her. So, she tried her best to keep her speed at the same level although she wanted so badly to push the pedal to the metal. She was hoping to ride until she spotted some cops. After driving for about ten more minutes without a police in sight sweat started dripping down her forehead.

Then right at a stop light the Acura pulled up on the side of her. She almost pissed on herself as the driver rolled down his window.

"Pull over, Falen!" Tino shouted.

Even with the red light Falen mashed her gas to the floor. She heard her car burn rubber as she tried to get away from Tino. She almost lost control as she sped down the street. She glanced behind her only to find that he was hot on her tail.

"Shit, shit, shit!" she screamed as she tried her best to lose him.

Tino blew his horn at her, signaling for her to pull over.

Falen found herself driving through a subdivision.

When she rounded the corner she turned her wheel too hard and the Lexus hopped the curb and veered directly into a tree. The car collided with so much force that her head flew into the steering wheel, creating a huge gash. Her adrenaline was rushing as she hopped out of her car and ran for the first house she saw.

Tino rounded the corner and stopped. His heart raced as he looked at Falen's car wrapped around the tree, but then he noticed her pounding on a door right across the street from the accident.

His car came to a screeching halt. "Falen!" he shouted as he hopped out of his car.

She turned to look at him and then continued to beat on the door. "Somebody, help me!"

Tino moved in closer to her. "Calm down." He gritted as he approached her.

Falen ran in the opposite direction as people slowly walked outside to check out the commotion. "Stay away from me!"

"Why are you running? Just let me talk to you!" Tino barked.

"Tino, stay away from me!" she cried as she backed away from him.

"Hey, she said leave her alone!" some white man shouted from his driveway.

Tino peered around and noticed their huge audience and knew that the police would soon be there. So, he backed away from Falen and jumped back into the Acura and skirted down the street.

Falen had a sigh of relief as she held her chest. "Are you okay, sweetie?" an older woman asked her.

Falen quickly nodded before looking over at her car. It was totaled out.

"The ambulance is on the way." the woman told her.

"Thank you." Falen said.

The paramedics and the police had a million questions for Falen. She told them that a strange man had been following her and that she'd crashed her car trying to get away from him. It was half the truth. The paramedics checked her for injuries and insisted that she go to the hospital to insure that she didn't have a concussion. She flat out refused. She gave the police a full report of the incident before she called Shan to pick her up.

"So, you was in a high speed chase with Tino?" Shan asked for the millionth time as she drove them back to her home.

Falen rolled her eyes to the ceiling. "Yes, Shan."

"But why? I mean I just don't get it."

"I don't know. He had been following me for a minute and then he tried to get me to pull over."

"Do you think that it had anything to do with the dope they say you stole from him?" Shan asked.

"What? Where did you hear that?"

"Everybody's been saying it. Junebug called and told me. People are even saying that Tino or Joe might have been the ones that shot Toya."

Falen had to laugh at herself. "Oh my God." She shook her head.

"What?" Shan questioned confused.

"Do you think that Tino did that to Toya?"

Shan thought for a few seconds. "I don't know. Tino is a nigga that don't play about his paper. You see how he handled Shun and 'nem and that was his cousin-n-law. So, when you get to talking about money and drugs you see a different side of a person. So, I don't know what he will or won't do. Shit, the same thing goes for you."

"What you trying to say?" Falen snapped.

"Aw come on, Falen. I would have never thought that you'd have the balls to steal from anybody less alone your baby's daddy."

"I didn't steal from him." Falen shook her head.

"Oh, you didn't, huh? Well, how did you get on, then?"

"That's our business."

"Well, it's a lot of people that feel that it's their business too."

"Fuck those people!"

"Aint no need to holla at me. I'm just letting you know. If you did take them niggas shit you know that you got a problem on your hands. Maybe since you're Tino's baby mama he might let you keep breathing."

"Whatever. I aint took nobody's shit."

Falen sat in her hotel room staring at the television set. After Shan drove them back to her home Falen and Tez caught a cab to her house and hopped in their Navigator. She couldn't stand being around Shan or any other person right then. She had to be alone and a small part of her felt that Shan would hint Tino off to her whereabouts, so she felt safer in an undisclosed location.

Now, Tino was blowing her phone up and she didn't know what to do. She was scared to even hear what he had to say. It couldn't be good.

Right when she was about to finally doze off her phone rang.

"Hello." She spoke into her phone.

"Falen, are you okay?"

"Crystal?"

"Yeah."

"Oh yeah, I'm okay." Falen said sitting up in bed. Her sister never called her.

"That's good. I was just calling to make sure that you were okay. I know that you're going through a lot right now, and I wanted you to know that I'm here for you."

"Oh for real? That's nice of you." Falen said surprised.

"Yeah. I know that we don't always get along, but we need to put all that shit behind us."

"I was thinking that same thing." Falen smiled.

"Right. So, I wanted to let you know that I've been hearing some shit about you."

"Like what?"

"Like, you stole Tino's dope."

"Aw man, that shit again? Crystal, you can't believe everything that you hear. People will say any damn thing."

"Yeah, people talk but that explains a lot, Falen. How did you and Toya come into all that money overnight?"

"We hustled. I never denied that."

"How did yall get in the game?" Crystal pried.

"Through a friend of a friend."

"Yeah, right. Falen, who do you think you fooling? I know you. You was green to the game, so how in the hell would somebody trust you with their work? Especially with the amount that they're saying that you got."

"What? How much are people saying that I have?"

"Keys. They aint saying no specific amount but they say that it's keys. Most niggas aint seeing that type of shit. Motherfuckas will kill over that type of weight. Shit, we both know niggas that's dealing in ounces and people calling them ballers, so what you think they saying about somebody holding them thangs?"

"Well, niggas do a lot of talking, but nobody knows what we're working with."

"So, what are you working with?" Crystal asked.

"Bitch, you nosy." Falen laughed.

"I'm for real. You can't tell your big sister what you working with?"

"Umm, let's just say that I'm sitting real pretty, but I'm trying to get rid of it all in the very near future."

"That's what's up. Just don't forget about your nieces and nephews when you get rid of your load."

"I won't." Falen giggled.

"Oh, and Falen."

"Yeah?"

"I love you."

"Aw, I love you too." Falen told her sister.

"Okay, now you be careful in these streets."

"I will." Falen said before hanging up.

Life never ceased to amaze her. She never thought that she'd see the day when her sister would treat her civilly. There was a God. Their little talk gave her some much needed reassurance. She was feeling like she was all alone in the world without Toya, but now she knew better. So, for once she went to sleep without the constant nightmares.

Chapter 18

The Flip Side

"So, have you had a chance to talk to her?"

"Naw. She won't answer my calls or nothing." Tino told his cousin.

"This shit aint looking too good. She's starting to look guiltier by the minute."

"Nigga, who you telling?"

"So, what do want to do about it?" Joe wanted to know.

Tino placed his head in his palms. "I don't know, man."

"You don't know?" Joe repeated in disbelief. "You gotta come better than that, man. The streets is watching. If we just let this shit ride then everybody gon feel that they can test us."

"I know that. But we talking about my son's mama, here. I can't just take her out like that."

"Well something gotta be done, dog. I've been hearing that they were bragging about taking our shit."

"What?! Who told you that?" Tino snapped raising his head up.

"It's been too many people to remember them all. Even her sister confirmed it."

"Her sister? You serious?"

"Yeah, she said that Falen was bragging about how she put the pussy on you and got you for your dope."

Tino shook his head. "Naw, that don't sound like Falen. She wouldn't talk her business like that."

"She really got you." Joe eyed his cousin. He had never witnessed Tino defend anybody the way he did for Falen. "Evidently, it's a lot about her that you don't know. Hell, I didn't think that she had it in her to get her hustle on, but we both know that that assumption was wrong. So, at this point I aint ruling out nothing."

"I aint either, but damn. This shit is crazy. Why all of a sudden everybody want to point the finger at her after over a year don passed? Something just aint right. And then all this is happening right after her friend gets shot. It's like somebody is gunning for her."

Joe shook his head. "I don't know. Maybe somebody got mad and decided to throw her under the bus, but that still don't change the fact that she took from us."

"You right." Tino nodded. "That's why I need to catch up with her and get to the bottom of this."

"And then what? Are you going to give her a tap on the hand and say "bad girl"?"

Tino gave his cousin a look. "What you trying to say, nigga?"

"I'm saying that this has to be handled properly. When you hold court in the streets issuing out love taps aint gon get it. You have to make her and everybody else feel you. I mean, if it's too much for you, I can handle her."

"So, you saying that I'm soft now? You saying that I can't handle my business?" Tino asked growing agitated.

"All I'm saying that this might be a conflict of interest to you, so I can handle it. I don't want your feelings to get in the way of us handling our business." Joe explained.

"Miss me, nigga. If we was talking about your baby mama doing some shit like this then I wouldn't be the nigga talking about handling it for you. If anything I would sit back and tell you to do what's best for you. Do what you see fit, you know?"

"And that would be all good if she had just taken my money. But Falen took from the both of us. What she did affected the whole family. There was blood shed, money lost, and penitentiary time issued out, because of her. Aint nothing she say gon change that!" Joe shouted losing his cool.

Tino was taken aback by his cousin's furry. It was usually never directed towards him. "Nigga, I think that you need to calm your ass down." Tino gritted. "Now, when I get to the bottom of this shit I promise to murk any person held liable. But not a minute sooner. And if Falen stole from us I will lay her down. You can take that shit to the bank."

"Why are you leaving?"

"Man, I have a lot of shit to handle." Booby said as he pulled his shirt over his head.

"When are you coming back?"

"I don't know, man. I have to turn a few corners, so aint no telling when I'm going to be finished." He said as he sat on the edge of the bed and placed on his Forces.

"You full of shit!"

He turned to look at her. "Crystal baby, I really got a lot of shit to handle. Now if I didn't have to go out and get this money then maybe I could kick it with you a little longer. And if you would just do what I asked you, shit would be a lot easier on a nigga."

Crystal pulled the sheet over her exposed breasts. "There you go with this shit, again." She sighed. "I told you that you have to be patient, and let me do this my way. I can't just get everything out of her, after barely saying two words to her in this past year. Let me warm her up first."

"Got damn, how long is that going to take? All you need to do is get her to talk about Tino and then you go in for the kill. Talk about everything as if you already know for a fact. Make up some outrageous number about the amount of dope they stole. Tell her that niggas is saying that she took like fifty bricks, you know. Use reverse psychology on her. Shit, use your head. Be creative."

"Why do you want to know how much they got so bad?"

"What I keep telling you? I want to know if it's even worth me going after. If she got less than a key left then I won't even bother."

"And you aint gon hurt her to get it?" Crystal asked for the umpteenth time.

Booby looked at the ceiling then blew out hot air. "For the hundredth time, I'm not going to hurt her. Okay?"

"Okay." Crystal nodded. "Well, when I called her last night she said that she was sitting pretty." She offered.

"And she wouldn't get specific with you?"

"No, but she did say that she was trying to get rid of it all at once."

"No shit?" Booby asked. His wheels began spinning. "Okay look, I want you to call her back in a couple of hours."

"For what?" she asked.

"Tell her that you know somebody that wants to buy six keys from her."

"And then what?"

"Just see what she says first. And then let me know and I'll take it from there."

"Whatever you say." She shrugged. "Are you still going to give me that?"

"What?" he asked with a raised brow.

"The money."

"Oh yeah." He said as reached into his pocket. "Here." He told her as he handed her two crisp bills. Two hundred dollars was such a small investment for the pay off.

"Thanks." She smiled as she leaned in for a kiss. She aimed for his lips, but he turned his face and her lips landed on his cheek. She couldn't help but feel rejected. It was written all over her face.

"What's wrong?" he asked reading the expression on her face.

"Why don't you like kissing me?" she wanted to know.

"Aw come on. I know you aint tripping on that? I just aint the kissing type."

"Whatever, Booby. Just admit it, if Falen didn't want to be with Tino, you'd be with her right now."

"Crystal, stop that. How long have we been fucking around?"

"Since I was sixteen."

"And in all that time you still don't know how I feel about you?"

"Jaylen." She gave him a look. "Don't try to play me like I'm crazy. The first time we had sex you admitted to me that you liked my sister, but she was just too young at the time."

"I still liked you, though."

"So, why nobody knows about us, then? How could you fuck me for all these years and keep it a secret, if you like me so much?"

"There you go. Let's not forget that you tried telling me that Lil' Ken was my son first. And then when you had him you named him after some other nigga." He reminded her.

"Oh, please. I did what was best for my baby. You was denying him anyway and Ken had a good job at the time. I aint seen you trying to step up to the plate for him, yet."

"And why should I? He's carrying some other nigga's name."

"So what, Booby? You of all people should know that a name doesn't matter. Tez has your name but that's little *Tino* all day." She laughed.

Before he could think Booby's hand slapped her

face. "That shit's funny to you, huh?"

Crystal held her face. "I can't believe that you put your hands on me because of that. Tez is Tino's son. You know that and I know that. Hell, a blind man could see that." She cried.

"Fuck Tino!" Booby roared. "I don't give a damn about him being Tez's daddy. I aint about to let you throw some bullshit in my face!"

"I hit a sore spot, huh?" she asked with a smirk as the tears slid down her face.

He bucked at her again and she flinched. "Yeah, look at you. Scary just like your stupid ass sister."

"Why does everything always go back to her? Huh, Jaylen? Tell me that."

"What the fuck are you talking about?"

"Why the hell are you always comparing me to my *little* sister? What is it? Does she fuck you better? What, she sucks your dick better?"

Booby shook his head. "Why are we having this conversation? You and Falen are two different people. You'd kill yourself trying to compare yourself to the next person."

"That's what you just did." She reminded him.

"That's different. Both of yall are scary. I aint comparing yall pussies or some shit like that. Why are you trying to compete with her?"

"I'm not trying to compete with that bitch!"

"I sense some hostility there." He chuckled.

"You damn right. I sure am hostile. All yall niggas see is Falen. I'm right here and it's like you're looking past me."

"If that's the case, then it aint got nothing to do with Falen."

"How so?"

"If you can't see if for yourself, then I don't know

what to tell you. Just stop blaming people for your short comings."

"You know what, fuck you." She snapped.

"Been there done that."

"And you keep coming back." She sassed as she slid out of bed. Booby eyed her thick body frame and couldn't help but get a hard on. She'd lost a few pounds and the weight loss agreed with her. She and Falen were both shapely with nice round asses. It was Crystal's lack of confidence and desperation that turned men off.

He stood unbuckling his belt. He slid his jeans down to his ankles. "Well, let me get one for the road." He growled as he pushed her body back on the bed. She gapped her legs open welcoming him in. He slid between her thighs.

"You know that she can't do you like me." Crystal moaned as he slid inside of her.

There he was standing there with his hand in his pocket, acting like he owned the world. Booby couldn't wipe the snarl off his face if he tried. It took everything within him to not pull out his strap and just start blasting. Tino was surrounded by fake niggas and bitches that just wanted to be around him. He was *that* nigga and Booby hated it with every fiber of his being.

Of all the bitches in the world Tino just had to fuck with Falen. Tino was a ladies' man that always had top pick, but he was stepping on the next man's toes. Why couldn't he give the common niggas a break?

Booby watched closely as hoes lined up to smile in Tino's face. He didn't seem impressed. In fact, it seemed as though he wasn't even there mentally. His mind was probably on…Falen. Booby knew that the rumors were rapidly spreading, so Tino had to know that it was Falen that had stolen from him. He had to know. Just then it hit him! He had just figured out a way to kill two birds with one stone. He whipped out his cell. Man, it was on now.

Tino pulled up at his condo and just sat for a few minutes. He'd just left Harlem Knight's and was completely wasted. He and a few niggas from the hood had popped bottle after bottle. The strippers swarmed them as they made it rain all night long. He needed that little brief moment of fun while dealing with all the drama in his life.

He found a piece of blunt left his ashtray. He lit it up while he listened to Master P's Ghetto Dope album. It was crazy how the song he was listening to was a reflection of his life. *Eyes on Your enemies* talked about not being able to trust anyone around him. He had to laugh at the timing of the song.

After finishing up his blunt Tino got out of his truck but not before stumbling. He could barely stand and never saw the man dressed in all black approach him. Although, he was oblivious to someone standing behind him he did feel the cold steel strike him across the head.

"What the fuck?!" Tino winced as he staggered while holding his wounded head.

"Shut your punk ass up!" the dude with the ski mask demanded as he pointed a gun at him.

"What you need, man? You want my car? You can take it." Tino slurred drunkenly.

"I said shut the fuck up?" the gunman gritted. "I came to deliver a message."

"What's that?" he asked as he found himself staring at the dude's Nike's. He had a major scuff mark in the front of one of the shoes.

"Falen said to know your motherfuckin place. And

stay in your lane before your mama have to buy that black dress."

Before Tino could say another word the gunman was gone. He stood still for a few seconds frozen in shock. He was actually caught slipping and it could've cost him his life. There he was tripping over Falen and she sends a nigga to get at him. He didn't see that move coming. Did she want a war? What was she trying to prove?

Suddenly, Tino was enraged. He wanted to find Falen and blow her brains out. Nobody was ever that bold to pull a stunt like this. She most definitely had to be dealt with. Baby mama or not she was about to feel him.

Chapter 19

Who can you Trust

Tino rolled around the streets of Houston with the same clothes from the night before. He was on a mission. He needed to see Falen in a real way very soon. He could've easily gotten one of his little niggas to do her, but this was personal. He couldn't even bring himself to admit to another soul that she'd played him. He never knew something so beautiful could be so wicked.

As he drove he tried calling Joe for the sixth time. There was still no answer. He didn't know what was up with this nigga. Of all the times, this is when he decides to be out of pocket.

Out of frustration Tino threw his cell into the passenger's seat. He cruised through Fifth Ward hoping to spot Falen, but she was M.I.A. Tino had less trouble finding seasoned vets in the game. Falen was definitely a person that stepped lightly, so he didn't even know where to begin to look. Outside of her home and Crystal's he was completely clueless.

As he drove he thought about all the things that Falen had altered when she stole those ten kilos. The only reason that he'd ended things with Jamie was because he thought that she may have known something about the missing keys. In all the years she was the closest thing he had to a wife and after taking that lost he walked away from her. But if he was being real with himself things hadn't been the same with them since the first night he'd slept with Falen.

He'd tried to treat the experience with her like any other, but it was impossible. It was something about her that he just couldn't shake. No matter who he was with or what they did he still thought about her. Falen's innocence drew him in and that tight pussy captivated him. Still, it went beyond that. No matter how brief the conversation with her or the encounter, he thought about it for days. Every moment with her seemed to be suspended in time. He found himself longing to see her smile or the feel of her skin on his. The connection they shared was damn near intoxicating and when he found that they'd created a life together it solidified their thing.

It was crazy to think that if Falen hadn't fucked up that he would have wifed her with no hesitation. He literally would have taken her hand in marriage, gladly. Even with all their history he'd never even contemplated making a lifelong commitment to Jamie. He tried to convince himself that it was because Falen gave him the little boy that he'd been longing for, but he knew that it went deeper. He didn't even know what he wanted in his woman until he'd witnessed Falen's work. He could see the desire in her eyes without the neediness. She wasn't infatuated with the street legend, but loved the man that lied beneath. Or so he thought.

At the end he still felt guilty about treating Jamie the way that he had. It was her who'd gotten the short end of the stick and she didn't deserve that. He would give anything to take back the hurt he'd caused.

After thinking on it for a while he decided to give her a call. Her cell rung just once and then he heard talking. "Who was that?" a voice asked in the distance.

"That was Tino." He clearly heard Jamie say.

"You sent him to voicemail?"

"Yeah."

"I wonder what that nigga want."

"I don't know." Jamie replied.

"Yall back on good terms?" the dude asked.

"Naw, I hadn't talked to him since the day I left his mama's house."

"You wouldn't lie to me would you?"

"No, baby."

Tino sat and listened to his baby mama call another man baby. He felt a slight twinge of jealousy.

"When are you going to move out of that nigga's house? You've been claiming that you gon make that shit happen for the past six months."

"Baby, I told you to give me some time. I don't want to remove Tia from her school in the middle of the year."

"Bullshit!" the man shouted. "That's an excuse that I'm getting tired of hearing."

"Well, it's the truth. Besides you're talking about moving into an apartment and that is going to be a major adjustment for me."

"Major adjustment? Baby girl, be for real. I know that nigga spoiled you, but damn. You act like I'm trying to move you in the projects or some shit."

"I didn't say that." She sighed.

"I think that it's about time that you tell him about us." He said.

"What? Are you crazy? He would kill us." Jamie panicked.

"Do you honestly think that the nigga gives a damn? He left the city for damn near a year and left you right here." The man said. Tino was wishing like hell that the man was closer to the phone so that he could listen to hear if he recognized the voice. He was beginning to get the feeling that he knew this man personally.

"But he's still my daughter's father and your." was all Jamie was able to get out before there was loud gunfire and glass shattering in the background.

"Aaahh!" Jamie screamed at the top of her lungs.

"Fuck!" the man yelled.

There was screeching tires in the background and then the phone went dead. Tino dropped his phone and damn near lost control of his wheel. He was crossed between feeling pissed and major concern. Somebody had just lit up a car with the mother of his child inside.

Tino pulled over on the side of the road and frantically tried dialing Jamie's number again. All her phone did was ring. He called her again and again with no answer. About forty minutes later his cell rung.

"Hello." Tino spoke into his phone.

"Tino!" Joe shouted.

"What's up, nigga?"

"Man, some bitch ass niggas just started blasting at me!"

Just then Tino got a bad taste in his mouth. Either somebody was trying to hit everyone close to him or Joe was the nigga with Jamie.

"Where was you?" Tino questioned with his antennas up.

"I was sitting in my truck." Joe said hurriedly.

"With who?"

"With who?" Joe repeated. "I was with this female. But anyway, these niggas just pulled up on me and started blasting."

"So, where is the broad that was with you?"

"What? Nigga, you tripping that's irrelevant. I'm trying to tell you about how I damn near got my head blown off."

"Okay, so tell me what happened again." Tino said although he tuned everything out. He'd known Joe all his life and could always tell when he was lying. He didn't know how it took so long for him to figure out that his cousin was fucking his baby mama. He was really slipping and it seemed that everybody around him was plotting.

Booby pulled up to the trap house on 36th Street. He had put Kay-Al on and he'd been manning their spot in Studewood. Kay had the smokers going crazy over their product. He was a natural born hustler that Booby had to have on his team.

After tapping his horn twice Kay-Al emerged from the house. He spotted Booby's car and walked right over to it. "What up, nigga?" he asked as he slid in the passenger's seat.

"Trying to get this paper, nigga." Booby sighed as he sat back reclined in his seat.

"I feel that, but when somebody gon drop something this way? We down to our last."

"I know, I know. Give me a little more time on that. Yall just get rid of what you got."

"Oh, you know that we gon do that, anyway." Kay nodded.

"So, did you handle everything like I asked?"

"Come on, nigga. You know me."

"A'ight, that's cool. But say, I might need you in a couple of days."

"For what?"

"You trying to get paid, right?" Booby asked with a raised brow.

"Already."

"Okay, well let me worry about that. You just be ready when I call you to get down."

Falen lied in the bed with her son as she watched BET. She was watching girls her age enjoy their selves on TV while she was living in hell. She was wishing that her life had taken another direction. She had never known what it was like to not have the weight of the world on her shoulders.

As the days passed by she found it harder and harder to trust anybody. Something inside wouldn't let anybody in. She felt like any mistake she made at that point could cost her gravely. She couldn't chance it so she was going to stay away from everyone.

As she channel surfed she received a call from Crystal. She was glad that her sister was calling her again.

"Hey, what's up?" Falen answered.

"Nothing. What my nephew doing?" Crystal asked.

"Girl, he's sleeping right now. Over here snoring like he's been at somebody's job." Falen giggled.

"Oh, poor baby. He's probably tired."

"From what? Eating, shitting, and sleeping?"

"No, he probably tired of looking at your ass."

"Fuck you."

"No, for real. Why don't you let me keep him for a while?"

Falen wanted to tell her sister hell no! She couldn't say that without hurting her feelings, but Crystal was the last person she would trust with her son. Her sister wasn't the best at caring for her own, so she wasn't about to put her child in Crystal's care. "Girl, Tez would keep you up half the night. Maybe you could keep him once he gets a little older."

"Umm." Crystal let out. She knew that Falen thought that her baby was too good to come over her house. "So, when was the last time you had a break, Falen?"

"When I let Tino keep him for a day."

"Well, I was just trying to help you out. I know that you've probably been under a lot of stress since Toya been in the hospital."

"And I have but I need my baby. He keeps me sane."

"I heard that." Crystal sighed. "So, what are your plans for the day?"

"Nothing too heavy. I'm going to go by the crib in a few and grab a few things."

"Oh yeah?"

"Uh huh."

"Well, call me if you change your mind about letting me keep Tez."

"Okay, I will."

"But, before I let you go I wanted to talk to you about something."

"What's up?"

"You know that I have a new boyfriend, right?"

"Oh, I didn't know that."

"Well you would if you came around more often." Crystal laughed. "Anyway, he got a cousin that's from Louisiana that's down here looking for somebody with the right prices."

"Oh, yeah? How much they looking for?" Falen asked.

"They want like six bricks."

"Six? Damn I aint got that. I got like four."

"What are they going for?"

"Twenty."

"Twenty? Well, let me tell him and then I'll call you back."

"Alright. Call me and let me know something."

"I will." Crystal said before Falen hung up.

"Booby, you still there?" Crystal asked.

"Yeah, I'm here."

"You heard everything?"

"Yeah, I did."

"Can you believe that she won't let me keep Tez?"

"Hey, hey, thank you for the three-way. I'm a hit you back." Booby said as he hung up the phone not wanting to hear Crystal's crazy rants. Hell, if he was Falen he wouldn't let her keep his baby, either.

Tino stepped inside of Joe's condo. It had been a while since he'd stepped into his cousin's personal domain. Usually, in his free time he was posted up somewhere with one of his bitches. He didn't have time to sit around the niggas that he got money with all day. As he searched the room with his eyes he noticed pictures of his daughter and few photos of him and his cousin at different clubs.

"Sit down, nigga." Joe said from the kitchen.

"Yeah, a'ight." Tino sighed as he sat on the couch.

"You want a glass of Henny?" Joe asked.

"Naw, I'm good."

"Nigga, I'm still tripping on these niggas shooting at my ass, dog."

"Yeah, that's some way out shit." Tino said blandly.

Joe picked up on his mood. "What's wrong with you, nigga?" he questioned as he stepped into the living room with a glass of Hennessey and Coke.

"Nothing, man. I'm good." Tino shrugged.

"That's what's up." Joe laughed as he took a seat in his recliner.

"Yeah, man you really fixed your spot up. One of your bitches fixed this bitch up for you?"

Joe glanced around as if it was his first time noticing his place. "Yeah, one of my lil mamas did it for me." He nodded.

"That's what's up." Tino nodded. "You know, I let Jamie decorate a few of my spots."

"Yeah?"

"Yeah. She did one of my spots just like this. It's damn near the exact same."

"Well, they say that great minds think alike." Joe chuckled.

"Yeah, that's what they say." Tino said as he sat up in his seat. "I think that I'm about to go to Jamie's in a little bit."

"For what?" Joe asked with a raised brow.

"What you mean for what? Shit, I'm about to get some pussy."

"Yall still been fucking?" he asked sounding confused.

"Hell, yeah. What, you aint know that?"

"Naw, I aint know that." Joe sighed.

"That's fucked up aint it?"

"What?"

"How she didn't tell you that she was still fucking me."

"Why would she tell me some shit like that?"

"Shit, I know that yall discuss shit like that."

"I aint following you." Joe shook his head as he looked at his cousin.

"Well, I figured that since you are fucking her, you'd want to know about any other niggas getting a piece of the pie." Tino said as cool as the other side of the pillow.

"Who am I fucking?"

"Jamie, nigga."

"What? Where, where you getting that from?"

"Oh come on, man. This Tino you talking to. So, leave the games at the door."

"Nigga, I don't know what the fuck you're talking about."

Tino nodded his head. "So, you gonna play me like some nigga off the streets?"

"Man, you my nigga if you don't get no bigger. You know that I would never come at you sideways, dog."

"So, you still gonna lie?"

"I'm not lying!" Joe shouted.

"Be easy, nigga." Tino said as he stood.

"What's up, Tino? You trying to roll with me?" Joe asked as he stood as well.

"Naw, nigga. I aint trying to square off with you, or no other nigga." Tino laughed as he lifted his shirt and pulled a .380 from his waist.

"So, you gonna shoot me, now?" Joe asked in disbelief as his cousin pointed a gun at him.

"What would you do if you was me, Joe? How would you handle a situation where the one person that you trusted betrayed you? How would you deal with a nigga that you get money with and trusted with your life? If I can't trust you around my pussy, then I can't trust you with nothing."

Joe was boiling hot. "Nigga, your pussy?! How the fuck is that *your* pussy? You barely even see her and now you want to pull a pistol out over her?"

"Fuck that! It don't matter how often I choose to fuck with her. What in the fuck does that have to do with you fucking my baby mama?!" Tino shouted.

"Who the fuck do you think was taking care of your family while you lived in Atlanta for damn near a year? Huh, nigga? Who looked out for your daughter while you was out there fucking with hoes? Who was here to protect your baby mama? Huh nigga?! Me! That's who, nigga!"

"So what?! That's what you were supposed to do! If you was the one out there doing what you had to do for family, then I would have looked after yours. That's what we do. You was being selfish and decided to do more than check on her."

"Selfish? You want to talk about selfish? You are the most selfish nigga on the planet. Everything always revolves around you, nigga! Who knew Jamie first?" Joe asked.

"What's your point?" Tino asked growing agitated.

"No, nigga you wanted to go there, so answer the question."

"You knew her first, but what do that have to do with anything?"

"Everything. I told you that it was a bad bitch at Wheatley that I had my eye on, remember? You didn't even know who she was, but when we saw her at the game who approached her first?"

"So what, nigga? You tripping over some pussy?"

"Come again? Nigga you the one that got a gun pointed at me!" Joe reminded him.

"That's cause you lied, nigga!"

"So, what, Tino? You fucked a few of my bitches or somebody that I had my eye on first. You did the same shit with Falen."

"Falen? Nigga, you have lost your damn mind!" Tino roared.

"Yeah, play that selective ass memory shit. You know that I told you that I had been trying to get at her, but she was slow at responding to a nigga."

"Okay, well that meant that she wasn't feeling you like that, it aint my fault." Tino shrugged.

"But it was cool for you to step on my toes, right?"

"Playas get chose, nigga."

"And that's why your other baby mama chose me."

"Yeah?" Tino asked as he cocked his gun back.

"So, you gonna shoot me over some pussy? You don't love her, Tino."

"And you do?"

"Actually, I do." Joe admitted.

Tino had to laugh. This was unbelievable. All the bitches in Houston and his cousin was in love with his child's mother. "So, what you expect for me to do while you lay up with my BM, nigga?"

Joe shook his head. "I don't know, Tino. It's fucked up but we can't change it."

"You can't change it?" Tino bit his bottom lip as he

moved in on his cousin. "I ought to blow your fuckin brains out." He gritted.

Joe balled his fists as they shared an intense stare down.

"But you know what? You can have that bitch." Tino said as he backed away and headed out the door. "Chump ass nigga."

Janah walked up to Crystal's doorstep. She hadn't seen much of her friend since the shooting. She was hoping that her best friend could cheer her up. Before she could even knock somebody opened the door.

"'Sup, Janah?" Booby asked her as he walked out of the apartment. "You cool?"

She gave him a funny look. "Yeah, what chu doing over here?"

"Oh, I was just visiting. How is Toya?"

"She still aint woke up." She sighed heavily.

"That's fucked up. But um, Crystal is upstairs in her room." He said as he headed down the sidewalk.

"Yeah, okay." Janah said as she walked inside of the apartment and closed the door behind her.

She then headed up the stairs. Crystal's bedroom door was cracked, so she could see that she was lying in the bed naked.

"Knock, knock." Janah said as she pushed the door open. "Why are you laying around ass naked?"

"Oh, shit." Crystal said as she pulled a sheet over her body. "How did you get in here, bitch?"

"Booby let me in." Janah said as she sat on the edge of the bed.

"Oh, is he gone?"

"Yeah, but I'm not sure of how far he's gone. But

anyways, when did you start fucking with Booby's cute ass?"

Crystal waved her off. "Girl, that's just something that I do from time to time."

"Yeah, okay. But I thought that he was your sister's piece of game?"

"Fuck that bitch and the horse she rode in on." Crystal snapped.

"Damn, it's like that? She was telling my mama that yall had been getting along lately."

"Yeah, in her mind. I aint fucking with Falen like that. She thinks that she's too much."

"I don't know, Crystal. She aint that bad."

"I know that aint Janah talking? I thought that you hated her?"

"I don't hate nobody. I had a few issues with her, but that was all petty shit."

"So what, yall friends now?"

"I didn't say all that. But this situation with my sister put everything in perspective for me. I put a whole lot of wasted energy into beefing with my one and only little sister. I was acting like she was a bitch off the streets that I couldn't stand. But that's not how it should've been. I should have had her back, no matter what." Janah said as her eyes got misty. "She's the only girl that experienced all the traumas with me. She held my hand when I got that abortion after my step daddy raped me. She was the one that defended me when people would say that I would be cuter if I was lighter. She was the same little girl that would follow me around trying to be just like her big sister. She was the little girl that I took baths with until I was eight." She sobbed. "I never thought that I would lose her, Crystal. I would do anything to have her back. All that petty shit just aint worth it."

Crystal sat stone faced. She didn't know what to say.

She'd cut off the emotional part of herself years ago. She'd been through so much that she was now numb.

"Janah, stop that crying, man." She said as she patted her back from a distance.

After a couple of minutes Janah was able to gather her composure. She had to laugh at herself. "I'm up here crying like a big ass baby."

"That's alright." Crystal sighed. "But Janah, have yall thought about the next step?"

"What next step?"

Crystal took a deep breath. "How long do yall plan on waiting before yall take her off of life support?"

Janah shrugged. "I haven't even thought about that. I can't think about that. If we had to bury her anytime soon it would kill my mama. Literally."

"Maybe it won't be as bad as you think. Like the sooner yall deal with her death, the sooner yall can heal."

Janah shook her head. "Naw, it's not time to let her go yet. She's not dead yet. Don't try to dig my sister an early grave." She snapped.

"Don't get smart with me! I'm just trying to help you deal with the facts! Your sister is dead, Janah! And the sooner you deal with that, the better off you'll be!"

"Bitch!" Janah lashed as her hand struck Crystal's face. "You aint God!"

Crystal held her face. "And you aint either, bitch! Not get the fuck out of my house!"

Chapter 20

Jamie sat in total shock as she talked to Joe on the phone. "Baby, I don't know how that nigga found out, but he knows."

"Are are you sure?" she stuttered.

"Yeah, he pulled a gun on me." Joe spat exasperated.

"Wow." She stressed. "He was that upset?"

"What you think?" he asked sarcastically.

Before their conversation could continue she heard footsteps outside of her bedroom. She knew that the only person that had a key to her home was her child's father.

"Baby, hold up. I think that somebody's here." She told Joe as she tried to listen closely. Suddenly, her door was pushed open.

"Yeah, tell *baby* that you're going to call him back." Tino said calmly as he entered the bedroom.

"Let me call you back." She spoke into the phone as she eyed Tino. She didn't wait for a response as she hung up. "What's up?" she asked him.

"You tell me." He said as he glared at her.

She shrugged her shoulders. "What's on your mind?"

"How long have you been fucking Joe?" he got straight to the point.

"What?" she asked faking confusion.

"You heard me!" he shouted losing his cool.

"Why does it matter, Tino?" she snapped.

"What the fuck do you mean?!" he asked in disbelief.

"You are never here for me anymore, Tino!" she cried.

"I'm not here for you? Look at where you staying at. I don't see nobody with a fucking job around here!"

"This is material shit, Tino. I never asked for any of

this. All I ever wanted was you! Can you say the same?"

"Come on, with that shit. I don't hear your ass complaining when you go shopping or drive that motherfuckin Benz you got sitting in the garage. I don't see you complaining when you hit up the beauty shop every week!"

"That shit aint nothing, Tino! You do all that for me because deep down you know that you treat me like shit! I was with you when you aint had shit, remember?!"

"Okay, so I'm the bad guy, right?"

"You know what?" she snapped as she hopped out of bed. "There is no bad person in this situation. I should have left your ass a long time ago. That was my fault. I could see it in your eyes that you didn't have the love that you should. Right then I should have walked away from your ass, but I held on hoping that you would change."

"So, I never loved you? Is that what you're saying?"

"Are you saying that you did, Tino?"

He stood there for a few seconds stuck. He hadn't even associated the word love with Jamie in years. She was a responsibility. She was the chick that all his boys wanted. She was the mother of his child, but did he love her?

Tino met Jamie when she was sixteen years old. She was going to Wheatley High school in the hood. It was Joe that noticed her first. He'd been going on and on about this sexy light skinned chick that the niggas were going crazy over. When Tino saw her for himself he thought that she looked good, but all the hype about her is what drew him in. So, he approached her while all his boys stood on the sideline. Jamie was staring at him with star struck eyes as he talked to her. He was twenty and had already made a name for himself in the hood. Most girls in her school talked about having crushes on him.

So, after just a few words Jamie was hooked line and sinker. Anything that Tino asked her to do, she was down for it. Nothing was off limits for him; not even her precious virginity. So after just two weeks of dating she let him have his way with her. Tino enjoyed her, but she didn't have that usual pizzazz that his girls had, so it wasn't long before he got bored. He never knew that right as he was about to kick her to the curb, she would tell him that she was carrying his baby. He couldn't play the *it's not mines* card, because he knew that she hadn't been with another man.

Tino wanted to run as far away from her as he could, but his mama had taught him better. So, he decided to take care of his responsibility like a man. The relationship they developed was kind of implied. She was head-over-hills him for him, so she didn't even think about getting another man. She'd wait until he finished hustling and take any little time he had for her and the baby.

As time passed Tino's pockets grew and he was able to provide just about anything that Jamie desired with the exception of himself. Being that Jamie was a misguided young lady she mistook him providing for her as him having actual interest. Tino was doing what he had to do, and didn't mind getting the ass whenever he wanted. All his boys thought that he had the baddest bitch alive, so he liked showing her off from time to time. Then after he played with her he'd put her back on the shelf.

He always knew that she'd be there no matter what. It was just a given. She was like this piece of property that he owned. He liked the fact that other niggas wanted her more than he liked actually being with her. It was Joe always saying that if he had a girl like Jamie that he'd marry her in a second. It was Joe that was impressed with the way that Jamie carried herself. It was Joe that noticed her first.

Tino hadn't realized that he was being selfish. He hadn't realized that he was holding her back from finding real happiness. He hadn't realized that the only things he loved about her was that she was the woman that had given birth to his first child. He knew what he had to do.

"You know what you can do whatever you want to do." He told her.

"What does that mean, Tino?"

"It means that you pack your shit up and move in with Joe. You're free." He said before he walked out of her room and her life.

Falen pulled up in front of her house. It still looked the same but she was having trouble getting out the truck. This was the place where someone damn near took her best friend's life. The house now had this eeriness about it.

Finally, she was able to gather her composure and step down out the truck. "Come on, Tez let's go get your stuff." She said to her baby as she removed him from his car seat.

She took a deep breath as she approached the house's door. She couldn't bring herself to look down at the pavement because Toya's blood had dried up into the cement, reminding everyone of her struggle to keep her life. She quickly glanced around before using her key to unlock the door.

As they stepped into the house she broke down. The enlarged picture of her and Toya at Booby's party was taunting her. Toya was smiling hard and she knew that it was genuine, because that was during the time where they both had a brief moment of peace in their lives.

"I'm sorry, Toya." Falen cried out as she held her son in her arms. Her body trembled from her head to her toes as she felt it in her soul. Why did this happen to them?

After crying for several minutes she pulled herself together so that she could gather her things. So, she headed out the back door that led to the back yard. She smiled to herself as she approached the merry-go-round Toya insisted that they get installed out there. That was one of the best ideas she ever had, Falen felt.

Booby sat in his rental car waiting. He'd been sitting outside of the house for three hours waiting on her arrival. He damn near creamed all over himself when she pulled into the driveway. He was that much closer to the big payoff that he rightfully deserved.

Falen was taking forever in the house. He figured that she was in there getting the money that she and Toya had hidden somewhere. He figured that it probably wasn't much. He wasn't really interested in the money. He wanted the dope and she was going to lead him right to it.

Finally, after an hour Falen reemerged from the house with Tez in tow. Booby was quickly reminded of how much he missed the little boy. He hated how Falen had torn their family apart with her selfishness. She'd forced his hands. He had no choice but to play the game dirty to insure his own survival.

Falen carried only Tez's diaper bag and a few outfits out of the house. He was kind of hoping to see her carry something a little larger, which would have told him that she may have had the work with her. From the looks of it she had only come to the house to get Tez's things.

He sat patiently as she loaded Tez and his stuff into the truck. She then stood and playfully kissed her son over and over. Just by looking at Falen you'd think that she was a young mother enjoying her baby without a care in the world. She was still beautiful and her body was calling Booby. He had to adjust his pants as he got a hard on.

After twenty minutes Falen finally pulled away from her house. She stopped at Taco Cabaña to grab something to eat before driving back to the hotel. Booby made sure to stay his distance as he watched her grab the baby and struggle with his things as they disappeared into the building. He hadn't seen anything too suspect but at least now he knew where she rested her head.

Tino pulled up to a house that was rumored to be Falen's trap. Since it was raining hard out no one seemed to be outside. So, he checked his waist to make sure that his gun was secure before he hopped out the car and made a dash for the house's front porch. He knocked twice and listened to the footsteps move closer to the door.

"What's up, Tino?" Kay-Al asked as he opened the door.

"What's good, Kay? Can a nigga come in or what?" Tino questioned.

"Yeah, yeah." Kay said as he moved aside and allowed Tino to walk inside.

"You here by yourself?" Tino asked as he looked around the room.

"Yeah." Kay said as he closed the door behind him.

"That's what's up." Tino nodded. "That rain slowing down your flow, huh?"

"Hell yeah. But you know those fiends. They still been coming through in the rain. Shit, a hurricane couldn't stop those motherfuckas." Kay chuckled.

"True that. But um, you know where Falen at?"

"Naw. She probably with that nigga Booby or some shit."

"With Booby?" Tino questioned with a raised brow.

"Yeah, they probably at their crib together."

"They live together?" Tino asked faking confusion.

"Yeah." Kay nodded.

"When was the last time you talked to her?"

"The other day."

"Oh, yeah?" Tino said as he stroked his goatee.

"Hell, yeah. She should be making her way around here soon cause we need to re-up."

"The money good around here?"

"Yeah, nigga. That's why I've been in the same clothes for the past two days. I've been bleeding the block."

Tino eyes looked him up and down. "I see you getting your grind on, nigga." He smiled. "But um, can I use your bathroom right quick?"

"Yeah. It's right around the corner." Kay said.

"A'ight." Tino said as he rounded the corner and found the empty bathroom. He then turned to see if Kay was watching before peaking in both backrooms to ensure that they were empty as well.

He stood in the hall for a minute before heading back to the living room. Kay-Al was chilling on a tattered couch.

"You kool-aiding?" Tino asked.

Kay-Al looked up at Tino. "What the fuck?" he asked in shock as Tino pointed a gun at him.

"I thought that we was better than this, Kay."

"I did too. So, why you got your gun pointed at me?" Kay-Al questioned in shock.

"You know most people don't know that I'm a neat freak, Kay."

"Oh, yeah?" he asked as he sat up in the couch.

"Yeah. My shit has to be perfect and I find myself bothered by the smallest smudge on my clothes or shoes. So, even while you had a pistol pointed at me I still noticed that your Nike's had a huge scuff mark in the front of them."

"What? What are you talking about?" Kay asked as he squirmed in his seat and beads of sweat slid down his face.

"Don't play me! You remember hitting me across

the head, nigga! My mama gonna have to buy that black dress, huh?"

"I don't know what you talking about, man." Kay said in a high pitched voice.

"Look at you. Squirming around like a little bitch." Tino gritted. "Falen sent you, right?"

"No, no." Kay shook his head.

Tino cocked his gun. "Okay, okay! It was Booby. He paid me to get at you!" he admitted.

"Booby, huh?"

"Yeah, he told me to say that the message came from Falen."

Tino shook his head. "I thought that you was a real nigga. But you the worse kind. A snitch." He chuckled.

"Come on, Tino man. I wasn't going to kill you or nothing. Please dog. I got kids at home." Kay-Al cried.

"That's why you should have pulled that trigger." Tino gritted as he squeezed. Five bullets left the chamber and violently tore into Kay's body.

Kay-Al sat in a state of shock as he looked down at the holes in his chest. Blood spewed from his mouth as he tried to catch his breath and stared up at Tino. His chest heaved up and down as his hands touched his wounds in disbelief. There was no remorse in Tino's eyes as he stood over him and placed the hot steel to his head.

"Now *your* mama gotta buy that black dress." He gritted as he pulled the trigger one last time. Kay's brain matter splashed all over the walls and Tino's white tee.

"Nigga, got my shirt dirty." He mumbled as he backed away from Kay's dead body.

"Bitch ass nigga." He spat as he made his way to the front door.

Tino gripped the doorknob with his tee and slowly opened the door. The rain was still pouring down and the thunder was roaring. There wasn't a soul outside as he closed the door behind him and made a run for his car.

"Falen, where you at?"

"Why what's up?"

"My boyfriend's boy trying to get with you." Crystal said.

"Oh, yeah? Did you tell him what they going for?"

"Yeah, and they're cool with that. They want to know when can yall make this happen."

"ASAP."

"Well, where can they meet you?"

Falen had to think for a minute. She'd never handled business without Toya or Booby, and all the other transactions were much smaller. This was the biggest lick and she was alone.

"I can meet them at the mall, and I will take the money first like I usually do."

"I don't know if they'll be cool with that, Falen. Just like you don't trust them, they don't trust you. I'm sure that they want an even exchange right then and there."

"Well, that's how I conduct my business." Falen said firmly.

"Okay, well let me call you back in a few minutes. I need to check with them on this." Crystal said.

"Okay." Falen sighed before hanging up.

"Why didn't you agree with her?" Booby questioned.

"Cause. If we aint got the money and she's trying to meet in a public place your plan won't work."

Booby shook his head. "Simple minded ass girl. If we can't get her to bring the work to the meeting we can at least lure her to a spot and ambush her. Then we can make her take us to the work."

"But she'll know that we were behind it all."

"Duh. Either way she'll know in the end. It aint like she gonna call the police on us, and tell them that we just stole her four kilos. That's Falen. What the fuck can she do to us?"

"You got it all planned out, huh?"

"Yeah, now call her and tell her that we'll meet her at the mall."

It was official. Crystal had come through for her and Falen was about to get rid of her burden. As much as it pained her, she was going to do this one last score and leave town for a while. She wanted to stick around until Toya came around, but she wouldn't be sane doing that. She needed some time away to let everything die down. She'd heard that Tino had been looking for her, so she had to get out of dodge.

In just a couple of hours she was going to meet with Crystal's boyfriend and his boy at the mall. Her only problem was that she didn't know where to leave Tez. It was sad how she had very few people in her life that she could trust with her son. She thought about calling Shan, but was still salty about their last conversation. There was no way in hell that she was calling Booby. It was something deep inside of her that didn't trust him anymore. Ms. Gloria was too grief stricken to take care of herself, less alone a baby. The only person that she completely trusted with her baby's safety was his grandma.

Falen knew that regardless of what was going on with Tino and herself that his mom would take good care of her baby. After thinking long and hard she decided to give Tina a call.

"Hello."

"Ms. Wiltz?"

"Yeah, this is she. Who's calling?"

"Um, this is Falen."

"Oh hey, baby. How are you and my grandson?" Tina asked cheerfully.

"We're okay."

"That's good."

"Is Tino near you?" Falen needed to know.

"No. I haven't heard from his hard headed ass in days. The last I heard, he was headed out of town" Tina sighed.

Thank God! "Okay, do you think that you can do me a favor?"

"Anything, baby."

"Could you keep Tez for a few hours?"

"Sure. Are you going to bring him out here?"

"Well, I was hoping that you could meet me somewhere in like thirty minutes."

"Yeah. I can do that. Just let me throw on some clothes. Where do you want to meet?"

"Let's meet near the Katy Freeway and 610 Loop at the Shell."

"Okay, I'll be there."

Falen grabbed Tez and her things and headed out the door. She hopped in the Navigator and headed to the Shell off of 610. She arrived at the gas station first which was to be expected since her hotel was closer.

After forty-five minutes passed she was beginning to think that Tina was a no show. Right when she was about to leave Tina's Lexus pulled into the lot. Falen gave her horn a honk to get her attention. Then the Lexus pulled up on the side of the Navigator.

Tina hopped out of her car. "Is that my grandbaby in there?" she asked as she approached the truck with a smile.

"Yeah, he's in here sleep." Falen said with a grin as

she got out of her truck and opened the backdoor.

"Oh, even when he's sleep he looks just like his daddy." Tina smiled as she glanced over Falen's shoulders.

"I know right." Falen giggled as she removed Tez from his car seat. "Here you go." She said as she handed her baby to Tina.

"He's going to enjoy his time with his granny, trust me."

"I know he will."

Booby and Crystal sat and watched the exchange between Falen and Tino's mom. Even though it was just Tino's mama, Booby still found himself feeling jealous. He didn't like the fact that Tez was having any dealings with anyone associated with Tino. He hated to even think about how Tino's blood flowed through Tez's veins. So, watching that little scene was a reality check.

"Tino's mama still looks young." Crystal commented.

"Yeah, but that old ass bitch is messy." Booby spat.

"What you got against that lady?" she asked with a raised brow.

"Nothing really. But I can still remember when she lived in the hood, and she told my next door neighbor that I broke into his car."

"Well, did you?"

"Yeah, but that bitch should've minded her own damn business."

Crystal let out a slight giggle. "Your ass is crazy."

"Yeah, I just might be."

"Umm hmm. Tino's mama is leaving. Let's follow her."

"Why should we follow her old ass?" Booby

questioned.

"For insurance purposes." Crystal said seriously putting her game face on.

"I got you now." Tino nodded as he watched Falen leave out of the parking lot.

That day had to be his lucky day. He had just finished giving his mama the run down when Falen called. He made sure to tell Tina to lie about haven't seeing him lately. He was sitting right on her couch when she agreed to go get Tez. So, he drove ahead of his mama and sat at the Shell's gas station. He watched Falen impatiently wait on Tina's arrival.

He knew that Falen was being extra-precautious so he knew that he really had to stay his distance as he followed her down the street.

Chapter 21

The Set up

After Falen dropped Tez off she drove to the hospital to visit Toya. She needed to mentally prepare herself for her last lick. She had been feeling uneasy about everything and was more than ready to be done with the drug game. She needed her piece of mind back.

"Toya, you've been sleep for long enough. It's time for you to wake up." Falen said as she stood at her friend's bedside.

The swelling in Toya's head had gone down tremendously. All of her vitals were fine and nothing seemed to be internally damaged, so the only thing she needed to do was wake up.

"I'm about to meet with Crystal's friends today." Falen said. For a slight second she could have sworn that a slight frown crossed Toya's face. "What's wrong? You aint feeling that?" she asked hoping that her friend would miraculously reply.

"Your friend is very much loved." A nurse said as she stepped into the room.

Falen turned to look at her. "I know." she nodded. "I just wish that she would wake up."

The nurse stared down at Toya. "Just keep the faith, baby. Having faith can get you through anything."

"I don't know much about that, but I need something to believe in right about now." Falen admitted.

"You don't know about God?"

"A little. I believe that there is a higher power. I wasn't really raised around religion, so I don't know much about the bible."

"Well, that's something that you can work on, you know that right?"

"Yes, ma'am."

The older nurse looked Falen over. She thought that she was a beautiful young lady, but there was a lot of pain in her eyes. She had a feeling that the pain was there long before her friend was shot.

"What's your name, sweetheart?"

"Falen."

"I'm Mrs. Smith." She smiled. "Well Falen, do you mind praying with me?" the nurse asked.

"Yeah, I can do that." Falen nodded again as Mrs. Smith took both of her hands.

"Lord, we come to you for guidance and strength today. These two young souls need you right now. God, I ask that you rid them of all the sorrow they have in their hearts. Help them get rid of the negativity that surrounds them, God. Help them to know that they're worthy, God. They're worthy. Let them know that being fruitful doesn't spell out mayhem. Help them to see that with you anything is possible. And please give them the courage to improve the things that they can change and the knowledge to accept the things that they cannot. And the wisdom to know the difference."

"Amen." Falen whispered as the silent tears slid down her face.

"What the fuck is taking her so long?" Booby complained.

"Just chill, out. I know my sister and she's coming." Crystal sighed. She was sitting inside of Starbucks waiting on Falen to arrive. She was talking to Booby on the phone.

"Her ass better come." He said right before he got an incoming call. "Say, hold on. I got another call." He said as he clicked over.

"Hello."

"Jaylen?" a female said on the other end of the phone.

"Yeah, what's up, mama?"

"Nothing, what's up with you? I haven't heard from you or seen you since the night your people got shot around the corner."

"Yeah, I know. It's been real crazy since then."

"Well, did they catch the person that did it?"

"Um naw, not yet."

"That's messed up." She sighed. "Well, I miss you."

"I miss you too, Ashley. But, can I call you back in a few?"

"Sure."

"Alright, then." Booby said before he clicked back over. "Hello, Crystal?"

"Umm hmm. You sure did have me on hold for a long time. Who was that?"

"A friend."

"Who? Was it LaQuita, Tasha, or the newest one, Ashley?"

"None of your business." He snapped.

"How the fuck you figure that it aint my business?! You fuck me damn near every night and you gonna sit your ass on this phone and tell me that it's none of my business?!"

"Lower your fucking voice before those people put your ass out and you fuck up everything for us." He gritted.

"Fuck these people!" Crystal shouted gaining a lot of attention from the other customers. "What the fuck are you looking at?" she yelled at a white man with thick glasses. His face turned beet red as he turned around. "You better turn your ass around." She gritted.

"Who the fuck are you talking to?" Booby questioned.

"This white man up in here looking at a bitch like I'm crazy."

"What? Bitch, don't make me come in there and drag your ignorant ass out of there! We are here to handle business. Stop drawing attention to yourself!"

"Whatever." Crystal rolled her eyes. "I'll be glad when this bitch gets here."

Booby glanced in his rearview mirror and spotted the Navigator entering the parking lot. "She just pulled in. I'm about to hang up. Remember the plan."

Falen hopped out of her truck after she looked around. She checked her purse for her gun one last time before she headed into the Starbucks. She and Crystal had made the decision to change the meeting spot before they made the deal official. She really didn't care as long as it was in a public place.

As soon as Falen stepped into the coffee shop she spotted Crystal. She was actually surprised at how nice her sister looked. Her hair was done, nails were done, and she had a brand new outfit on. Apparently, her new man was treating her for once.

"You looking good, girl." She smiled as she took a seat at the table.

"Thank you." Crystal sighed.

"So, where's your boyfriend and his people?"

"Those niggas claimed that they was hungry and went got something to eat. Since your ass was taking so long to get here."

"My bad. I had to make a stop first."

"Umf." Crystal tooted up her lips. "Where's Tez?"

"With his daddy's people."

"Whaaat? You cool with his people like that?"

"I don't know his whole family, but I'm okay with his mama."

"Really? She like keeping kids?"

"She keeps her grandkids." Falen shrugged.

"But it's somebody to help her with the kids, right?"

"No, I mean, she's still able to do that by herself. She aint that old."

"She lives by herself?"

"Yeah."

Twenty minutes passed by and then fifty. Falen was beginning to think that Crystal's boyfriend was playing games. She had drunk two cups of cappuccino and was restless. Every time another customer walked in she would turn to see if it was the dudes.

"Crystal, can you call them niggas and see what's taking them so long?"

"Yeah, let me call his ass. This shit don't make no sense. He's pissing me off, too." Crystal mumbled as she pulled out her cell. "Baby, where yall at?"

Crystal paused for a response. "The police pulled yall over? For what?"

Another pause. "Damn. They towed his car?! Let me ask my sister if she can come pick yall up." She spoke into the phone. Then she looked up at Falen. "You think that you can go pick them up from up the street? The police pulled them over and took the car because they claimed that it wasn't registered to either of them."

Falen took a deep breath. "Fuck. Where are they?"

"Around the corner at McDonald's."

"Alright, come on." Falen said as she stood to leave.

"We on our way." Crystal said into the phone as she stood up as well. "My bad, about this, girl." Crystal said as they made their way to her truck.

There was a black tinted Impala parked right next to Falen and just as she was attempting to unlock her truck the Impala's door swung open. "What's up, baby?" Booby asked as he hopped out of the car.

"Booby, what are you doing here?" Falen asked.

"I came to get it." He chuckled.

"Get what?"

"The shit you got." He said as he pulled a gun from his waist and pointed at her. "Take me to it, Falen."

"What, what the fuck are you doing?"

"I'm about to do some damage if you don't give me what I came for." He gritted. "Now, get your ass in the back."

"Don't do this, Booby." She pleaded.

"I aint gonna ask you again, Falen." He warned.

Falen reluctantly got in the backseat of the Navigator and he climbed in right after her. To her surprise Crystal slid in the front seat with no problems.

"Give me the keys, Falen." She said.

"You in on this with him?" Falen asked in disbelief.

"Yeah." Crystal sighed as if she was uninterested. "Keys." She said as she held her hand out.

"Here, bitch." Falen spat as she tossed the keys over Crystal's head.

Crystal simply shook her head as she retrieved the keys from the floor and started the truck up.

"So, where the work at?" Booby asked.

"It's, it's at the house."

"You better not be lying."

"I'm, I'm not."

"Crystal get on 610 to 45." Booby instructed.

Falen was sweating profusely as she sat next to Booby who still had the gun pointed at her. She thought about the gun she was totting in her purse. She knew that it would be hard to get to it without alerting him with her sudden movements.

"Exit right here." Booby said.

Crystal was already in the exiting lane before he ever opened his mouth. As they rode Booby realized that she knew where she was going without him having to say anything. This was strange because as far as he knew she had never been to Falen and Toya's house. When she found their subdivision without his help he knew that she had been playing games.

Booby was hoping that everything would go as plan. He'd already run into one glitch in his program. Initially he wanted Kay-Al to drive the Impala out the lot for him but he was M.I.A. He hadn't answered any of his calls that day and too much was going on to go hunt him down. And now something was telling him to keep an eye on Crystal.

Crystal pulled into their driveway. "How the fuck this bitch know where I live? You had her at my house before?" Falen snapped.

"And if he did?" Crystal shot back at her.

"Crystal." Booby gritted giving her the eye. "But no, I have never brought any girl to this house. Not even her." He told Falen.

"Why the fuck are you explaining yourself to her?"

Booby shook his head. "We not even doing this right now." He said as he opened the door. "If you try to run, Falen, I will shoot you. Do you understand?"

"Yeah, I got you." She answered as she slid across the seat and climbed out of the truck.

"Ladies, first." He said as he allowed her to lead the way.

Falen got half way to the door before she paused. "Oh, she got the keys."

"Crystal, bring the keys." He called out while never turning away from Falen.

Crystal brought over the keys and they made their way into the house. Falen's mind was racing. She was trying to think of a way to get to a phone or a weapon. She felt like her life depended on it. It was becoming crystal clear who tried to kill Toya. She couldn't believe that Booby had her blinded for a minute. That was the one time that she really wished that she'd listened to her friend.

"Show me where it's at." He said as he continued to point the gun at her.

"It's in the room."

"Well, take us to it, then." Crystal snapped as she roughly shoved her.

"Don't touch me again, you weak ass bitch." Falen gritted.

"Or what?" she questioned getting into Falen's face. "What are you going to do to me?"

"This." Falen lashed as she threw a mean slug knocking Crystal to her knees. She never had a chance to recover. Falen delivered blow after blow to her sister's face.

Booby just stood and watched them fight. He didn't want to get off task or have a slip up by trying to break them apart. He regretted his decision when Falen slung Crystal into him sending him flying to the floor. He lost the grip on his gun and it slid across the floor.

Falen was truly focused and knew exactly what she was doing. She quickly crawled over to the gun.

Once she griped the gun she slowly rose to her feet. "Yall better not make another motherfuckin move!" she shouted as she aimed the gun at Booby.

"Aint this something." Booby chuckled as he stood. "Pretty Falen got a gun pointed at a nigga."

"And *Pretty Falen* will use it, nigga!" she shouted. Booby took a step towards her. "I said stay still!" she roared as she pulled the trigger. The bullet ripped through his shoulder and his body violently hit the floor. "You thought that I was playing with you motherfucka!"

Crystal scrambled to the door. "Bitch, get back here!" Falen yelled as she turned and shot at her sister. She missed her by inches. "Fuck!" Falen vented as Crystal ran outside.

Crystal's heart was pounding in her chest as she

made her way to the Navigator. She'd hopped in and cranked the engine by the time Falen made it outside. Knowing that it wouldn't be a smart move to shoot her truck up she allowed Crystal to speed off. She decided to go back inside the home and call the police.

Once Falen was back inside the house she saw a huge puddle of blood where Booby's body once laid. Her eyes frantically searched the room. She saw a trail of blood leading to her bedroom.

"Booby, bring your ass out here!" she shouted not wanting to search for him. She didn't want any surprises.

"Booby!" she shouted as she tiptoed towards her room. Falen couldn't help but breathe heavily as she walked into her bedroom. She saw that the blood was leading to her closet. "Come out the closet, Booby!" Falen barked as she aimed the gun at the closet's door.

She heard her bedroom's door squeak but by then it was too late. Booby came from behind the door and lunged at her. On impact the gun slid out of her hand.

"I can't believe that you shot me, bitch." He gritted as he wrapped his hands around her throat.

"Get off of me!" she gasped.

"Where the dope at?"

"Let. Me. Go." She struggled to get out.

"I can't do that. Tell me where the dope at before I send you to meet your maker."

Falen's entire life flashed before her eyes. There were visions of her daddy smiling at her. She saw Tez's face and even Yolanda. She couldn't believe that it had come to this. This was the same dude that she considered a good friend. She trusted him. She welcomed him into her bed and he was about to take her out.

"Take me to the dope!" Booby screamed as Falen began to lose consciousness. Finally, he released the grip on her and reached over and grabbed the gun.

Falen was coughing desperately trying to catch her breath. "Now, take me to the dope before I place a bullet between your eyes." He threatened while placing the gun to her forehead.

"Okay, okay." She sobbed. "It's outside."

"Don't play games with me!" he shouted while he pressed the gun deeper into her head.

"I'm serious." She cried out.

Booby lifted himself off of her. "Get up and take me to it."

Falen slowly rose to her feet and headed out of the bedroom with Booby right behind her. "Walk up. I aint got all day." He seethed as he held his bleeding shoulder. He was continuingly losing blood and feeling weaker by the second. "Where is it?" he asked once they both stepped outside.

"Right here underneath the merry-go-round."

So that's why I couldn't find it the other day. Booby thought to himself.

"Well get to digging." He told her.

Falen dropped to her knees and sunk her hands into the soil. She clawed away at the dirt until she came across a small child's chest. She picked it up and placed it at Booby's feet. "There you go. It's all right here. The devil's work. You can have that cause I don't want it. This shit is bad luck and I don't need no more help with that."

He gave her a sinister look as he glared down at her. "It was just in the wrong hands." He said as he reached down and grabbed the box. "How do you unlock this motherfucka?" he asked her.

"You figure it out."

"Oh, I will."

"Now, can I go?"

He glowered down at her. He felt powerful, holding her life in the palm of his hands. She was the only person he ever really gave a damn about and she shitted on him. She had crushed his heart time and time again. Did she really deserve life after she'd damn near destroyed his?

"You got two choices…one you be with me and never talk to that bitch ass Tino again. Two I kill you right now."

That bullet wound must be causing brain damage. What kind of choices are those? "Okay, Booby, I'll be with you."

He stared at her intensely. She thought that it was all finally over, so she attempted to stand.

SMACK! The pistol went across her head. "Bitch, you must think I'm crazy!"

"What?" she sobbed. "You said that if I chose…"

"Shut the fuck up! I just wanted to see if you'd keep it real. A scary muthafucka will say anything when their back is against the wall."

"What do you want from me?!"

He lifted the gun. "I want your life." He smiled right before a bullet ripped through his chest. Booby couldn't believe that he'd been shot again and this time it wasn't Falen doing the shooting. He tried to catch his breath as blood spewed from his mouth. "F..f..fuck." he let out as the blood spilled from his lips. Before his body could even hit the ground another bullet tore through his stomach.

Falen sat in shock not able to move as she witnessed Tino aim the gun in her direction. Today was doom's day and she was wishing like hell that she could just close her eyes and disappear. She knew that she was next. So, she closed her eyes and accepted her fate.

"You okay?" Tino asked her as he stood over her.

Falen slowly opened her eyes. "If you gonna kill me just get it over with."

Tino tossed his gun on the ground. "I'm not here to hurt you." He said as he knelt down so that they were face to face. "I know that you took my keys, but I aint gon kill you. You gave birth to my seed and I would never take you away from him."

"I'm so sorry, Tino. When I took those keys I had no idea about who they belonged to."

He nodded "I know."

"Can you forgive me?" she asked as she gazed into his beautiful eyes.

As he stared at Falen he knew that he loved her. He loved her like he'd loved no other woman. She was his heart and that was…dangerous. She could cause more damage than any other person in his life. The fear of her hurting him was damn near paralyzing. Could he ever really trust her? Was she as innocent as she portrayed? Would she be his downfall? As much as he wanted to be with her he just couldn't chance it.

"I can forgive you but I can't forget." He told her as he heard police sirens off in the distance. "Let me get rid of this before these pigs get here." He said as he grabbed the toy chest.

As he walked away Falen knew that she would never have him the way that her heart desired. This wasn't a fairytale and he just wasn't her Prince Charming. Having a solid nigga by her side holding her down just wasn't in the stars for her. Bad luck was something that she always had, so why should this time be any different?

Falen didn't know what Tino did with his four kilos of coke and didn't care. By the time the police pulled into her driveway he was back at her side ready to give a statement. The police bombarded them with questions and they both told most of the truth with a few adjustments. They made sure to make the shooting sound like a home invasion gone bad.

As Falen told the detective how Booby and Crystal lured her out of Starbucks she remembered that her sister was still somewhere out there in her truck.

Chapter 22

The Crystal Clear Picture

"Who is it?" Toya asked as she heard a knock at the door. She figured that it was probably Booby trying to find Falen again. When she opened the door she was surprised.

"Crystal, what are you doing here?"

Crystal pushed her way inside. "I could've sworn that my sister lives here too." she snapped as he glanced around the room. "Where Falen at?"

"I don't know where that broad at?" Toya shrugged.

Crystal's antenna shot up. "Yall got into it or something?"

"Yeah." Toya thought about it. She didn't need Crystal in their business. "I mean, no."

"Yes or no? Which one is it?"

"That's not here nor there."

"Whatever." Crystal rolled her eyes. "When will Falen be back?"

"I don't know."

"You know where she at, so stop lying!"

Toya put up her hands to halt her. "Whoa, whoa. Hold up, now. Don't be getting loud with me cause I aint did shit to you. But what you want Falen for, anyway?"

"None of your business."

Toya nodded. "Okay, well since your sister aint here you need to leave. I'll let her know that you came by."

"Are you trying to kick me out?"

"I'm not trying, I'm doing it. Get out Crystal."

"I aint going no fuckin where!"

"What the fuck is so important that you refuse to leave until you see the sister that you can't stand?"

"I'm waiting here until this selfish bitch gets here. This shit has been going on long enough. A real sister

wouldn't be over here laying up with her sister's baby daddy!"

"I know damn well that your dizzy ass aint talking about Booby?"

"Yeah, that's right. I'm talking about him. Falen knows that he lil' Ken's daddy but that aint stopped her from fucking him."

Toya couldn't believe what she was hearing. "Crystal, I think that you are losing your everlasting damn mind. Your son's name is Ken Junior. He is named after some other nigga. Since I've been knowing yall Booby has had a crush on Falen. I never saw him look twice at you and if he does it's when nobody else is around and that should tell you something. So, if you mad at somebody it needs to be with yourself. You're the cause of your own grief. You turned your back on your own sister and put her out on the streets for a nigga that left you a few weeks after she was gone. It's your fault if you can't keep a man. Nobody wants a nasty chick that don't clean up and have low self-esteem."

Crystal's blood was boiling. "Fuck you, you little high yellow bitch! You don't know shit about me or Falen. She aint the person that you think you know. She's sneaky. That little bitch will pretend to have your back and then leave you hanging when you need her the most."

Toya shook her head. "If you talking about when Yolanda sold your virginity, you are really crazy. That girl was nine years old at the time. What was you expecting her to do?"

"She could've done something! I would have! She just sat her pissy ass in the other room and listened to that man rape me! She could have climbed out the window or something and called the police."

"She was a little girl, Crystal. She didn't know what to do. You are holding a grudge for something that was beyond her control."

"You would take up for her. You're her fuckin sidekick. Always kissing her ass. In your eyes she can do no wrong. Just wait 'til she fucks one of your niggas and then you'll feel me."

"That's not even Falen's character. She has only been with two niggas in her entire life."

"Yeah, that's what she told you." Crystal smirked.

Toya couldn't stop shaking her head. "What's with you and Janah? Why do yall put so much energy into hating your own sisters? What the fuck did we ever do to yall?"

"You bitches were born!" Crystal shouted. "Since, Falen tells you everything, did she tell you that it was because of her that our daddy is in prison?" she waited for a reaction. "Yeah, you aint know that, huh? She walked out into the streets in front of a car and a man damn near ran her over. My daddy got into a argument with the nigga and they started fighting. The man called Falen a bitch and daddy went into the house and got his gun and shot the man. It was all over Falen's stupid ass. She fucked it up for us all. If it wasn't for her my mama would've never started smoking that shit. She fucked up all of our lives."

"Now, I see why Falen don't fuck with you. You are delusional. Falen was a little girl but you're grown. Look at you and how you treat your own kids. You need to stop playing the blame game and take responsibility for your own actions. So, your childhood was fucked up. That's damn near every girl's story in the hood. That's an excuse to be trifling. You need somebody to blame and Falen was the easiest target. She might be a fighter but she has a kind heart. You took advantage and feared what you didn't understand. You're weak and pitiful. Just look at you. You barely say two words to your sister and now you come to her house for the first time to confront her over a nigga that she don't even want. Don't be mad because that nigga don't want your sorry ass. Shit, I don't blame him for denying *your baby. If I was him I would have done the same thing. Who'd want to be tied to your nasty ass? You fuckin disgust me!" Toya spat.*

"Bitch, you really think you hard, huh? I will get some goons to kick door on you simple bitches. You think you John Gotti or somebody?!"

"Hoe, I'm Toya and that's good enough for you and whoever you think you gon bring to kick this motherfuckin door in. Your low budget ass won't make it passed the front door. We got cameras posted everywhere for haters just like you, so try me."

"Fuck you!" Crystal seethed as she rushed Toya knocking her to the floor.

"I don't think so, bitch!" Toya growled as she flipped Crystal over so that she was now on top. She gripped her hair as she slammed her fist into her face. "Talk that shit now!"

Crystal was becoming desperate as Toya laid into her so she sunk her teeth into Toya's flesh.

"Ahhh!" Toya screamed in pain as Crystal bit her left breast. She rolled off of Crystal which allowed her to crawl to her feet.

Crystal was fuming as she raced to their kitchen. She went through all the drawers until she found a large butcher's knife. Her mind was racing as she ran back into the living room.

"Bitch, your scary ass had to go get a knife?" Toya asked in disbelief as she held her breast.

"Alls fair in a fight, hoe."

Toya didn't want to do Falen's sister like that but she had no choice. She scrambled to the couch and pulled back the cushion and grabbed a glock. "What now, bitch?" Toya laughed as she aimed the gun at Crystal.

Adrenaline ran through Crystal's veins as she lunged at Toya with the knife. Toya let a round off but missed Crystal. Once again Crystal knocked her to the floor as they fought to gain control over the gun. Crystal's hand was wrapped around Toya's wrist as she tried to force the gun into her face.

"Not today, whore!" Toya shouted as she tried to flip Crystal over. The two women rolled around on the floor until the gun went off. Time stood still as they stared into each other's eyes. Crystal didn't know what to do as they both lay in shock.

"Oh my God." Crystal sobbed as she pulled her body away from Toya. She slowly stood with the gun in her hand.

Toya was still breathing. Crystal didn't know what to do. I can't go to jail, she thought to herself. Something told her that the best thing for her to do was for her to finish the job. So she closed her eyes tightly and squeezed the trigger four more times.

Crystal slowly opened her eyes and saw the bloody body that lied before her. She couldn't afford to panic because her freedom was on the line. She remembered that Toya said that there were surveillance cameras around the house so she searched the house until she came across the monitors and tapes in Falen's bedroom. She removed any evidence of her being there and wiped down anything that she touched. She searched Toya's bedroom and found five thousand dollars. That day was definitely her lucky day...

The machine monitoring Toya's heart rate went into overdrive. Ms. Gloria just knew that her daughter was going into cardiac arrest. Toya's body shook violently.

"Doctor! Nurse! Somebody help my baby, please." Gloria cried. She grabbed her daughter's hand and for once she felt her grip her hand back.

"Oh my Lord! I think she's awake!" Gloria sobbed while she tried to figure out what was going on.

Toya snatched her hand away and began clawing at

the tube down her throat. "No, Toya don't do that. This is the feeding tube they feed you with. Let them remove it, baby."

Toya woke up not fully understanding what was going on with her. She didn't have a clue as to how long she'd been in the coma. The shooting seemed like yesterday to her.

One by one the doctors and nurses came in to welcome her back to earth and check her vitals. They told her to be patient and they would remove the feeding tube and catheter as soon as possible. All she could do was nod.

Gloria stood on the sidelines thanking God every second for bringing her child back to her. "Are you in pain, baby?" she asked Toya once the doctors cleared the room. Toya nodded her head.

"Did you realize that you were in a coma?"

Toya shook her head no.

"Do you remember what happened to you?"

She shook her head yes.

"Do you know who did this to you?"

Toya nodded her head over and over.

Gloria searched around the room. She spotted the easel that the nurses used. "Here, write the name on here, baby." She said as she placed the marker in her daughter's hand as she held the easel.

Toya slowly spelled out the letters C.R.Y.S.T.A.L.

Tina heard a car pull up into her driveway. She peeked out of her blinds and spotted Falen's truck.

"Tez, your mommy is back." Tina told her grandson as she totted him on her hip. "Come on let's go meet her at the door." she said as she walked to her front door.

"Fal..."Tina trailed off as she opened the door and

realized that the visitor was not Falen.

"How are you doing? I'm Falen's sister and she sent me to pick up Tez." Crystal smiled.

"Oh, she did?" Tina said inspecting her from head to toe. "She didn't mention that."

"Yeah, it was a last minute thing really."

"Well, let me call her. I aint trying to offend you but I got to make sure that everything is cool before I let you leave with my grandbaby." Tina said as she attempted to close the door.

Crystal stuck her foot in the door before Tina could close it. "That was rude." She growled as she pushed her way into the house.

"What the fuck are you doing!?"

"Shut up, bitch." Crystal whispered harshly as she pulled out a gun. "Now I'm going to need you to do exactly as I say."

"I'm going to head over your mama's house to pick up my son and you won't have to worry about us anymore." Falen spat with a lump in her throat.

Tino gave Falen a look. "What you trying to say? You would keep my son from me?" he asked her as he drove his car down the road. They'd both just finished giving the police an account of the shooting and were now headed towards Tina's home.
Falen decided not to answer him.

"Falen, I know you hear me talking to you." Tino snapped. He glanced over at her and she was staring out the window. "Falen."

She whipped her head around. "What?"

"I know that you fuckin heard me. I'ma let you have your little moment right now, but you need to listen and listen good. Regardless of what goes on between us I will always be there for my son. And I aint gon let you or nobody else stand in the way. So, if you think that you're going to be doing your little disappearing acts then you better think again."

"When have I ever disappeared, Tino?"

"You know what the fuck I'm talking about. I shouldn't have to chase you down to see him."

"Who said that you would have to do that?" she huffed as she folded her arms across her breasts.

"I'm just letting you know." he sighed as she drove through his mother's sub-division.

Falen thought that she was hallucinating as they pulled up on Tino's mother's block and spotted her Navigator sitting in Tina's driveway. "What the fuck?"

"What the hell is your sister doing here at my mama's house?" Tino asked confused.

"I don't know what that stupid bitch is doing here." Falen said trying to gather her thoughts. There were so many unanswered questions. Why would Crystal go to Tino's mama's house? How did she know where Tina lived? Then it hit her.

"Oh my God, Tino." She gasped.

"What?"

"She was asking questions about your mama earlier. She wanted to know who all lived here and how often she had company."

"What?" Tino spat as he glared at her. "So, your sister trying to get at my mama?"

Falen shrugged her shoulders. "I don't know."

Tino parked directly behind Falen's truck making it impossible for anyone to leave in it.

"Look, I don't give a fuck about her being your sister. If she fucks with my mama I'm gonna do her; period." Tino said as he hopped out of his ride.

"Whatever." Falen mumbled as she slithered out the car.

Tino didn't bother knocking on his mama's door because he had the key. So, he pulled out his pistol, then unlocked the door, and walked in. The living room was empty, but there was a pool of blood in the middle of the floor. His heart rate sped up.

"What the fuck." he whispered as Falen walked up behind him.

"Oh, my God. Where's Tez." she panicked.

"Shh." Tino placed his finger up to her mouth. "Be quiet. Whoever did this is probably still here."

Falen nodded her head before Tino pulled away from her and tiptoed to the hallway right outside the living room. There in the hall was Tina slowly crawling on her belly while leaving a trail of blood behind her. Seeing his mother in this condition made his heart drop.

"Mama." he uttered as he tried to help her up.

"The baby, Tino. She got the baby." Tina struggled to get out as he held her in his arms.

"Did she shoot you?" Falen asked on the verge on losing her mind.

Tina slowly nodded.

"Are they still here?"

"I…I don't know."

"Fuck! I'ma kill that bitch!" Falen seethed. "Tino give me your gun."

"My gun? No, I got another one at the top of this closet." he told her as he gestured at the hall's closet.

Falen snatched the door open and rambled through the closet until she found the .357. Tino instructed her on where to find the bullets and then she loaded the gun.

"I'll be back." Falen said as she headed towards the bedrooms while Tino dialed 911 for his mama.

As she headed down the hall she could hear Tez's

cries. She felt a small sense of relief knowing that at least her son was still alive. Still, there was no telling what Crystal's nutty ass had in store. Falen followed her son's voice and it led her to the last bedroom in the house. The door was closed and she stood there staring at it trying to think of the best move. Crystal could be standing there aiming the gun directly at the door for all she knew.

Suddenly Tez's cries became more intense. "Shut the fuck up!" Crystal shouted.

All reasoning went out the door when Falen heard this. She opened the door so fast that it crashed into the wall.

Crystal's head shot up as she held a gun to Tez's temple.

"Bitch, you just lost your fuckin' mind!" Falen screamed as she pointed her gun at her sister. She couldn't believe that anybody could be so heartless to the point where they'd aim a gun at their infant nephew's head.

"No, bitch I got my mind right. And if you make another step I will blow your baby's fuckin brains out."

Falen felt defeated. Her sister was about to murder the one good thing she had in life. Her own flesh and blood wanted to see her hurting. "He aint got shit to do with this, Crystal. Please let my baby go. If you want to hurt somebody, then kill me." she pleaded as she dropped her gun to the floor.

Crystal smiled deviously. "Kill you right? No, that would be letting you out too easy. No, I need you to live in hell on earth. I want you to wake up every day knowing that you wasn't woman enough to save your own child's life. I want you to suffer a slow death every motherfuckin day."

"What did I ever do to you, Crystal? What was so fucked up that you'd want to hurt me?"

"Bitch, please. Don't pretend that you like me. We both hate each other and you know it. The difference between me and you is that I just don't give a fuck. So, I'm about to put an end to this shit once and for all." *Blow*.

Falen stood in shock as Crystal's eyes grew larger. She sat with her mouth open before she fell back in the bed. The bullet wound left a huge hole in her head.

"Oh, God!" Falen screamed as she quickly removed Tez from her arms.

"Bitch." Tino gritted as he gripped his gun.

"You okay, baby?" Falen questioned as she checked her son for any injuries.

Tino held his breath as he watched her examine the baby.

"Whew, thank God." she finally said as they heard police sirens off in the distance.

"Tino!" Tina yelled from the other room.

"Fuck." he mumbled as he went to his mama. He had propped her on the couch and she was holding a towel on her wound.

"I…I had to make sure that the bitch didn't hurt you." Tina said out of breath.

"Don't talk, mama. Save your energy, okay." he instructed as he dropped to his knees in front of her.

Falen entered the room with Tez in her arms. She was still in shock as she stared at Tina lying there damn near lifeless. "Ms. Tina, I am so sorry." she cried.

"Girl, stop that. If it's my time, then it's all good. God got me." Tina waved her off and smiled weakly just before she closed her eyes slowly.

"Mama!" Tino screamed as he frantically tried to wake his mother. "Mama, wake up! Mama!"

He shook her body but she never bothered to open her eyes.

"Oh, God!" Falen screamed as Tino cried over his mother's body.

"Get up, mama!" he pleaded.

Boom! Boom! Boom1 "Police!" someone shouted

from the other side of the front door.

Falen made her way to the door and opened it. Tino was oblivious to what was going on around him. All he could see was his mother lying there breathless. He'd seen so much while in the streets, but nothing could compare to what was before his eyes. Everyone only had one mom and his was now gone. All the money in the world couldn't change that.

As soon as the officer saw the blood all over her he drew his gun. "Ma'am I need you to step back." the white man said as he aimed the gun at her.

"No, problem, but you aint gotta point that gun at me." Falen seethed as she stepped back and allowed him in with his partner right behind him.

The officer laid eyes on Tino hovering over a bloody Tina. "Stand up with your hands above your head!"

Finally, Tino broke out of his trance, lifted his head, and then placed his gun on the floor. He slowly stood with his hands above his head. "Okay, yall can take it easy."

"Handcuff him, Bob." the officer told his partner.

"Why are yall putting me in handcuffs? This is my mama. I didn't hurt her. The bitch in the back room did." Tino snapped as Bob placed him in handcuffs.

"There's another person in here?" the other officer asked Falen.

"Yeah, my sister but I think that she is dead."

"This is officer Cossack requesting back up and an ambulance to 1287 W...." he spoke into his walkie- talkie.

Falen stood as the officer went to search the house as the other officer took Tino out the door. He placed him in the back of the patrol car all the while Tino protested. "I'm telling you motherfuckas that yall got the wrong one!"

The officer ignored him as he went back inside the home to aid his partner. Just as he entered the house his partner walked back into the living room. "There's a young female lying dead with a gun still in hand."

Falen could hear several sirens approach as she watched the policemen talk. Finally one of them turned to her. "Ma'am I need you to tell me everything that just happened."

"Yall motherfuckas need to be tending to my son's grandmother!"

"Hey, hey. Ma'am we need you to calm down. The paramedics are on their way and they will do everything within their power to save your grandmother."

Tino sat in the waiting area as the doctors worked vigorously on his mother. He was about to go insane. He wanted to lash out and do some damage to the world. He couldn't do anything to Crystal because she was already gone. Still he felt this overwhelming anger towards her and any other person involved in the situation; including Falen. If he hadn't fucked with her in the first place his mama would still be fine. He couldn't help but sit and glare at her. She had come in like a tornado and tore his life apart.

Falen could feel Tino staring at her and she didn't know how to feel. Something inside told her that he blamed her, and she could definitely understand why. Her actions sort of had this chain reaction. She was the one person who set all the events into motion and she wishing like hell that she could go back in time.

"Tino, is she okay?" Jamie asked as she hurriedly walked over to him.

He shook his head. "I don't know."

Without thinking she knelt down to hug him.

Falen sat uncomfortably watching the two embrace.

"It's going to be okay." Jamie whispered to Tino. She was definitely comforting to him. After everything that had gone down she was still there in his time of need.

"I hope so." he sighed trying his best to keep it together. "I hope so."

Finally, Jamie released Tino and turned to see Falen. She gave her a quick smirk and then sat down right next to Tino.

"They need to come and tell me something." Tino told Jamie.

Falen had never felt more unwanted in her life. As time passed Tino continued to ignore her while Jaime tried to console him. Finally, she had enough. As she stood to leave a white gray haired doctor approached them.

"Mr. Wiltz?"

"Yeah." Tino nodded as he held his breath.

"I'm sorry. We did everything we could save her. She didn't make it."

"Ow, naw!" Tino bawled as he fell to the floor. "I need my mama."

"Tino, it's okay." Jamie cried as she hugged him.

"What I'm going to do, Jamie?"

"We gon get through this together."

Falen stood with mixed feelings. Her heart was hurting for Tino but she couldn't help being consumed with guilt and jealousy all at the same time. "Tino, if there's anything that I can do…"

He quickly shook his head. "No, there aint shit that you can do to bring my mama back."

She slowly nodded as she held back the tears. "I know that. So, I guess that I'll just go."

"Yeah, you do that." he seethed.

"Okay. You have a nice life." she said as she walked away while Jamie stared her down.

"What was that all about?"

Tino sucked his teeth. "Don't even go there."

Falen walked out to her Navigator as she allowed her

tears to silently fall. As she was placing Tez in his car seat her cell went off.

"Hello."

"Falen." a raspy voice said slowly.

"Who is this?" Falen snapped not in the mood for any more surprises.

"Who is it supposed to be, bitch?"

Falen froze. "Toya?"

"The one and only."

"Oh my God! When did you wake up?"

"Today. Those bitches said that I aint supposed to be talking right now, but you know that I had to call my bitch."

"Already!"

"Yeah, so what the fuck is up?"

"Everything, Toya." Falen cried.

"Bitch, don't do that. Stop all that crying in my ear and tell me what the hell is going on."

"For one Booby and Crystal tried to rob me."

"Why am I not surprised?"

"I mean, you not the least bit surprised? I know that Booby shot you, but Crystal? I have to admit that that one caught me by surprise."

"Well, not me. Besides, Booby didn't shoot me. It was Crystal's nutty ass."

"What?!"

"Yeah, she came to the house to confront you about Booby. She claimed that she was tired of you fucking her man."

"Are you serious?"

"Hell, yeah. That girl really had it out for you. Truthfully, I think that it wasn't really about you at all. She was just mad at the world and she wanted to take all of her frustrations out on you. Girl, you know that misery loves company."

"I know." Falen sniffed. "But I just thought that me

and my sister were better than that. Girl, she was playing so many mind games while you was sleep. She actually called me telling me that she loved me and that we should work on our relationship. She did all of that just to help Booby set me up."

"Wow. They are some cold blooded motherfuckas."

"Was."

"What you mean *was*?"

Falen took a deep breath. "Both of them are dead."

Falen's words sent a chill down Toya's spine. As much as she wanted some hatred for the both of them to seep through to her heart it didn't. She had trouble processing that two people that she'd grown up with were now gone. "How…how did that happen?"

"Well, for one I shot Booby when they tried to rob me, and then Tino came and had to finish him."

"Tino? He don't know about the work, do he?"

"Now see, Booby told me that he'd spoken to you right before you were shot and you told him that somebody told you that Tino and nem knew already."

"What? Hell, naw. I hadn't talked to that nigga. You know that me and him wasn't even rocking like that, so he'd be the last nigga that I would discuss the damn whether with. Now, finish telling me what happened."

"Well, after the police came to the crib when Booby was shot, me and Tino headed to his mama's. Ms. Tina was keeping Tez for me. Oh, and Crystal had stole the Nav. So, you know I was tripping out when we pulled up in front of Tina's house and found the Nav in the driveway."

"Whaat? Bitch, you lying."

"Real talk. Well, come to find out, that crazy bitch had shot Tina and was holding a gun to Tez's head…"

"Wait, wait. Back all the way up. Now, your sister had a gun to your baby's head? Where they do that at?"

"I guess in the land of crazy bitches."

"So, who ended up killing her? Please tell me that it was you."

"No, Tino ended up doing that, too."

"Tino, huh? So, that nigga was really there for you, right?"

Falen sighed heavily.

"What's wrong?"

"His mama ended up dying." she sobbed into the phone.

"Wow." Toya stressed. This was some unbelievable shit going on. "So, where is Tino?"

"He's in the hospital with Jamie."

"His baby mama?"

"Yeah."

"He still fucking with her?"

"I guess. The bitch is here. Besides, the only reason he was dealing with me was because he thought that she had something to do with stealing his issue."

"Damn. I know that you might not want to hear this right now, but everything happens for a reason. Let's just say that this was kind of poetic justice. They probably didn't need to be together and that's where you came in."

"Toya, please. He loves her. He's with her. It is what it is."

"Falen, stop fronting for once, okay. I can hear it in your voice that it's not what it is. You love him and that shit is hurting you."

"Okay, I can admit that it hurts like hell. But I'm immune to this shit. I've been living in hell here on earth from the beginning so this aint nothing that I can't handle. Besides, as long as I got you and my son, I'll be alright."

Chapter 23

Tino sat around feeling the lowest he'd ever felt in all his life. He didn't have a soul in his corner. For a brief moment he allowed Jamie back in, only to shut her down again shortly after. He could tell that she still loved him and that was the reason he pushed her away. He knew that he just didn't feel the same. Then he felt guilty knowing that his cousin was in love with a woman that was still in love with him. He'd had enough of the back and forth and just wanted to wash his hands with the entire situation.

There was no longer anyone there to vent to during stressful times such as this. His best friend/cousin had betrayed him. His mama was six feet deep and he'd pushed away the only girl he'd ever loved. He knew that he'd hurt Falen with the way he treated her. He was just wounded and needed an outlet to vent at the time. Unfortunately, she ended up being the person he unleashed his anger and frustrations on.

Now, with a clearer mind Tino wanted to talk. He at least wanted Falen to know that he didn't blame her for the death of his mother. If he was going to place blame on her then he may as well turn around and point a finger at himself. They all played key roles in their self-destruction. He could sit around and think of a hundred different scenarios, but that wouldn't change that his decision to get in the game had caused most of his heartache. He knew like no one else that the game didn't have no love, still never in his wildest dreams did he think that this would be the end result. He was always so sure that he'd eventually come out on top. The only thing he envisioned taking him off his note was his death or imprisonment. He could have gladly accepted those terms. He wasn't so sure if he could live with these consequences.

Everything that he held dear was gone. He didn't

have a friend or a parent. The only people he had were his kids, and at the rate he was going they were going to grow up never really knowing him. It had been eight months since he'd laid eyes on either child. Guilt was damn near killing him. He had to do something.

Tino called up Jamie and asked her to bring Tia over. She happily obliged. He was surprised to see that she was wearing an engagement ring. Not one ounce of him felt any jealousy, and that is what told him that he'd made the right decision in letting her go.

"Appreciate you bringing her."

"It's no problem." she smiled. "So, how have you been, Tino?"

"I been alright. How 'bout you?"

"I'm happy." she nodded.

"That's cool. So, how is Joe?"

"He's fine…and he misses you."

"Oh, yeah? Well, I might give that nigga a holla."

"Yeah, you should do that." Jaime said as she headed out of the door.

"Alright. See you later." he said as he attempted to close the door.

"Wait, Tino."

"What's up?" he asked as he slightly opened the door wider.

"Thank you."

"For what?"

"For being man enough to let me go. A lot of niggas would have continued to be selfish. I know that I probably would have never had the strength to walk away."

"Hey, no need to thank me. You just make sure that you don't allow another man to think that he can walk all over you. You deserve better, but that don't mean shit if you don't realize it."

She nodded and smiled. "I know."

"That's what's up." he smiled as he closed the door and turned to his daughter. "So, what does my baby girl want to do?"

"I want some cake, daddy." she grinned.

"Some cake, huh? Well, let me make a phone call and then we can go find you some cake."

He picked up his cell and took a deep breath before dialing Falen's number. "We're sorry you have reached a number that is no longer in service." the automated operator said.

"Fuck." he gritted.

"What's wrong, daddy?"

"Nothing, baby. Let's go get that cake you wanted." he said as he grabbed his keys off of his table.

"Falen, you want anything out of this store?"

"Yeah, bring me some orange juice."

"Tez, you want some candy?" Toya questioned as she glanced in the back seat.

Tez gave her a nod as he toyed with his Tickle Me Elmo.

"Alright." Toya said as she hopped out the driver's side of the Navigator. She was happy to be able to move around without the aid of crutches. It took a lot of physical therapy, blood, sweat, and tears but she was back to her old self. On the outside looking in no one couldn't even tell that she'd been shot five times. She was definitely a walking testimony.

She walked into the store as she turned a few fellows' heads. She was still the shit and nobody could tell her differently. She could feel the eyes glued to her backside as she stood in line to pay for the gas.

"Daddy, can I have some ice cream too?" Toya

heard a little girl ask. Something told her to turn around and she spotted…Tino and his little girl.

Tino could feel somebody staring at him so he looked up. As soon as he saw her a smile crossed his face. "What's up, Toya?"

"Nothing too much."

"Yeah, where your girl at?"

"I don't know. I haven't seen them in like forever." Those words caused Tino's heart to sink to his stomach.

"Damn." he mumbled.

"Well, it was good seeing you." Toya said after she made her purchases and headed out the door. She hurriedly walked over to the Navigator. She slightly opened the door. "Bitch, why is that bitch ass nigga in there asking about you?"

"Who?" Falen asked.

"Tino."

Hearing his name made her heart skip a beat. "He's in there right now?"

"Yeah."

"So, what did you tell him?"

"I told him that I didn't know where you was."

"Oh, you did?" Falen asked disappointed. She wanted Toya to insist that she speak to Tino so that she could pretend that she really didn't want to.

"I sure did. If you want to talk to him you gon do that on your own."

"What?"

"Yeah, you heard me. Your ass is always putting shit in my head that wasn't there until you started talking. You used to have me kick in it the hood while you supposedly would be trying to avoid him. I'm hip to your game. You aint gon use me as a scapegoat."

Tino felt defeated when Toya told him that she

hadn't seen Falen. Then he got to thinking. Falen and Toya were tighter than tight. When you saw one you saw the other. So, he couldn't see them not being around each other.

"Come on, Tia." he said as he pulled his daughter outside.

"But Daddy what about my cake and ice cream?"

"Daddy gon get it. Just let me see something right quick." he told her as he spotted Toya standing by the Navigator that she and Falen once shared.

"Say, Toya!"

She turned around. "Huh?"

"Let me holla at you." he said as he walked over.

She tried to slam the door shut but it was too late.

"Aint that Falen right there?" he looked over Toya. "No."

Tino gave her a look. "Come on, Toya. Don't play your boy like that. I saw her. I just want to ask her about my son. That's it."

"Well, if you want to see Tez, he's in the back seat." she laughed as she reached and opened the backdoor.

Tino walked around her and peeped inside. Tez had grown so much since the last time he'd seen him.

Falen looked back at him and all her words became lodged in her throat. She hated how she still became nervous around him.

"What's up lil' man?" Tino smiled while ignoring her.

"Hey." Tez spoke shyly.

"You remember me?"

Tez slowly shook his head.

"That's messed up. You don't remember your daddy?" he spoke as he glared at Falen.

She turned her head and it was now her turn to ignore him.

"So, whose baby is this?" he asked as he spotted the

newborn baby sleeping on the opposite side of Tez and his booster seat.

"That's Falen's baby." Toya spoke up.

"Falen's baby? When did this happen?"

"About six weeks ago."

Falen was suddenly agitated. "Damn, Toya! I can talk for myself."

"Shit, I can't tell."

"You would know if you shut the fuck up sometimes."

"Hey, aint no need to get mad at me."

"Yall chill out, main. So, Falen you had another one, huh?"

She shook her head. "I aint got shit to say to you."

"Oh, I think you do. I need to see my son."

"You aint been worried about seeing him. Why start now?"

"Come on, man. Let's not go there, okay."

"No, let's go there." Falen snapped as she folded her arms.

"Okay. I was grieving. I needed time to get myself together before I could deal with a little person."

"Whatever." she rolled her eyes to the ceiling.

"Say girl, don't be taking shit out on me cause that nigga aint acting right."

"What?"

"Yeah, you didn't think that I peeped how you still rolling with your girl with no nigga in sight. You got this newborn baby rolling with yall. Evidently, that nigga aint in the picture like he supposed to be."

"Is you serious, nigga?" she asked before thinking. "You know what? You right. You aint doing what the fuck you should. So, what's up? Tina need some pampers. What you got on it?"

Tino wore this look of confusion. "What?"

"You heard her, nigga." Toya added her two cents.

"So, you saying that this is my baby?"

"One hundred motherfuckin percent." Falen spat.

"So, why didn't you tell me?" he asked infuriated.

"Cause I wasn't about to beg no nigga to help me. If you hadn't even bothered to check on the first child, why would I call you about another one?"

"Falen, I was going through some shit. Damn. Don't try to turn this shit around. You kept them away because you was being spiteful. Just like the last time."

"You know what, fuck this." Falen uttered as she hopped out of the truck and walked around. She stepped to Tino. "You better not ever say some shit like that again. If you was being a man you would know about them. You could have gotten in touch with me. I guess that Tez wasn't important to you."

"Girl, miss me with that shit. I'm here now."

"Man, will yall just kiss and get the shit over with?" Toya interjected.

"Toya." Falen gritted.

"What? I'm just saying. All you do is talk about the nigga. You got two kids for his ass. You might as well stop playing."

Tino stood blushing feeling like a little teenaged boy hearing that the girl he had a crush on liked him back.

Falen was totally embarrassed. Toya had put her business all out there. "Toya, you down bad, man."

"Whatever. I'm just saying. I'm tired of yall with this shit. Tell the nigga how you feel and get it over with."

"Alright, Toya. Can I talk to her? In private." Tino finally said.

"Okay. Hurry up." she said as she hopped in the truck.

"Can I follow yall somewhere, so that we can sit down and talk?"

"I guess." Falen shrugged.

"You guess?"

She stared at him, pissed that he was trying make her give a straight answer. "Yes Tino, we can talk."

"Good." he smiled. "Where are we going?"

"To our crib. I'm tired." she yawned reminding him that she'd just given birth to a new baby.

"Alright. So, I'ma follow yall. Come on, Tia." he nodded as he headed to his car.

Tino followed behind the Navigator as his mind raced. Just a few days ago he was weighed down with so much disparity that he felt like his life could never recover. Now, all of sudden he felt that he could do this thing called life again.

Falen was internally smiling. She had fanaticized about this day for eight long months. Her dreams were the only place she could admit that she still desired him. That was the only time she could imagine them together as a family. Since she was convinced that she just wasn't one of those people that was going to have a happy ending, she'd placed her and Tino's relationship way deep back in her brain. Or at least she tried to. She didn't know what was about to happen but she was glad that he would at least have some sort of relationship with their kids.

"Let me get her for you." Tino volunteered once they pulled up to their house. "What's her name?"

"Okay." Falen sighed as she watched him carefully remove the baby and her carrier from the truck. "And her name is Tina."

Tino took the time to really look at the small baby. "Tina, huh?" he smiled. Even though she was still fresh, he could see the family resemblance.

"Daddy, can I see her?" Tia asked.

He slightly lowered the baby seat so that she could get a glimpse of the baby.

"She's pretty, daddy. Is she my sister?"

Tino couldn't help but smile. "Yeah, she is."

"Ooh, I want to hold her." Tia said excitedly.

"You can once we go in the house. You can sit down and hold her." Falen spoke up.

"Okay." Tia smiled as they all headed inside of the house.

Tino stepped into Falen and Toya's house and looked around. They'd moved into a much nicer house since the last time he'd seen them. "Yall got a nice little spot here." he nodded with approval.

"Thanks." Toya smiled. "Falen did all the work."

"And that aint nothing to brag about. Lazy ass." Falen mumbled as she placed Tez on the couch. "Yall can take a seat." she told Tino and Tia.

"Oh, I didn't know, feel me." Tino said sarcastically. "Sit down, Tia."

"Okay." Tia sat. "Now can I hold my sister?"

Falen smiled. "Yes, you can." she said as she reached and removed the baby from the car seat.

"Hey, Tina." Tia cooed as Falen placed the baby in her arms.

"Awe, they so cute together." Toya laughed.

"Yeah." Tino stood back and admired them before refocusing. "Can I talk to you?" he asked Falen.

"I guess." she shrugged as she headed to her bedroom.

He shook his head as he followed her. "Whatever."

They both stepped into her room. "So, what's up?" she asked.

"What's up, huh? You kill me, man."

"What?" she asked confused.

"Everything is everything, right?"

"What are you talking about?"

"You know exactly what I'm talking about. How

could you go through an entire pregnancy and don't bother to tell me shit?"

"It was easy. Any time I thought about calling you all I had to do was relive the day when you dissed me and blamed me for your mama's death."

"Really? So, you was mad about that?"

"Yes and no. A part me blames myself too, so I was madder at myself than anything."

"Well, don't do that. You had no control over your crazy ass sister and I was wrong as hell for placing the blame on you. If anything it was my fault. I was in the life and never stopped to think about how my lifestyle might affect my loved ones. I was just upset at the time and was lashing out. I was wounded, Falen but you didn't deserve the way I treated you. Don't ever think that it's okay."

"I hear you." she mumbled as she stared at the floor.

He stepped to her and tilted her chin up. "Look at me."

She stared into his eyes.

"I'm sorry. I never meant to hurt you."

She slowly nodded.

"Can you forgive me?"

She nodded again.

"No, let me hear you say it."

"I forgive you."

"Thank you." he pulled her into his arms and for the first time in a long time he felt good. The feeling that only she could provide rejuvenated him. "I love you." he whispered.

"I know." Falen cried. Even as Tino turned his back on her she never doubted the love he had for her. She'd stolen from him and she was still breathing which was proof within itself.

"I missed you." he admitted right before he covered her mouth with his. "Umm, I missed those sweet lips."

She grabbed the back of his head as she played with his tongue. "Umm." she moaned against him.

"Knock, knock." Toya said as she entered the room. "Uh, not to interrupt yall little fun, but did yall forget about the kids yall got in the living room?"

Falen pulled away from Tino. "Nobody forgot." she said as she wiped the edges of her mouth.

"Let's go check on them." Tino suggested.

"But, I thought that we had to talk?"

Tino smiled down at her. "Lil mama, we got a whole lifetime to talk. Let's just go see about our little ones."

"A lifetime? What that mean, Tino?" Toya pried.

"That means that you need to find yourself a man so that you won't be living in this big ass house by yourself."

"What?! Falen, you hear this nigga?"

Falen giggled. "Yeah, I hear him. You might want to take heed." She pulled Tino out to the living room.

Toya shook her head while her hands rested on her hips. "Well aint this bout a bitch."